THE
CATERPILLAR
COP

THE
CATERPILLAR
COP

James McClure

Pantheon Books
New York

Library of Congress Cataloging in Publication Data

McClure, James, 1939–
    The caterpillar cop.

    Reprint. Originally published: New York:
Harper & Row, 1973.
    I. Title.
PR9369.3.M394C3   1982   823   82-47887
ISBN 0-394-71058-4   AACR2

Manufactured in the United States of America

To
Bay and Ella

Chapter One

THE SOUTHERN CROSS marked the spot where Jonathan Rogers laid his dinner jacket and prepared to lay Penny Jones. Stretched out side by side, just their elbows touching so far, they could see the constellation framed directly above them by a small, wavering gap in the wattle trees surrounding Trekkersburg Country Club. And it seemed somehow so much more romantic than the moon.

That was the secret of the thing, after all—making out this was the Big Romance, soon to be filmed in fabulous Technicolor on a wraparound screen. Even if you, for one, knew nobody would be out fooling with a glass slipper come morning. Even if you were doing it only because they said it had never been done before. At least to Miss Jones.

Jonathan found her hand, gently broke its clasp on a paper tissue, and mated his fingers with hers. Then he had his thumb describe tight, tickling circles on the moist little palm.

"Don't!" she whispered.

Instantly he went limp as a scolded spaniel.

"I'm sorry," she said. "It was just I—"

"Never to worry."

"No, honest. I don't want you to be cross."

"I'm not."

"Promise?"

"Take your time, Pen."

She squeezed and sighed happily.

But don't take all night about it, darling—they had put a deadline on this one. The singles play-off would begin at nine sharp and the team were expected back in town at the hotel by midnight. Jonathan lad, they had said when they fixed him up with her, Jonathan lad, we give you until eleven-thirty, okay? They were a good bunch of blokes in the team, but never liked having any of their traditions broken. In fact, it was considered an ill omen if they were not all gathered together again for a final round before leaving. And as the law dictated that no female might venture into a South African bar, it meant Jonathan would have to get it all over and done with outdoors. Pronto.

He set his thumb to work again.

"What's it like?" she asked timidly.

"Hey?"

"Being a tennis champion."

"I'm not really that."

"You will be, though—tomorrow."

"Going to watch again?"

"Of course!"

His turn to give a squeeze, sigh, and say nothing. It worked.

"What's wrong? Don't you want me there?"

"Got to keep my eye on the ball, haven't I?"

She laughed.

"You say you've seen me spectating all last week?"

"Gave me a hard time of it, you did."

"Where was I sitting, then?"

He gave it a pat.

"Jonathan!"

Silence—the kind judges use before calling for a verdict.

"Now *you're* cross, Pen. Aren't you?"

"No."

"Sure?"

"I'm not."

"Can I kiss you then?"

"If you want to."

He tried another. It was no better than the first half-dozen; her lips were soft enough but they parted wrongly so their teeth clinked together and she had pretty hard teeth.

"Oh, Jonathan . . ."

He sat up slowly and looked about while he wondered if he dared risk his tongue.

It was surprising how bright it seemed inside the forest

8

once your eyes had adjusted from the fluorescent blaze of the ballroom. He could see very well, in fact. The wattle trunks rose quite distinctly above the bracken ahead of him. He could even pick out spiders' eyes glinting in tiny clusters on the invisible webs strung between them. And a strip of rag left on a sapling as a marker in some cross-country run. The moon was lurking about somewhere, that much was obvious, and doing its best to curry favor. Only he was impatient for it to edge its way through the trees and do miracles with a pair of bare, if otherwise unremarkable, breasts. He closed his eyelids to see what his imagination could find to project onto them.

That was the moment, as he so often said later, when he should rather have glanced back over his shoulder into the undergrowth. Just a quick glance and everything would have been so different. Horrible, of course, but not in the same way. Then he would shudder and think of Miss Jones, while his friends would try to make of their embarrassment a silent tribute to her memory. Poor old Penny Jones, spinster of the parish. Forevermore.

"What's the matter?"

He kept his eyes shut and his slight smile turned away.

"Nothing."

"You've gone all funny, Jonathan. Why are your eyes closed?"

"I was listening."

"Oh? Is there someone . . . ?"

"I told you we'd be all right here; there's not a wog for miles. It's something else—can't you hear it?"

"Music?"

"Yes."

"It's coming from the clubhouse."

"That's right. And the tune?"

Trust old Steve. Every team had its funny man and he had the ability to be funnier than most. Right now he was up on the bandstand doing a takeoff of Sinatra, belting out a ballad, and making damn certain it would reach his doubles partner in the woods. No doubt the rest of the crew were falling about the place busting a gut.

"Don't know it. But I never listen to the radio much, just the 'Hit Parade' when my sister's got it on."

Which was as well, perhaps. Steve was giving with the oldie "Have You Met Miss Jones?"

"It's our tune." Jonathan chuckled.

"Really?"

More than that: it was a challenge. On court or off, the lads depended on their captain to boost morale by doing the impossible. There was no going back now with his shirttail between his legs.

Jonathan began peeling the bark from a fallen branch, slyly twisting his body so that she could see nothing but his back. He waited. The singing petered out. He waited some more.

"There *is* something the matter!" she said.

He shrugged.

"You must tell me. What is it?"

"Hell. I suppose it's because you're different."

"In what way?"

"Just different, that's all. Not like the others."

"Who?"

"The girls at these dances for us—you know what I mean."

"No, I don't."

"Then you must have a very sheltered life. Haven't you heard why most of them come? It's like being a pop star. You know."

"You mean . . . ?"

"Yes."

"I see."

Count to ten slowly.

"No, you don't. I'm not talking about that. Not exactly."

"Oh?"

"Pen, I think I love you. Isn't that crazy?"

One, two, three, four, five, six—

"Why should it be?"

Seven, eight, nine, ten.

"So you don't think it's crazy? Even if we only met tonight?"

"I—I cut your picture out of the paper last year."

"Why?"

"Because you're different, too, Jonathan. I've told everyone that."

10

"How could you tell?"

"I know."

He flipped the branch away into the bracken.

"Are you going to lie down again, Jonathan?"

"No."

"But you said—"

"You're different, Pen. Different. It makes me scared."

"What does?"

"The way I still want to—kiss you, and that."

"Perhaps I'm like them."

"Don't be sick! I told you the way I felt. Never happened to me before."

"I meant . . . I love you, too, you know."

"It's a bloody mess."

Her hand stirred from the leaves at her side.

"I've taken them off, Jonathan."

Hell. Without her spectacles, Penny Jones looked suddenly very unlike a trainee schoolmarm. Now her thick, long lashes came into their own and so did the pert nose with its dusting of cute freckles. Myopia lent the finishing touch by introducing a wide-eyed, trustful innocence.

The total effect was really quite appetizing.

So Jonathan made a slow-motion descent, took the first part of the kiss with a wary pucker, worked gently at her jaw with his fingertips the way he did when giving a worm pill to his dog, and gained entry to her oral cavity.

For one terrifying moment he thought he would have to learn to talk with his hands. And then she abandoned herself to her first adult sensation and took his breath away.

Literally.

Using every muscle in his athlete's torso to subdue a coughing fit, he went straight into the next stage. Once again his superb fitness was of paramount importance as it allowed him to rest himself gently on top of her right half while taking the weight on his offside limbs. All he had to do now was keep her lips occupied while his body heat sneaked across.

She melted rapidly right down the middle and his knee sank into her warmth. He began a restrained rhythmic movement. Her thighs clamped on his leg so hard he involuntarily broke the embrace.

"You're strong," he murmured.

11

"Riding," she said. "I'm in the pony club."

God, you had to laugh. They both did. Only she apparently found humor in the absurd, while he saw it in the unwittingly apt. His laughter was also the release of tension caused by a final anxiety—if she had been pounding about on a saddle, then there would be no need to deflower and that was always a relief. Especially if you had a date with the lads.

"I love you, Pen," he said.

"Do you really?"

"All of you. Every bit. Can I look?"

Before she could lift her head, he weighed it down with his mouth and sent his left hand down the front of her quasi-Regency dress to twitch the long line of buttons free. His right skillfully disengaged her bra hooks through the thin material at the small of her back.

Then he sat up—startled.

Never, never look a gift horse in the saddle blanket. Underneath, she was incredible. Like cream poured from a jug—a continuity of changing shapes each retaining a perfection of form. It was impossible to note detail.

"You're . . ."

Words genuinely failed him.

"Aren't my bosoms too big? That's why I always wear dresses like this one."

"Hey?"

"But this isn't fair, Jonathan."

"What isn't?"

"You looking at me. I can't see you—can I?"

"Do you want me to . . . ?"

"I mean—without my glasses."

"Pen, I'm going to, though—all right?"

She nodded.

And when he was naked to his black socks she giggled and said, "You're still just a blur. You'll have to find them for me."

"Touch me instead, Pen."

She did so, hesitantly. Then like a sculptor running a hand over a work by Michelangelo; there was awe and an urgent lust to create.

He touched her, too, selectively, and forgot to keep saying how much he loved her.

12

Not that it mattered any longer.

She was drawing him down into her.

It was sheer instinct.

Instinct.

Like the primeval leftover that alerts modern man to a pair of staring eyes.

Jonathan brought his chin up onto her forehead and looked into the bushes.

The eyes stared back.

There was a face, too. The face of a youth with blond hair who was smiling at him through a low fork in a tree.

"Jonathan?"

Her voice was anxious.

A terrible rage lifted him from her and he rolled to one side. She grabbed at him.

"What's wrong now? *Please!* We so nearly . . ."

He pushed her away. He was shaking uncontrollably. His face expressed one thing: revulsion.

Before she could ask him again, he was gone—blundering through the bracken, sobbing, cursing, heading straight for the youth behind the tree.

Who never moved.

Until he was caught by the shoulders and hurled to the ground. Jonathan was drawing back his foot for a kick to the groin when something made him so dizzy and nauseated that he staggered three paces and fell over a log.

Seconds later, she came hopping, a thorn in her foot, into the glade. Bibbity-bobbing about like anything. Weeping, too.

"Love me," she cried. "I'm not different!"

And she threw herself down beside the dim male form and pulled a limp hand to her breast.

Then she felt the rigor of the flesh.

And blood where manhood should be.

"Jonathan!"

"I'm over here," he gasped, "by the log."

For her last rational thought, Miss Jones resolved never again to take off her spectacles.

Poor old Penny Jones.

Chapter Two

MURDER WAS NOT altogether a bad thing, mused Lieutenant Trompie Kramer of the Trekkersburg Murder Squad. It had its advantages. Every murderer thought as much—even if for only a second split like a tree in a brainstorm. And a surprising number of so-called victims did, too, judging by the way they egged the buggers on.

He throttled hard as his long black Chevrolet sloughed suburbia and joined the dual highway to the country club. He licked up a squelch of tomato sauce for an apéritif before beginning on the hamburger.

Then again, take the rest of the mob: ask them how much they would like to live without murder. Not much. Not at all, once they had thought about it. A man with iron in his soul did a lot for the anemic world most people inhabited; everyone from the pale justices, arranging their pens and pencils like knives and forks, to the pinch-cheeked crones with flasks in the galleries, felt better for being there—while the press boys, ever mindful of the public's needs, added it to all the other good things in the breakfast cereal spooned up over their words. And when the genuine article was not available, there were always the hundreds of murders committed for profit by writers. Yes, they kept things going, just like those pinups in Antarctic weather stations. So at the expense of one, two, say a family of persons, a large chunk of society was kept either too busy or too content or too both to cause trouble. Something that did all this could not be all bad. No, sir.

But wanton sex killings involving the young were quite another matter. Kramer sucked his sticky fingers and wondered why.

He found a partial answer in recalling the Widow

14

Fourie's reaction a few minutes earlier to the news of his assignment. He had given it to her straight, with an apology for spoiling their plans. When she withdrew abruptly into herself, he had apologized again. It was then that he noticed she was trying to keep her eyes from the door of the children's bedroom. And that was his answer: this sort of murder was the one kind that could happen to anyone. You and particularly yours were eligible, maybe not this time but next time, no matter how much care you took to avoid sordid situations, no matter how often you slept with a cop. Just to know there was a homicidal pervert at large was to find yourself perversely cursing the fact you had four fine, attractive kids. *Attractive!* Man, everything sweet turned bitter when there was an animal in the shadows.

An oncoming vehicle glared before dipping its headlights, reminding Kramer of the way expert witnesses always looked down suddenly whenever he said animal. To hell with them and all that crap about mumsy-love and arsehole fix-whatsits; he knew what he was talking about. Human beings you investigated, animals you had to hunt.

And because he was a detective, not a bloody game ranger, this always niggled. So much—

His foot had jumped from accelerator to brake.

Not a hundred yards ahead a Land-Rover had emerged from behind a tarpaulined bulldozer to make placidly for the center island. At its present speed, with the bulldozer already blocking some of the road, the Chevrolet could take only one line into the next bend and that was straight through the Land-Rover.

These were the discernible facts.

Instantly Kramer confirmed his reflex decision by stamping on the pedal and careering into a tight spin just as the other driver glanced round in surprise at such an intrusion. He was that type. The sort who try to make combustion engines leap for dear life. The Land-Rover stalled. Kramer closed his eyes.

Opening them again in a sudden quiet to find himself at rest, facing the way he had come. It was a relief, too, discovering the Chevrolet had followed him round. Everything seemed intact—especially the bulldozer. Kramer uttered a short, unorthodox prayer.

15

But the Land-Rover driver did not linger to join him in it. All Kramer got was the registration number from the back plate. Crazy bloody farmer.

Now that, thought Kramer, as he continued up through the wattles to the country club, was what got his goat about sex killings: they were hit-and-run jobs. Time and place were merely coincidental—the only link between the participants was a single, spontaneous act of violence. And so, with no history of emotional interaction to provide the x and y of an equation, his customary reliance on flashes of analytical brilliance became totally inappropriate.

No less inappropriate, in fact, than asking the intimates of someone flattened by a rogue rhino if the deceased had ever quarreled with the beast.

Oh, ja, little wonder game rangers were such an unsophisticated bunch.

Blood in moonlight looks black.

Constable Hendriks had noted this on numerous occasions without ever making up his mind as to whether it contributed greatly to the overall effect. Sometimes it just reminded him of treacle. Other times—possibly because treacle was something you ate—it made him queasy. That was most often when there were flies about to confuse the issue, but thankfully it was long past their bedtime. As it was his own and presumably that of the kid at his feet.

He yawned.

Then stiffened into an attitude of ostentatious vigilance at the sound of footsteps approaching. They stopped just behind the perimeter of the glade.

"All right, where do you want them?"

"Hey? Who's there?"

"Sorry, mate, don't speak the lingo—Station Officer Pringle, fire brigade, with the lights you wanted."

There were six firemen waiting at a respectful distance with Pringle; two carrying a portable generator, three juggling lamps, and the other draped in coils of heavy-duty flex. All of them trying to get a glimpse of what welcome tragedy had broken the monotony of grass fires and snooker.

"I hear it's a kiddie," the shortest fireman said in Afrikaans.

Hendriks shrugged but moved to his side.

"What's with this redneck?" he asked, hard-eying Pringle. "Another bloody English immigrant?"

"Oh, no, he's come down from the north. He's all right."

Pringle must have recognized the apologetic, having heard it made for him before. He added helpfully, "Uganda."

"Ja, it's very bad up there," Hendriks replied with grave authority—and in English.

Everybody smiled.

There was a pause. Pringle wriggled a finger through his tunic and pajama top to scratch a heat rash. The pair with the generator grew impatient for orders and put it down where they stood. Pringle lifted an eyebrow, letting it go after a moment's mature consideration.

"And why not?" he said. "Us lads were told not to get too close because of footprints et cetera. Shall we string the floods round the trees here?"

"Fine. Need a hand?"

"Manage best on our own, thanks. Carry on, Viljoen."

"Sir."

"I'll just prime the generator meantime," Pringle said. And as he did so, he explained to Hendriks that his hometown was Margate. Hendriks said that Margate was not bad but the shark nets cramped his style. Pringle explained that *his* Margate was the *other* Margate although, of course, the one on the Indian Ocean was by far the prettier. Hendriks said that he preferred Umkomaas for his holidays anyway.

It was not much of a conversation, still less a dialogue, but it succeeded in establishing an air of professional nonchalance. Mutual respect grew apace.

In under five minutes the lamps were secured to the trees and connected to the generator. Pringle yanked on the starting lanyard and the small engine took first time, startling a wood pigeon out of the branches overhead with a loud clatter of wings. When Hendriks and the others, who all looked up at the noise, brought their gaze back to

17

the glade, they gave a little gasp like children at a panto-
mime when the curtain rises.

First, a slow fade up on the fairy grotto, as the generator's coil worked up to maximum revolutions, and then
each twig, leaf, and stalk of grass was finally revealed with
a vivid, artificial brittleness against the black flats of the
deep forest. All wire and paper and paint, it looked. The
lights pulsed to the quick beat of the two-stroke, investing
the unreality of the scene with a flickering life of its own.

And in the center sprawled a naked fairy. It had to be a
fairy because, as everyone there could see, it was sexless.

If only very recently so.

Kramer found Sergeant Bokkie Kritzinger waiting for him
in the car park at the country club, indulging in an un-
seemly personal eccentricity.

"Still chewing it then, Bokkie?"

The big fellow spat out the end of his tie.

"Sir? Just feeling a bit jumpy, that's all."

"But why come outside?"

"I wanted a word with you before you saw them—
there's something really funny going on."

"Who's this you're talking about?"

"That boy and girl who say they found the kid. They've
got blood on them."

"So you said over the phone."

"I don't just mean the hands now. I've had a better
look—it's underneath."

"What?"

"Their clothes."

"But—"

"On their *bodies*, sir!"

Kramer reached out and tucked the damp tip of Bokkie's tie into the bulging blue shirt front. The sergeant
grinned, hiding fists behind his back.

"In there you mean, Bokkie?"

"Sir."

"Then we'd better start again with their story. Here, we
can sit in this thing."

They filled the front seat of the fire department's emer-
gency tender. Kramer lit up a Lucky Strike and found the

18

multipurpose contraption had everything save an ashtray for his match.

"Well, sir, it's the same as before really. The bloke is a Transvaal junior tennis champion by the name of Jonathan Rogers. Age seventeen, last year at school, and English-speaking. The girl's Penelope Jones, sixteen years of age, doing her matric, and she comes from over Greenside way."

"What have they said happened?"

"The boy claims he left the dance—a Trekkersburg Tennis Club do for the visiting teams—at approximately eleven. He and the girl wanted to look at the city at night."

"From inside a plantation?"

"His story, sir. Anyway, I asked him the same question and he said he thought there was a little hill down there where you went for the lights."

"Uhuh."

"They were going along when they saw this boy who seemed to be watching them. He had his head in the fork of a tree, like so, with his arms out either side and sort of leaning on it."

"And then?"

"Rogers says he asked the boy what he was doing there. When the boy didn't say anything, did nothing, they went up to him. They then thought he'd slid down the tree and got caught in it. That he was hurt. Rogers says they tried to lift him off and he toppled backwards on top of them and they fell underneath. That's when they realized he—"

"Took them long enough!"

"What I thought, sir."

"Blood?"

"Plenty."

"And how long do you think the boy's been dead?"

"He was still pretty warm when I got there around midnight."

"I see. And what does the girl have to say?"

"Nothing."

"Hey?"

"Shocked out of her mind. In the club secretary's office just sitting. You can't get her to open her mouth. When she looks at you, your arse goes tight. I tell you there's

19

something bloody weird about all this, sir. That's why I've kept her father away so far."

"Good man. Who's with her now—and the boy?"

"Constable Williams. He's having a hell of a job keeping them out."

"Who?"

"The secretary, Pipson; Mr. Jones, the father; and the Transvaal coach, Freddie Harris."

"What the hell?"

"Really doing his nut, this Freddie. Says his chances of the singles championship are ruined—doesn't think the rest of the team will be up to much in the morning either; all too upset."

"Bugger me, and there's a kid. . . . Any identification yet?"

"Central are looking after that; nothing so far. I've asked for the dogs and the extra men and everything, like you said. The district surgeon is on his way now."

"Uhuh. What about the rest of the dance?"

"All gone home or back in their hotels."

"Good."

"Do you agree there's some . . . ?"

"Look, Bokkie, I never agree until I have facts that agree. Maybe there is something strange, maybe not. You go back and keep those two quiet and I'll take a look-see in the trees. I can hear they've got the lighting going."

With the sigh of the subordinate who is so often right yet never heeded by his superiors, Bokkie slid off the seat and landed heavily on the tarmac. He paused to hitch his button-down holster round to its correct position.

"Bokkie," Kramer murmured, "has it perhaps not occurred to you it might be *her* blood?"

As the father of two preadolescent girls, Sergeant Kritzinger understandably appeared shocked.

It was true, the body was warm to the touch. Very warm although several hours must have passed for blood to congeal like that. Most peculiar.

Kramer rubbed his fingers in the sand and stood up.

"Good-looking kid," he observed.

Hendriks gaped incredulously at the swollen features

20

and pair of staring blue eyes. Somewhere there was a face.

"Got a nice smile," he replied gamely.

Which made it Kramer's turn to wince and cast an odd look.

"Come on, man. When you've finished poking your brains about, we'll get the rest of the notes down."

Hendriks removed the pencil from his earhole.

"Right. We've been once over the surrounding area and found bugger all. Now for the body—write 'one' in the margin."

"Body One."

"Boy strangled by wire twisted eight times at back of neck. No defensive wounds or bruises on arms, suggests he was attacked without warning from behind and that other injuries were sustained afterwards. Description of wire: ten-gauge baling wire as found round fruit boxes, soft, bends easily. No sign of rust and it has kinks in it at approximately four-inch intervals, which suggests it was carried to the scene of crime."

Kramer lit a Lucky Strike and waited for Hendriks to catch up.

"Two: Severe grazing under chin and on either side of jaw with fragments of Tree A's bark adhering to wounds. This is consistent with description given by witness Rogers that he found the body semierect against Tree A with chin wedged in fork. This is backed up by pool of blood at base of Tree A."

"And the blood on the tree, sir."

"How fast can you write? Okay, put it down, too, and add pressure mark along torso. Now Number Three . . ."

Squatting down, Kramer made another examination of the body before going on.

"Three: Multiple stab wounds in and around groin, genitals severed, later recovered beside Tree A. Wound characteristics suggest curved knife used while body was up-right."

"How come, Lieutenant?"

"He's not big, man. When these bastards get worked up they've the strength of a bloody ox. Easily hold him up against the tree with one hand. More notes now: Mutilations consistent with frenzied attack by pervert—more

21

misses than hits. Bleeding limited, but a smear indicates area handled after death. Got it?

"Then Number Four: Back marked by long cuts, three across shoulders, another bisecting them and traveling from nape of neck to left buttock. These wounds suggest a ritual killing.

"And lastly, Number Five: Brown birthmark on right shoulder."

A Bantu constable appeared shyly at the edge of the light, holding his knobkerrie as if he did not know what to do with it in polite company.

"What is it, man?"

"Sergeant Kritzinger says I must come for the clothes, my father."

"Got the plastic bags?"

Kramer took them and packed away the white T-shirt, khaki shorts, and Y-front underpants found near the forked tree. He put the contents of the pockets—a khaki handkerchief, pencil eraser, three bubble gum wrappers, and single-bladed penknife—in a separate container.

"There you are. Tell the sergeant that the body has a brown mark like a spoon on the right shoulder, if he doesn't know that already. And say there are no shoes because the little boss was going barefoot."

"Doctor coming now, sir."

"Bugger off then."

Kramer paused to wonder if there was not something else he should pass on to Kritzinger. Then he turned to Hendriks again and frowned: he was sick of being lumbered with pimply youths who put in every spare moment on their pus crop. Hendriks was working his way along a row just above the back of his collar, reaping the golden harvest on a corner of his handkerchief. It was enough to turn any man's stomach.

"What are you planning to do with that thing?" Kramer snapped. "Pour water on it like a tea bag?"

Hendriks blushed—he was young enough to do that, too, the backveld clown. You could see that he was beginning to remember things he had said about present company. So much to the good.

Kramer picked up one of the long torches the firemen had brought down before being ordered away with mutters to wait at the tender. The beam was so strong it seemed solid enough to tap the twigs off the trees. Another, just as powerful, was tossed across to Hendriks.

"Right. I'm going to take a look at where this bloke says he and the girl first saw the kid from. You stay here and go over the glade again."

"But, sir—"

Kramer was just stepping out of the light when he spun round and caught Hendriks in midgrimace.

"Maybe you'll make a better job of it if I tell you there *is* something for you to find," he said.

"How do you know, sir?"

"Because I planted it there. It's my cigarette stub, a Texan. Okay?"

And Kramer permitted himself a smirk as he moved carefully into the bracken. Hendriks should have noticed something wrong about that brand name.

But the joke was short-lived. Kramer had hardly made the most of a patch of curiously flattened vegetation before there came a triumphant cry.

"I've found it!"

"Hey?"

"Your Texan, sir."

Jesus.

"But have you done it all yet?"

"Almost. I've got two other blokes helping me now and Dr. Strydom's come."

Kramer sighed. He had just begun to enjoy himself discovering things about a young tennis star who should know better than to tell such lies. It was also a shame that his ruse, planned to inspire a feverish search, had been nipped in the bud.

He began to move back along a path someone had forced through the undergrowth while traveling on one foot; a normal footfall made no impression on the messy carpet of compost, but a body's full weight concentrated on a single heel was something else. By holding a torch almost flat on the ground, a series of depressions was thrown into relief. Hmmm. Interesting.

Dr. Strydom was already at work; crouched like a tubby garden gnome in civvies, complete with gray goatee,

23

but flicking an anal thermometer instead of a fly rod. He slipped it in and smiled at Kramer.

"Hello, there, Lieutcnant. The lad's got a bit of a temp. We'll soon see to that."

"He seemed very warm."

"Yes. Of course, it's quite common in cases of asphyxia due to constriction of the neck."

Hendriks and a couple of other constables, whom Kramer recognized from the Central, drifted across.

"*Ach,* really?" asked the one with his first mustache, which was longer than any hair on his scalp.

"Oh, yes, and cerebral hemorrhage produces much the same results now and then. Had a woman not long ago who hanged herself in jail and she was pushing the mercury up over the hundred mark three hours later."

"How about that?" Hendriks remarked, the marvels of science driving from his mind any thought of his own discovery.

"This young fellow filled me in on your conclusions with regard to the injuries, Lieutenant. They seem pretty fair to me: the usual sex killer's workout. Talk about circumcision . . ."

Dr. Strydom rummaged in his bag for cotton wool. He wiped the thermometer and tilted it to catch the light.

"There you are, my boys, let's see what this tells us."

Kramer snapped his fingers and pointed to the stub. Hendriks handed it over with a grin and then, like his colleagues, gave his full attention to medical matters.

The stub was a Texan and it was fresh and that was not all.

"Almighty God, but this isn't an easy one to guess, Lieutenant."

Kramer glanced up.

"What do you mean?"

"You see, if we go on the usual average of the body cooling at about two degrees an hour over the first twelve, it's easy. But here you have a naked body, that cools half as fast again. Got that? But—ah, another but—it's a hot night, which slows things down. On top of which, you were right—the body temp is above normal."

"So?"

"I've got to make some sort of allowance for the fact it's a child and pretty thin-muscled at that."

"Want me to do your sums for you, Doctor?"

"Please, just let me explain why I can't be certain. There are other factors, too. These dark stains indicate postmortem lividity but they're not as definite as I would expect."

"The body has been moved, remember."

"Ah, that helps. Let me see. . . ."

Dr. Strydom felt the limbs.

"Rigor's no guide at all on this occasion—it's hot and he's not a big chappie. Sets in faster, you see, especially if the metabolism is pronounced at death, which it would be if he'd been running to get away or anything."

"Just an estimate, for God's sake!"

"Make it around six last night. No earlier than five."

"Thanks. Now I've a little business at the clubhouse. Keep an eye on things here, Hendriks."

"Okay."

"One other thing, Hendriks."

"Ja?"

"What do you take me for? A bloody pansy?"

"Sir?"

But Kramer was gone, crashing away up the slope, carrying with him a Texan stub that bore a faint trace of orange lipstick.

Chapter Three

IT WAS 2 A. M. but far from the still of the night.

In the clubhouse hallway Freddie Harris, Mr. Jones, and Sergeant Kritzinger were caught in their own verbal crossfire and ricocheting their row off the walls right down to the ballroom. There a pair of dog handlers were trying to keep their charges away from the potted palms while about thirty uniformed men milled about discussing what they would do to the murdering bastard when they caught him. And from the kitchen came the harsh sounds of a team of Bantu detectives interrogating the club's ground staff—all of whom had been dragged from their beds in the compound and thought it must be a private nightmare.

The billiard room was the quietest spot Kramer could find. And it had become even quieter now that Jonathan Rogers had stopped bawling like a baby.

"Where should I put it, Miss Jones?" Kramer asked, using the rest for his cue. "The top pocket or the middle?"

Still nothing would evince the slightest response in her. The yellow ball cannoned off a loose red; one went in the top and one in the middle. Not a flicker.

"I should have known," Jonathan said.

"That's what I'm paid for," Kramer replied lightly, "putting the old two and two together—or, in your case, the two and one. Nice of you to round it off for me."

"But the detail!"

Kramer placed the corner torn off a small aluminum foil packet on the edge of the table. Jonathan whimpered.

"It's all right, son—I'm not a Catholic. Just thought you'd be interested. And so everything had an answer—even the blood."

"You do believe me?"

26

"Why not? Besides, you've got an alibi for the early part of the evening and that's all that matters. It's simply my job to tie up all the loose ends. Got a smoke? I'm out."

Jonathan fumbled a packet from his jacket and held it out.

"Texans, hey? Smoke a Texan and cough like a cowboy. Want one, too?"

"No, thanks."

Kramer lit up and chalked his cue.

"How come a tennis player smokes?"

"At—only at parties."

"Uhuh."

The brown shared a pocket with another red—always a tricky shot.

"When was your last, may I ask?"

"Cigarette? Afterwards, I think. To steady my nerves. Yes."

"And Miss Jones here?"

"She doesn't—"

"Not in the syllabus?"

"*Please!*"

"So you didn't try to snap her out of it with one little puff?"

"No!"

"Okay, okay. Think I could wipe off a bit of her makeup? Ask her for me."

Jonathan whispered to Miss Jones, who merely swallowed noisily.

"Go ahead, Lieutenant. I'm sure it . . ."

Kramer wandered over, tearing open a used envelope.

"Few things cleaner than the inside of one of these things," he remarked. "Remember a nurse telling me once it was almost sterile if you needed something for first aid. It'll do very nicely."

He braced Miss Jones gently with his left hand behind her head and then pressed the envelope over her lips. When the paper came away, it bore a large, sticky print in orange lipstick.

"She puts it on thick!"

"I told you, Lieutenant, she just wasn't very used to this sort of function."

27

"I bet."

One loose end dangled.

"What are you looking at me like that for?"

"You say you kissed Miss Jones?"

"Er—ycs."

"Hard? Often? Make a meal of it, did you?"

"We—"

"Come over here under the big light."

Jonathan hesitated.

"What's the matter? Think I'm going to give you the third degree?"

The youth came across. There was a tiny orange smear dead center of his upper lip—exactly where you would expect a novice smoker to pout for a draw. Simple, when you knew how.

"I think you can go now, and Miss Jones, too. I'll send somebody round for a written statement tomorrow. We'll overlook what you said to Sergeant Kritzinger earlier on."

"Then—are you saying that I haven't done anything wrong?"

"I'm Murder Squad, son, not bloody Vice Squad. Good luck with her pa."

Kramer stepped out of the billiard room, pulling the door shut behind him and absently tucking the envelope away with the stub. He carried more junk about in his pockets than nine kangaroos with kleptomania.

"I say!" said an elegant figure, tossing aside a copy of *Country Life* and rising from a deep leather armchair in the passage. It was that swanky specialist who went around with an Afghan hound in his Lotus and insisted on hot water bottles to warm his hands before touching an opulent abdomen.

"Yes," Kramer prompted irritably. "What do you say?"

"Gerald Jones got me out to take a look at his daughter Penelope. Where is she?"

"Second door down."

"Really? Quite finished with her, are you?"

A specialist in sarcasm, too.

"Yes—and worth quite a penny to you by now."

Without having once broken his stride, Kramer continued on his way.

28

Kritzinger accosted him in the lavatory a minute or so later.

"*Ach*, there you are, Lieutenant! I've been all round the building. They've got a possible identification for you."

"Oh, yeth?"

Kritzinger tactfully averted his eyes. Kramer was washing a denture under the cold tap.

"That's better; bloody hamburger had chips of bone in it. Got underneath. Go on, Bokkie."

"There's a boy aged twelve answering the description, including the birthmark, who was reported missing around midnight. Name's Boetie Swanepoel and the address is 38 Schoeman Road."

"Close by, isn't it?"

"At the bottom of the hill, over the river. They last saw him at lunch."

"But twelve years old and they only report it at midnight?"

"Told Central that they'd been to a special church meeting."

"Hey?"

"I know, sir. Perhaps we'd better send a bloke around to clear up the details right away."

"Isn't the father coming up?"

"Their minister asked if he could do it instead and the Colonel said yes."

"So the Colonel's here now?"

"In the ballroom, seeing to the briefing for you."

"Thank God for that."

Kritzinger grinned. Kramer's total aversion to working with a team, let alone organizing one, was well known. Legendary, almost. In fact, there was a joke about it in the NCO's mess which had for a punch line: "So the lieutenant says to her, 'But *of course* I came by myself, lady!' "

"What the hell's the matter, Sergeant? Did I put them in upside down?"

"Sir?"

"Never mind. Come, let's see what the Colonel's up to before we plan anything else. We could even get lucky and be sent home to bed."

"After you, sir."

29

They arrived in the ballroom just as the last of the search parties tramped off into the night across the wide veranda. Colonel Hans Muller was all by himself at a table littered with maps, snacks, bottles, and party hats. He was trying on the helmet of a London Metropolitan policeman.

Now there was a man who came damn close to being after Kramer's own heart. Tall enough to look you straight in the eye, and broad-minded enough not to go asking a lot of fool questions all the time. A real professional, in other words—and what a change from Du Plessis. He was also, as the papier-mâché headgear indicated, possessed of a winning cynicism that sorted the sheep from the goats.

As of that moment, Kritzinger was finding it almost impossible not to look like an astonished merino.

"Hello, sir," Kramer murmured casually, keeping his eyes perfectly level.

"Lieutenant Kramer—I was hoping you'd turn up. The men and the dogs are out but I don't think we'll get very far with them."

"Good for the papers, sir."

"Exactly. Now you must have a few things to tell me, but I don't think we need detain the sergeant."

"Bookie, go and see that the Jones mob push off."

"And then, sir?"

"Listen for the phone in the secretary's office."

The Colonel waited until they were alone.

"Right, take a seat, tell me about the blood on those two."

"Not material to the case."

"Don't waste time on it, then. I hear the murder was sometime around six."

"Thereabouts. Strydom isn't going to swear to anything more definite."

"And otherwise?"

"Usual bit of passion and panga."

"You mustn't get me wrong, Lieutenant, I want to get this bastard, but—hell!—it makes me bloody tired just to think of all the trouble it's going to be."

"And then we might not make it."

"True, too."

The Colonel picked out an unopened bottle of lager,

opened it, halved the contents, and handed a glass to Kramer.

"Cheers."

"Cheers, sir."

Kramer allowed his thoughts to rise with the tiny amber bubbles and pop unconsidered on the surface. The only sound was the swish of the big fans hanging from the ceiling. He wished it could stay that way for a while. He needed a break.

"Hmmm. Wrapped up the Shabalala case this morning?"

"Yes, sir. Remanded to the Supreme Court on the fourteenth."

"You're free, then?"

"Sir."

"Well, I'm a long way behind on the armed raids in Zululand so I'm giving this one back to you—it's all yours."

"What exactly do you mean by that, Colonel?"

"I don't want to know.".

"Until I've got something?"

"No, got *someone*. Okay?"

Kramer raised his glass to him—and noticed the funny hat was gone.

"So let me show you what I've arranged here tonight. . . ."

The Colonel took a sausage and placed it carefully on the already stained map.

"There is the body."

He arranged a handful of cocktail sticks around it so they radiated out down the hill.

"I've put teams out to search along these lines—the dogs are just picking up what they can. You'll see that the fellows going along this way must meet the others along that stick and so they'll cross over and double-check on the way back here. Like you, I haven't much hope they'll find anything so you'd better start working through known weirdos first thing in the morning. Any questions?"

"Have a nut, sir," Kramer said, offering him a bowl of them. "Make sure you get the right one."

Swish-swish went the big bright blades overhead.

And then the Colonel smiled with great care, as if his

31

teeth were bad. They were not. It was just the awkwardness of a well-mannered man who sees only his own jokes.

But the point had been made.

"Don't worry, I know the problems," he said. "Every mother in the town will be screaming for your blood if—We've got a visitor."

The middle-aged man advancing recklessly across the slippery dance floor wore the solemn garb of a minister in the Dutch Reformed Church. His smooth, flat face was paper white, making his mustache somehow not quite part of it—rather like a black postage stamp affixed beneath the blunt nose. This illusion was heightened by the way he kept pressing at it with the back of a hand.

Predictably he went right on by to be sick in the azaleas before returning to introduce himself.

"I'm Dominee Pretorius," he said. "Please forgive a moment's weakness. The Almighty has never before made such demands."

Kramer immediately gave up his chair.

"Was it Boetie?" the Colonel asked.

Dominee Pretorius nodded woefully.

"And have you known him long?"

"Since a babe in arms. Since a movement in his mother's womb."

What you might call a real friend of the family. Kramer brightened.

"But can you tell us anything about him as far as to-day—I mean yesterday—is concerned? Have you seen his parents?"

"Seen them? I've been sitting up with them until half an hour ago, going over it again and again."

"What."

"Where he was—what might have become of him. Dear God, we never imagined anything like this."

"Then can you tell us his movements?"

"Look, I must be going," the Colonel interrupted. "I'm sorry if I seem rude, Dominee, but there's work waiting at HQ. Anyway, Lieutenant Kramer is in charge of the case—I know you'll give him all the help you can."

"Of course."

"And you are sure that you're quite free, Lieutenant?

32

There are no little jobs left over I could delegate in the morning?"

"I don't think so, sir, thanks. But wait—there is one: here's a registration number I'd like Traffic to check for me before I forget. I'll give them a statement about it later. A bloody fool farmer tried to kill me with his Land-Rover near the bottom of the hill tonight."

"Oh, yes?"

"Came out of his place and right across the dual highway. Maybe you saw where I mean—there's a bulldozer parked by the side of the road."

"Man, I saw the tire marks. But that track doesn't go to a farm—it's for the wattle lorries. What time was this?"

Kramer almost flustered.

"After midnight. Twleve-thirty, perhaps. Half-past twelve."

The Colonel looked at his watch.

"Hmmm. A long time to hang around, I agree. But suppose I get Traffic to follow this one up straightaway?"

"If they don't mind, sir."

"I'll ask them to do it as a special favor—from you."

Hell, the Colonel was a bloody good bloke. But one oversight was all that you were ever allowed and Kramer had a sudden, unpleasant feeling that his score was two.

Hendriks was on the verge of joining the Trekkersburg Fire Department. From what Fireman Viljoen told him, as they shared a log in the now deserted glade, the pay and conditions compared more than favorably with his own. You spent twenty-four hours on fire duty, twenty-four on ambulance duty, and then had the next twenty-four all to yourself. With a set rota like that, the dollies at the post office could take you seriously when you asked for a date. On top of which, you got a decent room of your own (to take them back to), your own washbasin with hot and cold, and proper meals at a private hotel down the road. This, too, was an excellent source of female company, he was vividly assured. Oh, and another thing: it was perfectly natural to appear only half-dressed at the machines when the bells went down, so there was no need to limit yourself to one night in three. All this and an extra twenty rand a month.

33

"How are you off for blokes?" Hendriks asked, attempting merely polite interest and failing.

"Three vacancies."

"Really, hey?"

Hendriks wandered across to the generator. Viljoen watched him uneasily.

"Of course, it's not the same as the police," he said quickly. "Different regulations and all that."

"Jesus, you're not telling me it's tougher, are you?" Hendriks scoffed. "You should have been at police college."

"No, but different."

"How?"

"Little things—heights, and so on."

"Huh! When I was so big I used to hang by my hands from the top of my pa's windmill. You just ask him sometime—he nearly took the backside off me with his belt when he caught me. Said I'd have all the Kaffirs laughing at him if I fell off."

Viljoen made no reply.

"Isn't that good enough for you lot?"

"Fine! Only, you see, I meant heights this way." The fireman put his hand on his head. "Five foot eight."

He said it as nicely as he could but Hendriks reacted as if to a raucous jeer. He reddened and stumped off behind a tree, where he took oblique pleasure in urinating on a toad.

So that was it. But if the South African Police thought five foot six inches was man enough, then he knew where he belonged. And he decided to keep an eye on these fire brigade bastards; men with such amoral standards were capable of anything.

Certainly it was safe to assume that Dominee Pretorius never used notes for a sermon. Man, he could talk. He did for molehills what hormone advertisers claimed to do for flat chests. And the truth of the matter was that Kramer had long since ceased listening.

"Pardon?"

"Boetie won the hundred yards in the swimming gala last year."

"You don't say."

"Yes, and he was going for the record this very week. The ways of the Almighty—"

"Sorry, Dominee, but I think this man has a message for me."

The hovering constable proudly announced he had discovered what appeared to be the boy's bicycle down at the bottom of the plantation, just off the footpath, and hidden outside the fence. Kramer noted the position on the map then dismissed him.

"Well, that's something," he said. "Boetie presumably met up with whoever it was at this spot. Tempted into the plantation—perhaps the bloke promised to show him a rare animal or the like—they headed up this way. Then, sensing trouble, Boetie made for the clubhouse. That's why he was killed there—it's just out of earshot; another fifty yards and you're on the pitch-and-putt course."

What he did not say was that the bicycle had been found very near to the point where the Land-Rover emerged in a manner so precipitate it seemed now the kind of thing a man with other things on his mind might do. Murder, for instance. Kramer silently cursed Traffic for taking all night to trace the owner.

The Dominee sighed.

"Beats me how you fellows work these things out," he said.

"Ah, but so far just guesswork. Would you agree with the reason I gave for Boetie going into the trees?"

"He always had an inquiring nature."

"Too inquiring?"

"But what do you mean?"

"I'm trying to ask a question you won't like but his parents would like less: have you ever had any reason to suppose that Boetie wasn't—shall we say a normal, healthy boy with normal, healthy interests?"

"Lieutenant," replied the Dominee most gravely, "as God Himself is my witness, this boy was all that is pure and divinely inspired about the Afrikaner people. Let me tell you—"

Again Kramer cut him short.

"No, it's best I try to recap and you can check if I've got the main facts right. I'm pleased to hear what you say

35

about Boetie, by the way; it's just we must know as much as we can."

"I understand. Please proceed."

"Boetie went around to his friend Hennie's house after school and the two of them went out shooting. They came back after five. Boetie said he'd better get home for supper, leaving on his bike. The parents were not at home, having left early to go to a meeting in the church hall. When the servant girl had waited up until eight without him returning, she imagined he'd stayed at Hennie's for a meal. It was not until midnight that Mr. and Mrs. Swanepoel returned and found him missing. Normally he always informed them of his movements and this was why they contacted the police."

"Correct. It was a very long meeting on the Synod resolutions."

"Yet how do you explain him finishing up over on this side, a mile from his house that was just around the corner?"

"Very simple, I would think. The boys like to cut across the stream and take the footpath round here because it makes an exciting ride. That's probably what Boetie was up to. There was still plenty of time for him to get home for his meal. He knew it was just the servant girl waiting."

"Hmmm. How do they get back, then?"

"They push their bikes over the railway bridge. As a matter of fact, that's why I know about this practice of theirs—some parents are very concerned about the hazards involved."

"Understandably."

"With the trains, I mean."

Kramer got up to stretch.

"Boetie was a good pupil, a regular churchgoer, and a credit to his parents."

"They trusted him implicitly."

"Then this must have happened out of the blue. That's basically what I needed to know."

Sergeant Kritzinger was beckoning with a piece of paper from the far side of the hall. Traffic had finally surfaced.

"Thanks a million for your help, Dominee. I must go now—sorry."

But the minister insisted on the last, pompous word.

"I would that it had only happened to an old sinner like myself," he intoned. "Don't smile, Lieutenant. I have known them all—and vanquished them, every one."

Except perhaps gluttony. Someone had guzzled the sausage marker.

The Chevrolet was almost opposite the bulldozer on its way down again when the hair on Kramer's neck lifted slightly: he was not alone. He thought about it for a fast quarter mile and then wound up his window. He sniffed carefully. The cheap pomade, so pungently sweet it was capable of fertilizing a pawpaw tree at forty yards, proved unmistakable. He found the other hamburger and tossed it over his shoulder.

"Fizz-bang, you're dead," he said.

"Very nice, too," replied Bantu Detective Sergeant Mickey Zondi, who fitted exactly across the back seat but chose, for reasons of his own, to lie on the floorboards.

"And what are you doing in my car?"

No answer. Merely a steady munching.

"Were you questioning the Bantu staff in the kitchen?"

"No, boss. I got a lift up with Dr. Strydom."

"He didn't say anything about that."

"He didn't, boss?"

Kramer saw the point and laughed.

"You're going to get me into trouble one of these days—you know that?"

"*Hau!* I am very sorry."

Then they laughed together, as they often did when on their own.

"Is this a Bantu case, boss?"

"Since when have Kaffirs gone around committing sex killings on white kids? Of course not. Perfectly straightforward and I think we're already on to the bugger that did it. Want to get off here and go back to Central?"

"I'll come with."

Kramer ignored all the traffic lights through the city center—it was still very early in the morning—and took the Durban road, watching the street names on the left.

He swung into Potter's Place. The homes round about were modest bungalows succumbing, in their middle age, to an ill-becoming trendiness; bright colors had been painted over the exterior woodwork and all sorts of rubbish, old street lamps and wagon wheels, littered the small frontages. No. 9 Potter's Place was untidier than most and a child had been scribbling on the garage door. This door was closed, but the chunky tracks of a Land-Rover could be seen clearly in the dried mud of the short driveway.

The Chevrolet stopped two houses further on. Kramer and Zondi walked back and up the path. Somebody was singing in a low bass on the walled veranda.

"Stay here," Kramer ordered, mounting the steps.

A Zulu houseboy jumped up, his knees red with the floor polish he had applied so lavishly, and went bug-eyed. He did it very well, considering the hour—which was, according to the grandfather clock in the hall passage, a minute after six.

"Police," Kramer cautioned. "You shut up or I'll call my boy."

The Zulu peered over the wall at Zondi, dropped to his knees again, and slipped a hand under the brush strap. He went on scrubbing away.

"Every man to his job," Kramer remarked with satisfaction, stepping into the house.

All was quiet; but nobody would think of stirring until the veranda shone like a tart's toenail and the tea was brought in. There was ample opportunity for a preliminary survey.

Behind the door, where they had been dimly visible through frosted glass panels, were a collection of coats and other outdoor garments. The driver of the Land-Rover had been wearing something greenish. A scruffy sports jacket came as near to the color as any—and it had been hung up last of all.

Kramer lifted one sleeve to inspect the cuff. What he noticed there halted his breathing.

He wet a finger and dabbed at one of the brown specks, seeing his spittle turn pink. He gave it the nose test.

The same with the other cuff.

Blood.

It was too easy. Too easy and too like what happened when the gods played silly buggers. An alert sounded within.

Right then someone behind him said, "Stick 'em up."

Chapter Four

KRAMER STUCK THEM up. He waited a moment and then turned around, lowering one hand to lay a finger on his lips.

"Don't shoot," he begged in a whisper.

Bang.

"I said—"

"You're dead," the small boy informed him. "And when you're dead, you can't talk."

"Quite right."

"I know. I'm not stupid like Susan."

"Who's that?"

"My baby sister. She's three."

"And you are?"

"Fi—no, six. It was my birthday yesterday. Guess what I got?"

"A cap gun?"

"*And* a microscope."

So this was how a mad scientist appeared during his formative years.

"I say, Mungo?" The sleep-slurred voice came from behind a door on the bedroom side of the house. "What in heaven's name are you doing? Not trying to frighten poor Jafini, are you?"

"No, Daddy, it's a man."

"What man?"

Mungo appraised Kramer, sizing him up thoroughly the way children do when they can see how tidy a fellow keeps his nostrils. Then he paused to wrinkle his brow and select a category.

"It's an uncle-ish sort of man with very short hair and big front teeth like a rodent."

Kramer snorted.

"Aren't you an uncle?" inquired Mungo politely.

"No, I'm a policeman."

"Oh, good! Then show me yours and I'll show you mine."

"Hey?"

"*Your* gun, of course!"

He damn nearly did.

"Get your father!"

"Will you?"

"Scoot!"

Mungo retired with dignity and there were whisperings. Kramer stepped back onto the doorstep. Things had got out of hand. Nor did they add up. Still, there was undoubtedly blood on that jacket and some family men had been known to live extremely private lives.

From the bedroom emerged a shock-haired, bearded weirdo in a tartan dressing gown and Wellington boots. He was about thirty-five, slightly built except for the hands, and like a tick bird in his movements—jerky yet enormously precise.

"Yes?" he said, bringing to his face a half-smile which never left it again. Kramer was immediately reminded of the anxious expression worn by travelers being addressed in a foreign tongue.

"CID. I'm Lieutenant Kramer."

"Yes?"

"Philip Sven Nielsen?"

"Correct."

"You are the owner of a long-wheelbase Land-Rover registered as NTK 1708?"

Nielsen nodded.

"And you were driving this vehicle in the vicinity of the Trekkersburg Country Club at 12:30 A.M. this morning?"

"But—"

"Were you?"

"Oh, yes. I was out collecting."

"What exactly?"

"Excreta."

"Pardon?"

Nielsen looked to one side as if sneaking a peep at a phrasebook.

"Shrew shit," he said.

41

Now there was something to conjure with.

Danny Govender did the job because his father, mother, three sisters, two brothers, widowed uncle, half-cousin, and half-witted grandfather needed the money. It was as simple as that, they told him, and would hear none of his protests.

Such was the price of success, limited though that might be for a twelve-year-old Indian.

In the beginning, Danny had been fired with ambition. Something all too obvious to the dispatch foreman at the *Trekkersburg Gazette* who gave him his first newspaper round. A bleak, slothful man himself, he had hoped to break the persistent little bastard's spirit by awarding him the Marriott Drive area. This toy-block scattering of multistory apartment houses, with very few auxiliary lifts marked FOR NON-WHITES, was generally too much for a full-grown coolie, let alone a bandy-legged runt.

But somehow the foreman's plan had gone wrong—or right, depending on which way you looked at it. All of a sudden there were no more calls from irate subscribers down Marriott Drive way. Danny was getting up and down those stairs like a rock rabbit.

And more. He was rolling his papers neatly, being careful not to upset milk bottles, whistling silently, and winning the affection of every housewife up early enough to return one of his betel-nut smiles through her kitchen window. Someone even wrote a *Letter to the Editor*, saying what a joy it was to encounter a child who so loved his work.

That inadvertently chucked a handful in the fan, all right; the foreman was summoned to the dispatch manager's office and there upbraided for squandering such an asset on mere flat dwellers. After all, he was forcefully reminded, it was the manager who dealt with the irate Greenside subscribers who invariably began their calls with: "I would have you know that the managing director of your paper is a personal friend of mine. . . ."

Danny shot to the top overnight—the Boxing Day handouts in Greenside were enough to keep you in Cokes for the year. But, curiously, the boy he deposed seemed only mildly aggrieved. Perhaps there was a snag.

There was.

Danny discovered it the hard way: the bigger the property, the longer the drive leading up to the house, and the meaner the dogs—creatures so incredibly stupid they could not distinguish between an aquiline profile and a flat one. If it was two-legged, dark-skinned, and not employed on the premises, they attempted a disembowelment.

The big house coming up now on his right retained one of the most serious threats to his survival; an enormous, long-fanged, tatty-eared hellion called Regina by the family.

He called her "nice doggy" and ran like hell.

That was on the first day, and he got all of fifteen paces before going down screaming. Luckily the head garden boy was out early, dampening the lawns before the sun got going, and he had called the bitch off with a casual, almost regretful, word of command.

On the second day and thereafter, Danny never arrived at the high wooden gate without a bone cadged from the butcher's near the market that opened at five. Regina still pursued him, all right, but, being so incredibly stupid, kept the offering clenched in her jaws and this took care of her bite.

Danny leaned his bicycle against the gatepost. He unwrapped the bone and tossed it over.

There was an indignant yell. Then the head garden boy came charging out, rubbing his shoulder.

"What you do that for, you damn fool?" he demanded.

"Me?" said Danny, quick as a flash.

So the Zulu hurled the bone at him and missed. It hit the bicycle lamp instead and broke the glass. Now came Danny's turn for indignant histrionics.

"You damn fool!" he shouted. "That bike he belonging newspaper Europeans. Big trouble for you now."

A lie, but all the lovelier for it—vendors were required to provide their own transport.

"*Hau*, sorry, I buy new one—you not say," the Zulu urged, very shocked.

"Maybe, we see. But you better having it tomorrow, my boss he is a terrible man. Worse than the dog by this place."

"The dog is dead."

That took a few seconds to register.

"A car hitting it?"

"No."

"God's truth?"

The Zulu nodded.

"Why are you waiting by the gate, big chief? Did they send *you* to bite me?"

This bared the big bully's teeth but he knew what was good for him.

"Me for paper," he muttered. "Want quick today."

Danny handed it over with a flourish.

Then, as he pedaled on up the hill to make his last delivery, he looked back and noted that the curtains in the big house were still drawn across every window. When the servant had said the paper was wanted in a hurry, he thought it must be later than he imagined, but here was evidence to the contrary. Which posed the interesting question: Who had asked for the *Trekkersburg Gazette* so early and why?

He was freewheeling downhill past the big house again when a second question occurred to him: why had the dog, in such robust health two days before on the Saturday, died so suddenly?

Danny decided to have a word with the lad from the Central News Agency who delivered the Sunday papers.

Mungo had to take most of the credit for saving the situation, Kramer acknowledged generously—he himself had only made certain that a respectable citizen would not be protesting an infringement of rights.

"Because that's bloody nearly what happened," he told Zondi as they drove back into the center of Trekkersburg. "I was committed, you see. It was in the bloke's house and he wanted to know the reason. You can't go fooling with people like that even if they are polite face to face. The Colonel does not like that kind of trouble. He can tell them to get lost but he doesn't like it."

"Who could say you were in his house without asking first, boss?"

"This kid Mungo. He told them."

"But you could have said you were just talking to him."

"The trouble was I was stroppy with Nielsen when he

came out. I came on hard—Phillip Sven Nielsen? You know."

"Why, boss?"

"Because I'd already found blood on his jacket sleeves."

That took ten miles an hour off the speedometer.

"Boss Nielsen's?"

"Uhuh. That's where Mungo stopped me making the all-time boo-boo. Thing was I said to Nielsen I wanted to ask him some questions and we'd better go somewhere and sit. He said he'd have to tell his wife what was happening because she'd got a fright, and put me in his study. In the meantime Mungo comes in and wants to look at my gun. I let him and ask if he knows what his father's job is. Of course, he says—not like a normal kid at all, this Mungo; bloody microscopes, hell! His dad's an ecologist and he catches things. Kills them, too. Rabbits, mainly, he tells me, just as his old man walks in."

"And then?"

"He hears what the kid is saying and he adds, I need the blood, you know. Really, I say. He explains he uses it to catch meerkats, carries it around in one of those plastic bowls with a lid—like you put in the fridge. Splashes it all round his traps with a rag."

"His jacket, too."

"Yes, that's about it. By now I'm getting the picture. I tell him we believe he was up in the plantation catching things for ecology, and he says you could put it that way. He is doing a study of one small section and learning all he can about how the food goes from one animal to another. Like what the shrews eat and what eats the shrews. That's why he was working so late; shrews die if they are kept in a trap for too long and he has to empty them every eight hours."

"For how long, boss?"

"He says he's been doing it three years."

"You believe him?"

"There's a place in England, so he tells me, where the scientists have spent twenty-seven years in a forest nonstop."

"White men!" Zondi chuckled.

"I feel the same, Kaffir. Anyway, he asks me what my questions are. I say, as if I know already, Mr. Nielsen,

45

you visit this plantation at eight o'clock in the morning, four o'clock in the afternoon and at midnight? Ja, he says. All right, then, I say, did you notice anyone in the trees at all yesterday?—and I tell him why. He thinks for a long time and then says there was nobody. But, I must remember, he just goes to a small part down near the dual highway. Thanks very much, I tell him, and take my gun back from Mungo."

"So?"

"Then he says, Just a minute, is that all you want to know? He looks at me all suspicious. I don't say anything. Because if it is all, then he wants to ask a question. Go ahead, I say.

"He's no fool, this one. He says, It seems strange to me, Lieutenant, that you feel at liberty to walk into my house, unannounced, to ask a single question which, according to your theories on sex killers, could easily have waited an hour or so. You could have telephoned—or knocked on my door—at seven, when I generally get up.

"Man, I had to think fast. I said, It is urgent, man, because I wanted you to take a look at the murder scene for me before it rains or whatever. Why him? he wants to know. Well, because our forensic experts, ha ha, haven't been able to find anything there of any use to us. He knows the plantation better than anyone; there was just a chance he would spot what we wouldn't.

"But why hadn't I said so in the first place? he wants to know. Look, it's a favor I'm asking, I say. When you ask a favor, you try not to cause any inconvenience. I'm in a hurry, right? Surely it's better I come round and see if he is already awake? And, if not, wait a while in the car outside? I arrive, I see the kid in the passage, I hear he's awake, I ask to see him. Then, because it's a favor, I dither about before asking him because it could be a big waste of time."

Zondi gave the sort of grunt that implied he could not agree more. He picked up speed again.

"The main thing is to let Mr. Nielsen feel important and then send him away happy," Kramer said, really trying to convince himself, rather than Zondi, it was worth all this to avoid a fuss.

"Maybe he will find something, boss."

46

"True but unlikely. I'd thought of that; either way we can't lose."

They arrived at CID headquarters.

"I want the car for an hour, Zondi. See you here at eight and we'll be up at the country club by the time he's finished with his traps."

"Where do you go then?"

"One more bit of unfinished business before I really get stuck into this case. Cheers."

As Kramer drove off, he cursed himself loudly and viciously for having been so impulsive. From here on in, caution was the watchword. What a start to a sodding lousy morning—with the prospect of many more to come. This was definitely not his kind of case. Sod it.

The Widow Fourie presented her cheek to be kissed much as a bishop might his episcopal ring—there was no promise whatever of more intimate communion.

As Kramer never kissed women on the cheek, he ignored it. He pinched her instead.

"Trompie!"

Now that, too, was unlike her.

"What is it?" he asked. "Time of the month?"

"Yes," she said.

"The curse?"

"That's right."

But which curse? A good question. Right from the moment he entered the flat, with just enough time for bed and breakfast, he sensed a definite change in her. It was as though she dreaded something dark she could not quite see over his shoulder.

"Where are the kids?"

"Out."

"So early?"

"I asked Mr. Tomlinson down the passage to take them in the car—he passes the school on his way to varsity."

"It isn't raining, you know."

"I know."

"And so?"

"Nothing."

A whimsy caught Kramer unexpectedly. In the good old days, this would have been his cue to bash her one with a

47

club and drag her off by the hair. Hit her hard enough and temporary amnesia would take care of her troubles. But this was the twentieth century, Western civilization, and she was wearing a wig.

"I'm waiting," she said.

"What for?"

"Did you get him? Or are my kids still—"

"*Ach!* Don't worry, we will."

Strained silence.

"How did you get your hands so dirty?"

"I'll wash."

The Widow Fourie shuddered and went into the kitchen, pausing just inside the doorway until she heard the taps running. Her shadow was a dead giveaway.

It was shorter than she was, squat and broad and a little bowed; come to think of it, rather like the shade of some primitive ancestor apprehensive at the mouth of her cave.

Now a hunter sought admission but, having come from where the sounds of the night were made, his scent would lead the unthinkable right to her litter within.

Suddenly he saw it all.

"I've fried you a couple of eggs. There's no bacon left."

The plate stared balefully up at him with its two yellow eyes, waiting to be blinded by the knife.

"We know who the kid was. He—"

"I don't want to hear."

"But usually—"

"It's repugnant to me."

"Repugnant? Where did you get that one from? The crossword?"

"That's what Mr. Tomlinson called it and he's right. Repugnant."

"Ah, yes, our English-speaking university intellectual."

"He's a very nice man."

"Not repugnant."

"No, but—"

"Go on. Were you going to say . . . ?"

She responded eagerly to the kettle's whistled summons.

And returned with his coffee to find the room empty. Kramer had got the message.

48

The fresh-water crabs must have thought themselves especially favored when enough food to last them through two generations landed in their irrigation ditch. It came sealed in a big brown wrapper. After a week of high excitement, they had just started to get this off when it vanished.

And wound up on the next slab along from Boetie Swanepoel in the Trekkersburg police mortuary.

"I'll start on the Bantu male," Strydom told the attendant, Sergeant Van Rensburg. "No sense in trying to concentrate with a stink like that hanging around."

Van Rensburg had already made the preliminary incision from throat to crotch. All Strydom had to do was reel off enough routine observations to fill up the form. The plain fact of the matter was that a rural Bantu had died because he ate too little.

"Natural causes," Strydom concluded, moving on to the other table.

Boetie lay awkwardly on the channeled porcelain; the headrest was chiefly to blame for this—like the headrest on a barber's chair, it was not designed for the young. But his spare frame left plenty of working space all around him, which made a nice change.

Van Rensburg wheeled the light over and the examination began.

"Yes, someone definitely put their fingers in this lot," Strydom murmured, indicating a smear running up the belly from the lacerated loins. "Yirra, and look at this mark in the leg, man!"

Strydom had spread the legs apart and exposed a bloody mark on the inner thigh.

"That's the shape of the weapon we're after—remind you of anything?"

"No, Doctor."

"Well, it does me. Funny how the end is chopped off nearly at right angles like that."

"Could be the point snapped."

"Hmmm. Anyhow, I think I'll just save this for closer examination before you wash down."

Strydom flayed the area with his scalpel and laid the skin in a small dish. On a flat surface, the dominant characteristic of the weapon's imprint was even more pronounced. They both peered at it closely.

"That thing had a real curve on it," Van Rensburg said. "It wasn't a sheath knife for sure. What about one of those Arab daggers?"

"Not very likely. The width of those blades gets smaller all the way down to the tip. This one stays the same. Also it seems the blade was very flat or it wouldn't have made a clear mark like that. Finished?"

The blood was gone. The wounds were short, deep slashes that gaped like the mouths of smiling babes, each with a rim of subcutaneous fat to give an illusion of toothless gum within.

Strydom found them beguiling; he was sure they could tell him something. And would, given time.

Van Rensburg watched for a while and then helped his Bantu assistant remove the other corpse. A splintery coffin, made by a timber firm that also churned out fruit trays for farmers, was waiting for it in the refrigerator room.

As he measured and probed, Strydom could hear the widow being cursed for having come alone with her small son. So she had brought the coffin along on her head, Van Rensburg bawled, but how the hell did she think she would take it away again full? Still, that was her problem. No, he would not telephone for a taxi. The box scraped over the concrete floor, one bent nailhead screeching, and then the hot draft through the outer door ceased to blow. The fly screen beyond clattered.

"Damn fool," Van Rensburg grunted, taking up his clipboard for notes.

"And a lot of damn noise," Strydom rebuked him.

"Sorry, Doctor."

His tone was so surly that Strydom looked up in surprise. Van Rensburg had always been unbearably sycophantic—this was indeed a welcome indication of personality inversion. The big bruise of a face, purpled by drink and normally sensitive to the slightest touch of criticism, was without expression.

"Something the matter, Sergeant?"

"No, Doctor."

Strydom was sure then that in some way he had offended the great oaf. Exactly how was tantalizing, but best left unexplored if he was to make the most of the situation. Obviously Van Rensburg was desperately seeking a confrontation that would leave him the injured yet forgiving party. The hell with that. A diversion was indicated.

"Look at these wounds," Strydom said, "and tell me if the pattern means anything to you."

Van Rensburg shrugged.

The pattern had not meant a thing to Strydom either—until he started talking.

"Let's start by assuming that the object was mutilation—and mutilation of the genitals. But it is immediately apparent that most of the blows fell on either side and just above. What does that suggest to you?"

"He kept missing?"

"Right. But *why* did he? You use that ballpoint of yours and try a stab—see? You got it spot on."

"He could have been all excited."

"Then why stop once the severing had taken place? Why not go on—mutilate some more? Now use my ruler and hit the plug hole here by the foot. Quick!"

Van Rensburg missed by a good inch—enough to make the difference between a wound in a child's groin and one on the thigh. He tried again and hit his target.

"Now that's exactly what I'm talking about," Strydom said. "You had to have some practice because the longer the instrument you use, the greater your error can be. It's exaggerated, you see. You have to hold a pen near the nib, don't you?"

"And so? It was a long knife."

"Ah, but *you*, Sergeant, pointed out that it curved so much it was like part of a not-so-big circle. What sort of knife is that?"

"Which was he—left- or right-handed, Doctor?"

Two could play at diversions.

"From the wounds—they slope towards the right—I'd say left. But the wire is wound to indicate a right-hander."

"There were *two* of them?"

"Not necessarily."

"But it's difficult to hold a knife wrong."

"Back to the weapon again. Let's have your board and we'll try and draw what it looks like."

Strydom, whose mother had always said he was artistic, made an accurate scale representation of the weapon's imprint. Then he extended the natural lines of the curve until they ran over the edge of the paper.

"We need a bigger sheet," he said, and went through into the office, where he started again on Van Rensburg's blotter.

"Hell," said Van Rensburg softly.

After Strydom had made the blade about two inches longer, bringing it up to the conventional five inches, he tried to draw a hilt on it. The angle was very difficult, the arc being too tight. It finished up more like the end of a boat hook than anything else.

"It could have been on a long handle," Van Rensburg suggested.

"The force would have been increased proportionately, yet those wounds aren't very deep."

Strydom then discovered that by placing his drawing hand in the center of the paper and using his other hand to rotate the blotter, he could bring the edge of the blade around to almost meet. This left him with two concentric circles—or a ring of flat metal.

"But it can't do that," Van Rensburg objected, "or there would be no sharp end."

"I know. I'm just fiddling with the idea," Strydom replied.

"The nearest it can get is halfway, Doctor. Otherwise it's coming back to stab you yourself."

"Then let's mark it there if it pleases you," Strydom replied testily. "A blade that's half a circle is bloody ridiculous, man! I was only—"

That was when he saw it. By drawing a line at right angles across the extended blade, and then thickening it with a flourish of irritability, he had put the hilt—or handle—almost precisely where it belonged.

"A *sickle!*"

"A bloody sickle," sighed Van Rensburg, as if he knew already none of the glory would ever be shared with him.

"You know something, Sergeant? I've had a sickle at the back of my mind all along."

Van Rensburg, who looked as though he could cheerfully have put one there for him, lifted the telephone receiver.

"Shall I tell the lieutenant?" he asked.

"I will—don't want to bother you any more than I need to."

That did it, whatever it was.

When Kramer's car radio informed him that the district surgeon wanted him urgently, he stopped at the first call box and rang in. He then said nothing to Zondi about the conversation until they were at the country club car park waiting for Nielsen to appear.

"The bastard used a sickle," Kramer said, handing over a ready-lit cigarette.

Zondi looked understandably surprised.

"Where for, boss?"

"Seems it left a picture of itself on the inside leg. Doc Strydom also points out that sickles are easy to hold squiff and that's why the stab wounds came from the wrong side. He's quite sure about it."

"But that is a strange thing!"

"You've said it. Only time I remember a case was when two farmboys got in a fight. A sickle's hard to carry without someone noticing."

"Unless it is for your work."

"Changed your mind? Think a black bugger did it?"

"Never, boss."

Funny how you could tell some things when others were impossible to see. But statistics would bear him out on this one: There was virtually no likelihood of a white child being sexually murdered by a black. In fact, Kramer doubted there was a single example on record. Funny that, too.

Zondi was making stabbing motions, bringing the point of an imaginary sickle down on his knee.

"Look, boss," he said. "My hand is here and the sharp part is here. That is a big space between them."

"About nine inches."

"And where does the blood go? Because the blade is turning in it shoots that away."

"Not bad, man! You've got a good chance of not being splashed. That's probably why he chose it. By the way, the only fingerprints on the bike were Boetie's own ones."

A Land-Rover roared up beside them, stopped,

lurched, chipped a bollard, stopped. The engine died fighting.

Without even a sideways glance, Kramer said, "Mr. Nielsen has arrived. Right on time, too—he's keen."

"Makes you feel bad, boss?"

Kramer cuffed Zondi and they got out.

"Lovely morning," Nielsen said affably, shouldering a haversack. "Could turn into another scorcher, though. Shall we go?"

There was nothing for it—they went. Down the terrace, across the third green of the pitch-and-putt course, and into the trees.

The glade seemed exceptionally dull in daylight.

Twenty minutes later Kramer had waited long enough. He left Zondi beside the small stream, where they had been passing the time taunting tadpoles, and strolled back to Nielsen. The ecologist was crouched, staring intently at the ground just to the right of the forked tree.

"Man, I'm sorry but we'd better be getting along," Kramer said.

Nielsen pointed. A party of ants was dragging something through the litter of fallen twigs.

"Ants?" Kramer said.

"I've just finished timing them."

"Really?"

"And now let's have a proper look at their trophy."

The tweezers brought the back half of a hairy caterpillar to within six inches of Kramer's face.

"Very nice," he said, squinting politely.

"Anything else?"

"Interesting."

"Isn't it? A bird's beak couldn't have made such a neat job of slicing it in two like that."

"You don't say. Now I'll just call my—"

"It must have come from there somewhere," Nielsen said, looking up.

"*Ach*, yes, I know the kind you mean. They lie in a line along the top of a branch—something to do with the way eggs are laid. Like trains."

"So, you're quite a naturalist on the quiet!"

"Me? Any kid who's ever climbed a tree can tell you

54

the same. They're proper bastards when you come from underneath and squeeze your hand over them."

"Not that they stay stationary for more than a couple of days, though, but we may be lucky."

The use of the plural pronoun put Kramer to flight. As he retreated he added. "Thanks a lot for coming, Mr. Nielsen. We appreciated it."

He stepped backwards onto Zondi's foot.

But the protest was never made. At that instant Nielsen uttered a strange whoop.

"Just look at what I've found!"

"Oh, yes?"

Reluctant, yet curious, Kramer joined Nielsen on a stump beside the wattle nearest to the tree with a fork in it. Across a branch in front of them, which was just low enough for a man to touch with his fingertips from the ground, ran a long, deep cut that went quite a way into the bark on either side.

"What on earth would leave a mark like that one, though?" Nielsen asked, bemused.

"A sickle?"

"That fits the bill exactly! Why did . . . ?"

"The killer used one. Any blood? Hair?"

"No, not a suggestion; just a greenish smear where it bisected our small friend."

The gash was right in the middle of the gap in a straggling line of newly hatched caterpillars.

"I know what," said Kramer. "He just hung it up here while he had his hands full with other matters."

"Simplicity itself, Lieutenant. I do the same with tools when I'm gardening; keeps them out of the children's reach."

You could see, a second later, Nielsen wished he had not said quite that.

"Every little bit helps," Kramer said, jumping to the ground. "Now we really must be off, man."

Nielsen chuckled.

"You surprise me, Lieutenant."

"Why's that?"

"Are you usually happy with just half a body?"

"Hey?"

55

Zondi stepped forward and bent down to examine the area under the branch.

"You won't find it there, boy," Nielsen said. "I had a good quiz over the whole area when I found the first piece. That's why I was checking on the time the ants took to move such a weight."

"You think they were coming back for more this time?"

"It's a possibility. Shall we explore a little?"

Zondi, who was standing behind Nielsen, grinned heartlessly. He was thoroughly enjoying such an uncharacteristic display of restraint on Kramer's part. He knew it hurt.

"Why not?" Kramer replied, shrugging. He would deal with Zondi later.

"What we're after is their nest," Nielsen explained confidentially. "It shouldn't be too difficult to find as they try to travel in a straight line when they're lugging a load. Now this is the way they were heading. . . ."

Kramer followed him into the brambles a short distance.

"And here's a nest of them! Boy, bring me my bag, will you?"

Zondi slouched up with the haversack. Nielsen took from it a small trowel and began to dig. Furious ants poured out of the ground and pumped formic acid into anything soft. It was all very uncomfortable—yet obviously unscientific, let alone unmanly, to shift your position.

Finally, Nielsen held up a lump of earth resembling a gritty bath sponge.

"Their food store," he said, breaking it open gently. Out of the holes dropped a weblike cocoon. Nielsen peeled off the white covering.

"And here we have the rest of the caterpillar—the two halves match up precisely."

"What's the stuff around it?"

"The ants' way of preserving it for later."

"I see."

Nielsen shook his head solemnly.

"I'm not sure you do. Wrapping up their bits and pieces takes quite some time. Also, these ants never forage after dark. Therefore, according to my calculations, they must have got hold of it yesterday morning."

"Morning?"

"No later than lunchtime, I'm afraid."

The implication sank into Kramer like a depth charge. At first nothing happened as it moved down through the warm superficialities of a sunny day and fairly companionable intercourse. Then it entered the colder layers of his mind where, finding its critical level, it exploded—buckling the plates of a watertight assumption and bringing confusion to the surface.

"But—but that means the killer was here long before ... It was ..."

"Premeditated."

"Right!"

Zondi stepped in a pace. There was not a sound in the forest. No wind. Silence.

"I thought you said this species of murderer acted spontaneously," Nielsen queried.

"I did."

"And that, particularly with child victims, it was a case of their meeting up with a stranger quite by chance?"

"Yes."

"Yet the boy *must* have arranged to be here last night, in this one glade out of hundreds like it all around. How else could the murderer have known where to leave the sickle handy?"

Kramer was ordering his own thoughts.

"Maybe I'm wrong," he said, at last, sitting down on a boulder. Nielsen lit the cigarette for him.

"Never mind, you're not the only one to have a pet theory upset by the facts, Lieutenant. They've cost me my doctorate once already."

"Hey? I meant wrong in applying the bloody thing in the first place."

"But the mutilations! No ordinary murderer goes in for that sort of thing, surely."

The cigarette was handed over for Zondi to take a light. Kramer retrieved it before replying.

"Unless, of course, he's a very smart cookie. How's that for a theory? The facts fit it all right."

"Good God!"

Nielsen sat down, too, on the other rock.

"Are you actually suggesting that whoever's involved is not necessarily a pervert?"

57

"I'm sure of it."

This intuitive leap was too much for strictly disciplined thought processes: it plainly annoyed Nielsen.

"Oh, come on. Wouldn't you expect to have found at least some sign of squeamishness? I might be driven to kill, but I doubt if I could go in for—you know, that sort of disgusting behavior."

"What sort? All he did was strangle the kid and stab him. Stabbing is stabbing, whatever part you do it in. He just got the effect he was after by going for the crotch—and there are a lot more disgusting things he could have done than that, man."

"You're forgetting the legs, aren't you? I thought it looked like a frenzied attack."

"That was before, while we were seeing what we thought we saw. Now I'd say the lack of any proper pattern in the wounds shows he could have tried to do it with his head turned away."

"Because he was squeamish? Well, maybe."

"There's the time factor as well, remember. The body was carefully positioned and he made quite sure nothing incriminating was left behind. You can't tell me he was in such a hurry that he had to skip a part of his plans—there is no evidence of any sexual interference, besides the wounds."

"Then the whole thing's a fake!"

"Except for the fact, Mr. Nielsen, that the victim is genuinely dead."

Nielsen stared at Kramer and Kramer stared at Zondi and Zondi looked from one to the other.

Sex had been such an acceptable motive for child murder—yet any alternative was bound to prove twice as engaging.

"You're right," said Kramer, "it is a lovely morning."

Chapter Five

EVERY SILVER LINING has its cloud. Kramer forgot that in his new-found enthusiasm. He picked up a pair of winter vests, bust size forty-four, and edged around to the cash register.

"A present for my ma," he said loudly.

"I'm sure she'll like them, sir," replied the Widow Fourie, opening a hairclip with her pearly front teeth and sliding it in above one ear.

Kramer glanced around for the supervisor and then leaned forward.

"I've got some news for you," he whispered. "The boy was murdered after all—really murdered, I mean. Not sexually."

"Oh, yes? That'll be one rand sixty-four cents."

The Widow rang up the sale and held out a hand for the money.

"*Ach*, listen! There's no reason for you to be frightened now. It's all straightforward. Tomlinson needn't take the kids in his car anymore. I'll come round to the flat tonight and explain properly. I know that you—"

"One sixty-four, sir."

"But we found out this morning—"

"That it wasn't sexual?"

"Not exactly . . ."

"Well!"

"Well what?"

"Nothing's changed, has it?"

"Bloody hell!"

"Now the super's coming. If you get me into trouble, boy, that's you finished. Pay up."

"You know sodding well I haven't *got* a mother!" he protested.

59

The supervisor pounced, taking him from behind.

"Is the customer not entirely satisfied with his purchase?" she inquired menacingly.

Kramer turned with a smile the supervisor closed like a zip. In the manager's office at Woolworth's, Miss Hawkins was a gawky giantess who kept a moist eye on underwear, soft goods, and haberdashery—a decent enough old soul, given to overefficiency. But shoplifters, shopgirls, and swains recognized a dangerously repressed morbido when they saw one. Some even trembled.

"They're lovely vests," Kramer said. "No trouble at all."

Miss Hawkins breathed heavily.

"I was just saying to the assistant that I thought she'd undercharged me," he added, looking to the Widow Fourie for support. He got none.

"Is that the correct figure, Fourie?"

"Yes, Miss Hawkins."

Kramer handed over two rand notes. His change was returned without so much as a formal smile. The bag was dumped before him. The Widow Fourie moved away to serve a bare-breasted Zulu matron in a mud headdress.

This was hardly the way to treat a gentleman.

"Just a minute!" Kramer called out.

The Widow Fourie somehow caught the bag of vests he tossed over to her. She was bewildered.

"On second thoughts, they'd better be for you, popsy, seeing you're going to be all alone these cold nights."

Miss Hawkins indulgently let him pass unimpeded.

The Swanepoel family lived behind the station at one end of town. This did not, however, place them on the wrong side of the tracks. Far from it, they were part of a most influential community. Proof of this was to be found in records of Trekkersburg's recent history: before the vast railway township was abruptly (some said illogically) transferred there from the loyalist hinterland, the city had always managed to return an opposition member of Parliament—it had never succeeded since.

Of course the swiftness of the operation left its mark on the place. The Swanepoels' home was basically similar to the thousands surrounding it because this simplified construction, although an element of variety had been introduced by building the bungalows in pairs and making one the mirror image of the other. Each stood square on its quarter-acre plot, well fenced in by stout wire mesh, with its silver corrugated-iron roof covering a lounge, dining room, kitchen, bathroom, stoop, and three bedrooms. A separate structure, also in yellow brick, served to accommodate a car, a servant, and gardening equipment. The land in front of the dwellings was leveled for threadbare lawn and that at the back left rough for maize or pumpkins. When you really came down to it, the properties were as unremarkable as rows of passenger coaches in a marshaling yard.

A single tree would have made all the difference, Kramer mused, noticing another pack of sulky dogs patter by.

"Something wrong?" Zondi asked quietly, turning the Chev into Schoeman Road.

Hell, it showed so that even Kaffirs could tell. No reply.

"Sorry, boss," Zondi mumbled in apology.

But he was smart. He knew. He had guessed when Kramer erupted from Woolworth's and ordered him to get his finger out and the show on the road, and then sat beside him gazing with glum intensity at Railway Village as if he had never seen it before. Being a family man in his own right, Zondi understood the importance of a warm woman and a flat full of friendly children. He deserved better than a silent rebuke.

"Just a pain in my arse, man—it'll go away."

Zondi laughed hopefully.

The Swanepoel house had a white police constable lounging outside it in a van and the curtains still drawn behind the burglar-proofing.

"Good morning, Lieutenant, sir."

"What's up? Why're you here?"

"Colonel Muller's orders, to keep the neighbors and press away."

"Any trouble?"

"No, sir. Only one old dear being nosy so far. Dominee Pretorius is inside—the doctor's just been."

"Oh, yes?"

"The parents are both under sedation."

61

"Jesus! What is this, a radio play? I've got questions to ask."

"Bonita's all right, though."

"Come again?"

"Bonita Swanepoel—the boy's big sister."

"Okay, I'll start with her. Sergeant Zondi's going to take a look at the Kaffir on the premises. Don't let anyone in till I'm finished."

"Sir."

Kramer ignored the path, the doormat, and the brass knocker shaped like the Voortrekker Monument near Pretoria. He rapped softly with his knuckles.

The door immediately opened a crack.

"Dominee? It's Lieutenant Kramer."

The minister silently bade him enter.

"I want to see Bonita."

"Shhh! Not so loud. Bonita? Well, I'm not too sure that she's—"

"Don't waste time, please. This case is probably more serious than we thought last night."

While he was gone, Kramer opened the curtains and the windows. In no time at all the faint smell of ether from the injection rubs vanished. The room became a size larger with the sun in it and the vases of plastic flowers—mostly arum lilies—lost their funeral parlor gloom.

There was a large number of framed photographs scattered among the African wood carvings and miniature sport trophies. The small Instamatic ones on the radio-phonograph gave tilted glimpses of a holiday by the sea—Boetie must have taken them because he featured in none. On the bookcase, empty except for a pile of women's magazines, three copies of the Holy Bible, and a ready reckoner, was a selection of infant dimples and senile smirks that suggested a gallery of relatives. The wall opposite the window gave pride of place to pictures which marked major events in the Swanepoels' past—ranging from a large wedding group to a stillborn baby, hand-colored. Kramer paused to study the latter, not expecting to discover anything significant but remembering the day when just such a print in another home had given him the vital clue in an infanticide case. Then he passed on to the collection on the mantel shelf and had time to memorize the faces of the immediate family before Bonita presented herself.

She was truly a genetic amalgam of her parents, the poor girl. Her mother's sharp, almost pretty, features were ill suited to her father's broad, flat skull. The curly brown hair came from her mother, too, but she had her father's bull neck save for the Adam's apple. The maternal inheritance very properly dominated as far as her thighs, sadly giving way to knees, calves, and ankles identical to those of the engine driver snapped on the footplate. The mixture that produced the handsome Boetie must certainly have been more vigorously stirred.

"Hello, Bonita. I'm Lieutenant Kramer."

"Pleased to meet you, sir," she said, dry-eyed and somehow self-important.

Which struck Kramer as odd until they had completed an exchange of inanities appropriate to the occasion. Then it occurred to him that she was behaving as if Boetie had become a pop star, rather than a corpse, overnight. The impossible had been achieved. This wholly unremarkable young woman had become *someone*: no less than the blood sister of a posthumous celebrity soon to have his pictures in every paper. They would certainly want hers, too, no doubt artfully improved by holding a lacy hanky in the right place. She could tell her story of their happy childhood together and tug heartstrings loose from Table Mountain to the Limpopo. She could— *Ach*, maybe he was being too hard on her. Grief did funny things to people.

"You must understand I loved my brother very much," Bonita declared clairvoyantly. "We were very close."

"So you knew a lot about him—his friends and all that?"

"Oh, yes."

"Can you tell me who his main ones were?"

"There's Hennie Vermaak. He lives around the corner at 21 Retief Road. He's twelve, too.

"And how old are you, Bonita?"

"Sixteen."

"Who else, then?"

"His schoolmates."

"Uhuh?"

63

"I—I don't know all their names."

"Just some of them?"

She bit her lip.

"His teacher, Miss Louw, could tell you."

"Fine. Now did he have any other friends?"

"What do you mean, sir?"

"Any older people? Menfolk, for instance."

"Men?"

"Never mind. It's just some lads get friendly with an old chap and listen to his stories and that."

"He knew Uncle Japie but he's dead now."

This understandably broke the flow.

"Did Boetie make friends easily? Get on well with people?"

"Oh, he was very popular—everyone said so."

"Did he have any hobbies? Collect birds' eggs?"

"Just reading, I suppose. And puzzles—he really went for puzzles."

"I see. How had your brother seemed lately? Did you notice anything different in the way he acted?"

"A bit jumpy."

"Really?"

"Well, it's exam time."

"But I thought they were finished."

"Only just."

Kramer doodled another stick man on his notebook, behind the smaller one in the fork of a tree, and placed a question mark above him.

"That's all for now, Bonita. If you think of anything else, just give us a tinkle."

"Is it all right for me to ask you a question, sir?"

"Please—go ahead."

"Does the paper know about poor Boetie yet?"

Zondi was catching up on breakfast two houses along. He was eating porridge out of a pot with his fingers and complimenting his host, a Zulu cook boy named Jafini Majola, on its excellence. Majola was enormously flattered. He pushed over a can of sour milk with just the right sort of lumps in it. Zondi drank deeply.

"Hau, that was good." He sighed again, wiping his

64

mouth with the back of his tie. "Now we will go where this servant woman can be found."

Majola led him out into the street and around the block to a traffic island in the middle of an intersection. On it were gathered about a dozen domestic servants, enjoying the morning break in a working day that lasted from 6:30 A.M. until well after dark. Plainly this was an Afrikaner area as very few of them wore the uniform of canvas breeches and tunic favored by English-speaking employers. Zondi, who had been a houseboy in his youth, had never finally decided whether one's own rags really did add a touch of dignity.

As he and Majola approached, the group fell silent. If the face was not familiar, then the snap-brim hat and zoot suit were always enough to identify him.

Zondi gave the formal Zulu greeting and was grudgingly awarded the formal response.

Majola stepped forward.

"This is Sergeant Zondi, CID," he said. "He is not interested in passes or matters of that kind. He has eaten with me and now wants to speak with my friends."

Zondi sat down on his haunches like the rest of them. Nothing further was said for a while. And then a large house girl of roughly menopause age spoke.

"My little master is really dead?"

"Truly."

"Who did this thing?"

"We will know soon."

"And what will happen?"

"He will die, too."

A couple of youngsters at the back whispered, then giggled. Zondi speared them with a finger.

"You two! What is the matter?"

No reply.

"They are pleased," said the Swanepoels' girl. "They did not believe me before."

"Pleased? That the boy is dead?"

"Of course," muttered someone.

And, one by one, everybody there nodded their head. Zondi remained outwardly calm with an effort; no child he had ever heard of was capable of antagonizing as many adults to that degree.

The other thing was these adults were all black.

When he rejoined the constable on duty at the gate, Kramer had already made up his mind to be alone for a while. So it was most convenient to be told Zondi had wandered off and the man was buggered if he knew where.

"Tell him I'll be back," he said.

"When, sir?"

"If he asks that, you can also tell him not to be so bloody cheeky."

That would give the pair of them something to think about.

The day was indeed a scorcher. Getting into the Chev, which had been left locked with the windows up, afforded an idea of what a Sunday joint went through. The steering wheel felt like a boiler pipe. The seat was warm enough to set his bowels fidgeting. None of this improved his mood; there were times when even a man's body was unwanted company.

Kramer took off hurriedly and the artificial breeze caused by the Chev's motion helped a little. His destination was the Boomkop Lower School, only half a mile off, but he knew a long detour he could take. He had to think.

Starting with the Widow Fourie . . .

The radio squawked. So much for the sodding privacy of a public servant.

"Yes?"

"Control here. We've got Colonel Muller on phone link-up for you."

"Ta. Hello, Colonel?"

"No fingerprints on the bike, other than Boetie's own, and nothing in Juvenile Records, Lieutenant. Bit of a long shot, wasn't it?"

"Yes, sir. But you know how these ministers are sometimes; they get a bit carried away. Any luck with the check on the local station?"

"No, not tried it yet. I think you'd better drop that one before word gets back to the family and we have some unnecessary problems on our hands."

"Okay, sir—it doesn't really add up anyway."

"What doesn't?"

"The idea Boetie could have been mixed up with a bad

lot. They'd have knocked him off in an accident and no bother. This way, if there was any police history, we could trace them pretty easily."

"What I was thinking. So now how do we go about finding a reason?"

"By finding out more about him. I'm still not satisfied with what I've got. I'm going round to the school now to see his friend Hennie Vermaak. News of last night isn't common knowledge yet, so he's probably there."

"That's the kid he was with before it happened?"

"Uhuh. I'll get my questions in before he knows why."

"Tread carefully, Lieutenant."

"As always, sir."

"Hmmm." The Colonel rang off.

Kramer found he had driven directly to the school after all. It was coming up on his right and a lorry, assuming from his position he was about to turn, was overtaking him on the inside. So he had little choice but to enter the gates over the carpet of old bus tickets.

Mindful of how headmasters felt about these things, he did his swearing in the car before going round to the office. The secretary there, a proper old bag in a black dress, was taking her spinsterhood out on the typewriter. She totally ignored him until, out of the corner of a downcast eye, she noticed the intruder wore long trousers.

"Yes?" she said. "Have you come about the smell?"

"Not exactly," Kramer replied. "I'm from the CID. I want to see the principal."

"What about?"

"Can I see him?"

"Mr. Marais is down at the Education Department this morning. The deputy's got chicken pox."

"I see. Well, I want to have a word with one of the pupils—Hennie Vermaak. It won't take long."

"Break is just over."

"Fine. It'd be better alone."

"Do the parents . . . ?"

Kramer seemed to nod.

"Has Hennie . . . ?"

He shrugged.

Her imagination took over and the result seemed to delight her in a predictably unpleasant sort of way. She slit open a smile.

"What was the name again?"

"Vermaak, Hennie. He's twelve."

She waddled over to the door.

"I'll get Miss Louw; she teaches the twelves. Please take a seat."

Kramer sat down in her chair and read the letter she had been working on. From it he learned that all the school's attempts to get an English teacher had now failed. Then he looked through the desk drawers.

"Damn."

There was no correspondence whatsoever concerning Boetie Swanepoel, not even in the file marked STRICTLY CONFIDENTIAL.

Footfalls had him at the window admiring the featureless playing field. A dozen or so Bantu prisoners knelt weeding it under the supervision of a warder armed with spear and club. They wore the regulation white shorts and red-and-white-striped jerseys and looked like a soccer team who had lost the ball.

Christ, his mind was all over the place.

On the other hand, every part of Miss Louw was precisely where nature had intended. It made her one of those young women who always pause in a doorway because a doorway has a frame and a frame sets off a pretty picture. One rendered prettier still in this instance by strong sunlight shining through the light summer frock from behind to define the long legs in gentle silhouette. The glare from the quadrangle also gilded a rim around the bounce of blond curls, and cast a shadow that crossed the floor to smooth itself up against Kramer. If only it had reached high enough to shade his eyes, he might have been able to see the face properly.

"Hello," she said.

"Miss Louw? I'm Lieutenant Kramer of—"

"The secretary told me and we've discussed it," she cut in. "I don't really see why not. So I've put Hennie in the remedial classroom because it isn't being used today. Third door down as you go out of here. Sorry, I must get back to my class."

"But—"

Kramer was caught off guard. For a moment he considered chasing after her, and then vetoed the motion on the grounds that she had already made him feel old and enfeebled. Miss Louw was young in a way that hurt.

So he got back to business and tracked down Hennie Vermaak.

The boy was short for his age and not very bright by appearances. His hair had been cut so close he was almost bald, he had a snub nose, and under the small brown eyes, teeth like maize pips. He also bit his nails.

"Catching up on your reading, Hennie?"

The boy dropped the placard with DOG printed on it.

"Who are you?" he asked gruffly.

"Just a policeman."

Hennie edged away but Kramer moved with him, placing an arm around his shoulders.

"What's the matter, then? Don't you like cops?"

"Yes."

"Hey?"

"Yes, I do. They keep the communists away."

"That's what pa told you."

Hennie inclined his head.

"Good boy. So it's all right if I ask you a few questions?"

"What about?"

"Your mate Boetie Swanepoel."

The small shoulder blades squeezed together.

"He isn't at school today."

"I know. He isn't at home either."

Hennie looked up warily.

"Where is he, then?"

"They say you're his best friend. But do you know if he has any other friends he might go and visit? Special friends, like you."

"Everyone's at school."

"Grown-up friends maybe?"

"Huh?"

"Tell me, what did you blokes do together yesterday afternoon?"

"We went shooting birds with our air guns."

"Up near the country club?"

Hennie scowled.

"We never go there! It's too far. Besides, you're not allowed."

"How many did you get?"

"An Indian myna."

"Not bad! They're a smart lot. And did you have any plans for today? Were you going shooting again after school?"

"No, it's swimming. We've got to practice for the gala. Boetie and me—"

"Yes?"

"Nothing. We're in the interhouse relay."

"Is that what you talked about last night before he went home?"

"Maybe. I don't remember."

"Try hard, please."

"He just said he'd better be going a bit early before it got dark because his tire was flat."

"But he lives close by, doesn't he?"

"It was something like that."

"What time was this?"

"Sort of six o'clock."

"You're lying to me, Hennie! Want to know why?"

The boy ducked and ran for the door. Kramer grabbed him.

"Shall I tell you? Because Boetie's air gun is there in his bedroom, but he didn't go home last night. *Not at all!*"

Hennie's top lip trembled like the lid of a saucepan brought to the boil. Any minute he would spill over.

"Now take it easy, son! Just tell me how it was that you and Boetie were shooting when—"

"His gun's broke."

"And so?"

"He borrowed my big brother's."

Kramer's hands fell to his sides.

"Oh, Jesus," he sighed. This line of inquiry was getting him bloody nowhere fast, it really was. Maybe he should get back to the sick men with dirty fingernails, no sense in upsetting everyone, including innocent kids. But he had one thing left to do: flash his trump.

"Hennie, I've got some bad news. Boetie isn't going to be in the gala."

"Why?"

70

"Are you asking me?"

"Yes."

"And you'll tell your ma and pa that you asked me this question—straight out?"

"Yes."

"Boetie is dead."

Adults collapse, children can only gape.

"He was murdered, Hennie, killed by a very wicked man."

The convicts outside began a low chant, singing of their cattle and their wives and their children back in the reserves; it helped them bear the weight of a grass roller they were unloading from a truck. A window opened and a nasal voice screeched for silence. It went deathly quiet.

Kramer stared at Hennie incredulously. He had expected the boy to register shock but not fear. Not fear so great it smelled worse than the puddle of urine expanding on the classroom floor.

Beauty Makatini, as Zondi now knew her to be, was preparing lunch in the Swanepoel's kitchen. She opened two tins of pilchards in sauce, sliced six tomatoes, washed a lettuce, and grated some carrots. For dessert, she halved two pawpaws and squeezed lemon over them.

"Too much," murmured Zondi from his seat on the bread bin. "You heard the priest say the boss and the missus were sleeping."

"This morning I make porridge and eggs for four people, Detective Zondi. Bonita and the priest eat it all and I have to find toast for them, too. They are very hungry, I think."

He chuckled. For a while he had suspected she was up to the old trick of making sure there would be leftovers to supplement her own meal of boiled beans. But you could not get away with that one in every household and, from what he had heard about Mrs. Swanepoel, hers was no exception.

Dominee Pretorius poked his head in.

"Boy, your boss is outside now. Beauty, what's wrong with the bell? I rang it three times from the front room."

"*Hau*, shame! I hear nothing."

71

Zondi sidled past, giving her a secret pat on the bottom, and went out the back door.

He was just in time to see the Chev drive off without him.

Kramer brought it back a few minutes later with what almost amounted to an apology. He explained that after Hennie disgraced himself in the classroom, it had only been right to take the poor little bastard straight home before his pals saw him. In his hurry he had forgotten to inform the school and, on realizing this, had shot around the corner to use the call box.

"He was very frightened, boss?"

"Poop scared. But he wouldn't tell me why—and he wouldn't tell his mother. You see, I don't think he really knows himself; it's just a feeling I got."

"This is strange."

"But bugger-all use to us. Could be he just fancies he's next in line because they were great mates. You know kids."

"This Boetie fellow was also strange, boss," Zondi said softly.

"Why's that?"

"The servants all around here say he made life very hard for them. He looked at their passes."

"He *what?*"

"Checked their passbooks. Wanted to know if they had bike licenses. Went to their rooms at night to see if there were strangers sleeping there unlawfully."

"Never!"

"He also arrested three Bantu youths for loitering with intent."

"I don't bloody believe it."

"My people did not lie to me, boss. I sat with them for an hour."

It seemed to Kramer longer than that before he found his tongue again.

"Man, I've heard of playing cops and robbers . . ."

"Playing? It was not toys he showed them."

"Hey?"

"Beauty says he had everything—truncheon, whistle, and handcuffs. Real ones."

72

Kramer snapped his fingers. A subliminal image had started to nibble at the wall of his conscious mind. It was not going to make it, but a strong impression filtered through: Boetie's bedroom was the place to be. Something there had already made sense of all this.

"Back into the house," he said, pushing at Zondi to open the car door and sliding out after him.

Once back in the room, Kramer stood in the center of it. He was searching for a cue rather than a clue. He simply let his eyes pan uncritically over everything within the four walls. They stopped dead on a neat pile of magazines by the bed.

"Of course!" Kramer said, scooping one up and ruffling through it. He found what he sought on page three—a three-column panel headed DETECTIVE CLUB.

Zondi took another issue and they sat down on the bed together to read them.

Kramer found that the panel was made up of three parts. There was a chatty article by a senior police officer, a section for members' letters, and a block explaining the Detective Club rules with an application form included in it. Membership was open to all Afrikaner boys aged between twelve and sixteen who had never committed a criminal offense. They had to get their parent or teacher to sign beside their own signatures. If they were accepted, then they would be sent a card, initialed by the head of the South African Police, that gave them the right to "co-operate" with local representatives of the force.

Just what this meant was obvious from the letters. A boy writing from the Orange Free State said: "I spent nearly my whole holiday working as a member of the Detective Club. The station commandant said I was very useful to him as I arrested nine Bantu altogether and one Colored female. I also went on raids in the van. It was very nice." Another, this time a thirteen-year-old in the Transvaal, wrote: "In our English-language oral exam I had to pretend that I was a member of the Special Branch finding out if a man was a liberal. Because I belong to the Detective Club I knew the proper way to ask questions. The inspector said I was so good that I made him feel like a real communist!!! Thank you, Detective Club!" The editor had added in italics: "Glad that the Club is bringing

73

you good results. Remember, the rest of you, courage and loyalty is not everything a good detective needs—he also has to have brains."

Zondi whistled low.

"Well, are you thinking what I'm thinking, Kaffir?"

"Too right, boss."

Being a detective was one sure way of getting yourself thoroughly disliked.

Chapter Six

THE COLONEL PUT it another way when he arrived in Railway Village some minutes later. He said, "Man, it's funny, but having a policeman sniffing around can do something extra nasty to a mind that's warped already. You know what I mean?"

Kramer knew; one of his early colleagues, investigating the death of a racing driver whose car was suspected of having been sabotaged, had his face held in the radiator fan of an engine running on a test block. Things like that stick.

"But you did say *policeman*, sir."

"I take your point. So you can't find any trace of his membership card or the handcuffs and things?"

"Zondi and I have been all over—the garage, too. The only place left is his folks' bedroom but he wouldn't have kept them there."

"Could he have had them with him yesterday?"

"Hennie didn't say."

"And that's not all he kept quiet about."

"Of course, we are taking it for granted that Boetie *was* in the Detective Club."

"A reasonable assumption, Lieutenant."

"Then the next step is to contact Pretoria and have them ask this magazine for its list of members."

"Better still, ask his sister."

"Oh, she thinks he might have been playing about with some silly game, she says."

"Then ask Hennie. You're going to see him again."

"It would be an advantage if I also knew his position beforehand. Why can't we—"

The Colonel turned over the magazine he had been studying and showed the back to Kramer.

"Always read the small print, Lieutenant. Down at the bottom of the page . . . That press is owned by a cabinet minister—and so is the magazine. Send a man around there and you'll attract a lot of attention from high up."

"But—"

"Which would be a pity if this affair has only a slight connection with the Detective Club. And it would be more than a pity if it had nothing to do with it. Remember, the English-speaking press has its spies everywhere, too—they would make a meal of a morsel if they got the chance."

"What about the trial, sir?"

"Ah, thinking well ahead, I see. Well, I'll expect you to have enough evidence by that time to make your preliminary inquiries irrelevant."

"How do I go about it, then?"

"Keep it in the family. Ask the local sergeant a few casual questions."

"And what do we tell the papers meantime?"

"That there's a madman on the prowl. It's still the truth, to my way of thinking."

There was a tautness in Kramer's face that the Colonel could not help noticing.

"*Ach*, I know I'm probably making your job harder this way, Lieutenant, but I must be fair. Every time one of my men does something that's not in the book, I try to see the whole force doesn't take the blame in the eye of the public. Am I right?"

"Yes, sir. We appreciate it."

"Good. Now you just get going again and keep me in touch. Need any extra help?"

"Sergeant Zondi and me are doing all right so far."

"I bet."

Boetie Swanepoel was indeed a familiar name to the station commander, who had just returned from a fishing weekend to start his two-to-ten shift behind the counter in the township's charge office.

"That little bastard," he snarled. "He threatened me. The bloody cheek of it!"

"When was this?"

"Why?"

"I'm just asking."

76

"There must be a reason."

"He's in dead trouble."

"You've made my day. It was back last month when I took over this place—got transferred down from Vryheid. First night he comes in here with his mates and says he wants to go out on the vans. Shows me a bit of paper and says he's a detective! I didn't bother to read it. I just told him that this wasn't kids' work, thanks very much."

"You threw him out?"

"Well, it isn't kids' work, is it? It's bloody dangerous when a Kaffir gets filled up on white lightning!"

"I'd have done the same."

"Of course you would. You know what? He comes back in here *again* and says Wolhuter—that's the sergeant before me—let him go on raids, even. And then he says that if I don't let him 'cooperate' I'll be surprised what happens."

"Jesus!"

"I nearly knocked his bloody block off, I can tell you."

"See him again?"

"No, nor his mates neither."

"Look, Sarge, it might be useful if you can tell me when this was."

"November the first, the day I started. Then two days later."

"And was a kid called Hennie Vermaak with him?"

"Buggered if I know."

"Ah, well, that's how life goes," said Kramer, turning at a sound and seeing a housewife enter, dragging a small Bantu boy by the arm. "Looks like business is hotting up. See you."

"This little swine has been at my orange trees," the housewife declared. "I want to—"

"Just a minute," the sergeant interrupted.

"I can't stay, man."

"But you didn't say what sort of trouble the Swanepoel boy was in."

"Oh, somebody knocked his block off."

"Hey?"

"Murdered him," Kramer mouthed from the door, and then added aloud, "Not in front of a lady."

People often ask policemen what it is like to go around

77

breaking the news of sudden death. It can be a lot of laughs.

Japie Vermaak was also an engine driver, a somewhat more prosperous one than Boetie's father because he was in command of an electric unit. This in turn meant that the car in his garage was American rather than English and twice the size. But that was not what he was pointing to.

"There's Hennie," he said. "You can just see his feet. Been in there from when his ma gave him a bath, she tells me. Now don't ask me why because I don't know."

"He's upset!" his wife said.

"Naturally," soothed Kramer. "I'm sorry—"

"No, man, it was best he should know. Maybe it'll stop him going off without telling his ma or me what the game is."

Mrs. Vermaak clucked. She made a good hen to his rooster, what with her small, bustling body and his slow strut and red hair. Sad they had managed only the one egg.

"Besides," Mr. Vermaak continued, "it was rather you than me who had to tell him. He and Boetie were big pals—that was half the trouble."

"What was?"

"Them charging about at night God knows where. I'm working then, you see, and it was a worry for the wife."

"Has this been going on long?"

"What do you say, Lettie?"

"Not recently it hasn't, but it was very bad at one time."

"Whilst he was in the Detective Club?"

"Oh, no, that was only Fridays."

"I see."

"Suppose he's been spoilt a bit," Mr. Vermaak admitted. "Always difficult when they're on their own. They need company their own age."

"He seemed a very nice, well brought-up boy to me, sir. Sure I can talk to him again so soon?"

"Man, it's our duty, isn't it, Lieutenant?"

"I'm not so . . ." began Mrs. Vermaak.

78

But Kramer was already striding down the drive toward the garage.

The Security Branch offices lay out of earshot at the rear of the stone-faced CID building. The Murder Squad occupied the rest of the first floor, apart from a small section for Housebreaking, with most of its barred windows overlooking the street and the raw material passing by.

There was a window and a pair of men to each room; a system sound enough in theory, as they were assigned opposing shifts, but one at best congenial in practice. Which was why Kramer had pinned his name to the door of one of the interrogation rooms and called it his own.

Zondi went in ahead of him and opened the blind. The sun straight in his eyes made him sneeze. It was odd, that.

"Time?"

"Half-past five, boss."

"God, I was a long time at the Vermaaks' place. That kid wasn't easy."

"But you haven't told me what he said yet."

"I'm still thinking about it."

Kramer sat down at his desk. He took a toffee tin from his pocket. He placed it carefully before him.

"*Hau*, what's that?"

"All in good time. Run down to Records and get me a crime summary for last month."

As soon as Zondi had slouched out, Kramer dialed the Widow Fourie's home number. There was no reply. He used a finger to depress the telephone's disengage button and then tried again. Still no reply. He prodded the button automatically. Suddenly an idea occurred that both surprised and pleased him enormously. What a resourceful fellow he was. Leaving the receiver to purr like a cat in his lap, he opened the directory.

This time the response was immediate.

"The headmaster, please.... Oh, Mr. Marais?... Yes, they would all be gone by now but I guessed you'd be catching up on paper work left over from this morning. ... That's right—Lieutenant Kramer. ... Terrible, terrible. ... Naturally. ... As a matter of fact, you could: I'd like a word with Miss Louw tonight—do you have her home address handy?... Thanks ... Flat 36, Aloe Mansions. Fine. Of course I will. Bye now."

It was always a pleasure to deal with a genuinely busy man when you wanted something in a hurry.

"Nothing big, boss," said Zondi, reappearing with the summary. "What special do you want?"

"Serious crime while we were away on that job in Zululand."

"Murders? Five of them."

"Forget the Bantu stuff. Just concentrate on Greenside."

Zondi looked mildly surprised. The posh suburb of Greenside was seldom of any interest. As Kramer had said often enough, when you had the money, there were other ways than murder, all as effective.

"Only one grievous bodily harm on the first—sorry, Bantu employee on Bantu employee—and eight housebreakings. *Hau*, this skelm didn't do badly! Same m.o. each time and nearly a thousand rand in stolen property."

"Yes, I know about him already. Anything else, though?"

"One firearm recovered and the owner charged as well."

"Uhuh. When was the last housebreaking?"

"On the fifteenth."

"Damn."

Kramer took the paper and stared at it moodily. He had entertained high hopes for what it might contain.

And, inviting Zondi to take a seat opposite him, he began to explain why.

Hennie's story was that he, Boetie, and five of their classmates had joined the Detective Club back in July. The club encouraged its members to form gangs with colorful names and so they called themselves the Midnight Leopards. Sergeant Wolhuter, who was station commander in Railway Village at the time, had a daughter at the school and had seen copies of the magazine sponsoring the club. He made them welcome and gradually allowed them to do more and more. It had been very exciting.

Then at the beginning of November the station changed command. The new sergeant told them to get lost—and he collected up the equipment that had been loaned. They had all been very upset by this, but Boetie took it worse than anyone. He had two rows with the sergeant and then suggested that everyone's parents should get together and do something. This backfired when the parents said that with exam time coming, and a good pass needed to get into high school next February, it was probably just as well. Their kids had to get down to some hard swotting. However, Hennie had not told his parents of this and Boetie's parents were too busy with their church activities to take his entreaties seriously.

The Midnight Leopards became extinct. Or so it seemed until one afternoon when Boetie told Hennie he had a brilliant plan that would have them reinstated with full honors. He had noticed that the *Trekkersburg Gazette* was publishing story after story about police failure to put an end to the spate of housebreakings in Greenside. There had even been an editorial about it. His idea was for Hennie and himself to begin their own investigation up on the hill. While the burglar might be keeping an eye open for any grownup, he was hardly likely to feel it necessary to hide in a hedge when two boys came round the corner. There was no need to make an arrest, Hennie was assured—just a good description would do. Although, of course, what Boetie hoped for was actually seeing the crook climb in through a window; then they could ring the police and have him caught red-handed. Boy, after that they would be welcomed back, all right.

Hennie finally gave in and the pair of them cycled over to Greenside every evening after doing their homework. They saw nothing but learned that it was a very suspicious neighborhood. Big as it was, there were not that many roads and they had to cover the same route several times on each patrol.

In fact, Hennie had been on the point of announcing his resignation after a week of this when a police van cut them off and two white constables jumped out. They said they had received a complaint that two strange youths kept riding past a bank manager's house. He wanted to know what the hell it was all about—and so did they.

Boetie did all the talking; humbly, apologetically, and without giving any indication of their true mission. Exactly what he said Hennie could not remember, for it was a very confused story. The constables had been bewildered but impressed, nevertheless, by Boetie's attitude toward

81

them. Especially after he excused himself for asking if
they were not, as he felt sure they were, two members of
the police A rugby team that he watched every Saturday.
They preferred not to make a reply and stepped aside to
hold a whispered conference. All Hennie caught of it was
a giggled suggestion that the hunt for the housebreaker
was over. And then the constables turned on them with
a promise that if ever they were found making nuisances
of themselves in Greenside again, steps would be taken.

The two boys had sped off as fast as they could pedal.
When they reached Railway Village, Hennie told Boetie
that his father was on to him for not doing enough studying for the exams. Anyway, he thought the patrol in
Greenside was a silly old idea. He quit.

Boetie had called him a sissy. Boetie had said he was no
longer his friend. Boetie had ignored him at school for a
whole fortnight. And then he had come round the day before to go shooting.

This was a surprise, Hennie had conceded. He just had
to accept the fact that Boetie wanted to be friends once
more. They had had a very good afternoon. Boetie had
not said anything out of the ordinary.

This was his story until Kramer discovered what had
drawn the boy to the garage in the first place.

Hennie had been sitting with his back against the far
wall, resting his head on his hands on the bumper of his
father's car. Later, while he was talking, Kramer had noticed first a black smudge on Hennie's cheek and then
black marks on the palms of his hands. He looked around
and saw a crude brush on a long piece of thick wire, such
as was commonly used for sweeping the chimney of a
slow-combustion stove. It was soot Hennie had on him.

And there was more soot on the wall just beside the
huge old wardrobe converted for storing car tools.
Kramer had pressed his head against the wall and looked
behind the wardrobe to see a toffee tin, bound carefully
with an excess of insulation tape, hidden behind it in the
corner.

Two simple assumptions later and Hennie confessed to
having been bent on removing it when disturbed. He also
divulged what else had transpired the afternoon before.

When they returned from shooting, Boetie told Hennie

that he had carried straight on with his investigations up in Greenside—and had seen something that would shake the police solid if he was right about it. There was one more thing he had to do first, though, and he was going to check up on it that night.

"*Hau!* What thing?" Zondi demanded, breaking his absorbed silence.

"That's the bugger of it, man, we don't know," Kramer replied. "We're dealing with kids, remember. They go in for secrets and all that crap in a big way. Hennie didn't press him. You could almost say that would be bad manners. It was the same again when Boetie asked him to hide this for a while."

Kramer tapped the tin.

"You've opened it, boss?"

"*Ach*, yes. Hennie looked like he thought a bloody mamba was going to jump out. If I hadn't got there when I did he would have chucked it in the fire. That's why he was so scared, you see—there *was* a connection and what made it worse was that he couldn't understand it!"

"But if—"

"Look for yourself, man."

Zondi drew the toffee tin towards him and carefully prised off the lid. Inside it were four items: a membership card of the Detective Club made out to Boetie Swanepoel and three small squares of tissue paper.

Zondi took one. It was covered in closely packed lines of letters. There were no spaces between them—and no recognizable words in any of the three languages he spoke.

"They're all much the same," Kramer said.

"I have never seen such a thing. More children's rubbish?"

"It's called a coded message, you ignorant bloody Kaffir," Kramer said kindly. "At least, I think it is."

Bonita had remarked her brother loved puzzles.

Danny Govender became the Masked Avenger by the simple expedient of hitching the collar of his T-shirt up over his nose. Then, with a borrowed death ray clamped up to the front of his bicycle, he swooped.

Out of the yard behind his family's tin shack, down the footpath strewn with broken glass and other fiendish obstacles, and along a tarred road mined by deep potholes that led eventually into Trichaard Street.

To the people thronging the thoroughfare it was just that—a street. At the very most, *their* street, because all the faces were dark. There was nothing else particularly remarkable about it. Neon can cost up to forty rand a foot so it lasted for only about thirty shop fronts, both sides, before the final flourishes in pink and blue. From there on down to the municipal beer hall, the less affluent Indian traders settled for big letters on bright backgrounds and plenty of wattage. All of them, however, had domestic neon strips flickering over the fruit, clothing, suitcases, and blankets stacked on the dusty pavements; this kind of light made the eyes dance and the color of their goods twice as vivid—a most important factor when you had customers who favored tartan suits and oranges with blood groups. It was a street: busy, crowded, friendly.

Danny saw it differently because he was twelve.

When he arrived at the top end, he assessed the situation carefully. Outside the beer hall, in the shadow of a sign that read BANTU LIQUOR OUTLET, his friend who delivered the Sunday papers was waiting. But that was half a mile away and between them Evil in all its most dreadful forms lurked ready to pounce. For, as any literate person knew, the prime function of Evil was to deal severely with any champion of righteousness who happened to pedal by.

The Masked Avenger remained calm. He was chewing on a wad of bubble gum that turned him invisible for short lengths of time. It was just the thing for getting through the Gauntlet of Death unharmed.

When the traffic light shone green he would be ready.

Green.

As the bicycle rattled and bounced down Trichaard Street, its rider noted with satisfaction that everyone looked right through him.

And then, with a quick tug, he became the mild-mannered newspaper boy Danny Govender again before Rampaul Pillay could discover his proud secret.

"Where have you been all day, Rampaul, man? I look for you every place."

"Harvey Street Clinic."

"What you doing by that side?"

84

"Privates."

Danny stared rudely at Rampaul's flies, wishing he could cheat and use his X-ray vision.

"Privates," repeated Rampaul. "I am not telling you."

"Then you are not my chum anymore."

Rampaul thought about this.

"Okay," he said. "I falling off my bike and hurt my knee."

"And so?"

"If Chatterjee hears of this, he will be asking for my job on Sunday. My father he says to me, keep this very privates, Rampaul, or we lose money."

"Who will ride for you?"

"My brother."

"I do it, Ram. Easy."

"How much?"

"Ten cents."

"Five!"

"Seven!"

"Okay."

They shook hands solemnly.

Then Danny relaxed, grew confidential, and spoke in Tamil, their mother tongue: "I'll tell you why I left a message for you to be here tonight. I want to know what happened to that dog in Greenside—you know, Regina."

"She's dead."

"But how?"

"The servant said she'd been killed by a burglar."

"*Really?* He didn't tell me that."

"The boss found it early in the morning and told him to bury it. He said there had been something round its neck. Like a wire."

"I didn't know the house had been robbed!"

"No, it wasn't. The servant thought the bloke must have run away in case there was another dog."

"When was this?"

"They found the dog on Sunday."

"I thought so."

"Is that all? It's a funny question to ask, Danny. I thought it was something important. Let's see if Gogol will give some old bananas."

"Know something? I really got to like that horrible

85

dog," said Danny suddenly, as surprised by his outburst as Rampaul.

And it looked like a job for the Masked Avenger.

A thunderstorm of appalling ferocity was inevitable at the close of such a day.

Trekkersburg, which lay in a hollow on rising ground like the dent a head makes in a pillow, felt the final stages of the fever coming on just after seven. The weight of hot air pressing down on the town turned chill, then hot, then chill again. It started moving restlessly from side to side, setting weather vanes spinning. Strange, dislocated sounds were heard. Limbs of trees shivered. A thick, stifling blanket of black cloud was drawn up to blot out the bare bulb of the moon. The hallucinations began: it was as though, far above, a gigantic tin roof was being bombarded with boulders; as if each flash of lightning was a sear of pain through a reeling mind. A shuddering climax was reached. The rain came like a muck sweat.

Kramer stirred.

He sat upright behind the wheel of the Chev and opened his window a little. The night smelled as fresh and clean and inviting as Miss Lisbet Louw. A few minutes more and the downpour would ease off enough for him to dash across into Aloe Mansions. It was a great pity he had not been able to park any closer to the flats any sooner.

But the storm had forced him to rest and that was, perhaps, a good thing. He had been on the go for nearly forty-eight hours, counting the time spent half-dozing in court the day before. And really a man owed it to himself to keep enough energy in reserve to cope with the unexpected challenge. Miss Louw, for instance.

The rain belted down.

Kramer shifted his knee to avoid a drip that had found its way in under the rubber seal around the windscreen. The water was astonishingly cold. He found another leak in the same place on the other side. That was the trouble with police vehicles: you never knew where they had been.

The rain tried even harder.

Kramer watched it glut the gutters and then overflow over the road, creating huge, splash-pitted mirrors that tried vainly to reflect an orderly pattern of warm lights from the flats above.

The rain was remorseless.

The hell with having no coat. Kramer leaped out and ran.

To arrive at No. 36 soaked through—although it was not until after he rang the bell that he realized this. His thin suit had put up as much of a fight as a cigarette end in a urinal.

The door swung inward.

Miss Louw was also sopping wet. She had a towel round her body and another round her head.

"Oh, you poor man," she said and pulled him inside.

"But, miss—" he began.

"Quick, through there before you ruin the hall carpet."

Kramer found himself shut in a steam-filled bathroom, blinking rapidly, and unable to examine his expression in the misted looking glass. He was certain, however, it was a winner.

"I'm going to dress now," Miss Louw called out. "The lady next door has a tumble dryer so you put your clothes outside and I'll take them round. That's everything, mind. It won't take long."

"Hey?"

"Come on, Lieutenant. Be sensible."

She clattered off in her wooden sandals.

Well, well, that was the first of his three wishes granted—in her flat five seconds and she was yelling for him to get them off. The trouble with wishes was you had to be so specific or they sometimes misfired. Not that this was physically possible with the other two he had in mind.

The suit jacket was easy enough to remove but the trousers and shirt had Kramer grunting and hopping about. If only he had worn underpants that day he would have felt much happier. As it was, she might think he was withholding some ghastly secret. So he added his shoulder holster to the soggy pile as a distraction.

And pushed it all out into the passage.

"Won't be two minutes," Miss Louw told him as he sat on the edge of the bath warming his feet in her water.

She was back even sooner.

"I'm sorry," she said, "but Mrs. Turner's just put in a

load of nappies she must have. She'll do yours straightaway after. Why not come out and have some coffee meantime?"

The Smith & Wesson .38 made one hell of a fig leaf.

"In what, miss?"

"Oh, damn, all the towels are damp. Isn't there something behind the door?"

Kramer looked at it and shuddered.

"Maybe you could lend me a coat?"

"Not one that would come near to fitting you. You'd tear them."

"You live alone?"

"Of course."

That was promising anyway.

"Okay, but no laughing, hey?"

Miss Louw looked most beautiful when she laughed. The pupils of her blue eyes were like eclipses of the moon with a sparkle of stars all around. Her teeth were narrow and neat and just right for the wide, sensuous mouth. Only the tip-tilted nose stayed serious, although the nostrils dilated a fraction.

He had to laugh, too. It was not every day a senior CID officer made his entrance clutching the voluminous folds of a nylon negligee about him.

Then their laughter halted abruptly.

Kramer experienced a different sense of embarrassment and so, apparently, did she. There had been an uncanny exchange of something intimate between them, too subtle for him to catch.

"Nice place you've got," said Kramer, finding an excuse to take his eyes off her.

"Thank you, Lieutenant. Shall I get the coffee now?"

He sat down, crossed his legs firmly, and watched her pour two cups in the kitchenette alcove. Zondi would have given his full approval to such a rump. What a perfect complement it made to the full bosom. That was better.

"Did you come to see me about Hennie?"

"No, Boetie Swanepoel. You've heard by now, I suppose."

"Yes."

"And . . . ?"

"I think its horrible. An innocent child like that."

88

"Is that how he struck you?"

"What on earth do you mean?"

"Just that: what did you think of Boetie?"

Miss Louw frowned. She handed Kramer his coffee and stirred her own slowly.

"Then the paper isn't giving all the details?"

"We are having to be very careful. This could happen again."

"To whom?"

"Hennie."

"My God!"

"Or to any of his classmates, probably."

She went on stirring, staring at Kramer.

"Can I know why?" she asked finally.

"Miss Louw, you answer my questions first and then I'll tell you. If we do it the other way around, what you say could be affected, if you know what I mean."

"All right. Go ahead."

"First, describe Boetie to me as you knew him."

The coffee was just the way he liked it.

"He—was a nice kid. A bit on the serious side with definite ideas about right and wrong. If, for example, some child was cheating in a test, Boetie would tell me right then and there. This is what made him different to any other boy I've come across in five years of teaching."

"Why did you stress 'boy' and not say 'kid'?"

"Because girls sometimes are like that, although in their case it's generally spitefulness."

"Was he perhaps . . . ?"

"I'd say not! Whatever gave you such an idea? Anyway, he's got a girl friend he dotes on. Little Hester Swart."

"Sorry."

"This is worse than filling in reports; you can't get a proper idea of Boetie from all this."

"What are his best subjects?"

"Mathematics, English, and art."

"English?"

"Unusual, isn't it? He's got a thing about English, speaks it better than me. He says—said, I mean—it was essential if you want to do well because all the big business in this country was run by English-speakers."

"He sounds a very bright lad."

"Only in some ways. In others he was naïve."

"For example?"

"I know the others teased him about dirty jokes because he hardly ever got the point. This wasn't his being serious so much as ignorant."

"Or innocent, like you said."

"Yes."

"The strong church background."

"Everything very sacred—marriage and all that. The Ten Commandments."

"I notice you speak a bit impatiently, Miss Louw?"

"You would if your father had been a minister—and a damned hypocrite at that. Dirty old man."

The bell rang. Miss Louw closed the living-room door behind her before answering it. Kramer really liked her for that. In fact, he liked her for many reasons.

"But what about your job?" he asked, when she returned with his clothes. "Aren't you expected under Christian National Education to be a practicing one yourself?"

"What about you, Lieutenant?"

"At weddings and funerals."

"Huh! And yet who swears on the Bible in court that everything he says is true?"

"Touché. You must scare blokes away with a brain like that."

"Of course. I like to pick and choose. But this isn't anything to do with Boetie."

"One last question, then: Have you noticed any change in his behavior over the last month, going right back to the beginning of November?"

He could have done better in his exams, that's all."

"Thanks very much, then."

Kramer took his things and made for the bathroom.

"But you said—" she exclaimed.

"Why not finish this in a quiet corner over at the Tudor Tavern? I noticed you hadn't cooked your supper yet, Miss Louw, and I can't talk any more until I eat."

And so he *made* her pick him—even if it was only to satisfy the curiosity he had aroused over Boetie's death. But she did not hurry back home afterwards. By then they were coconspirators with an ingenious plan for the morrow.

Chapter Seven

ZONDI TRIED TO oversleep. But when the fourth person left his bed, fought the others over the clothing strewn around it, and ended up chanting multiplication tables, he knew Wednesday had begun for him, too.

He forced open an eye.

His wife, Miriam, was through in the living-room-cum-kitchen spreading sweetened condensed milk on wedges of bread. She piled them on an enamel plate and then poured six mugs of black tea. It would have been seven if she was expecting her husband at breakfast, so he had a chance of at least staying where he was for a while.

The twins, being the eldest, were also trying to oversleep on their mattress unrolled beneath the window—and having as little success.

Zondi grunted at them.

"Good morning, Father," they said together.

"Up!" he ordered. "What do you think I pay all that money to the teacher for?"

"So he will not beat us, Father," one of them answered.

"So he will give us good reports," said the other.

It was too early in the morning for that sort of thing. Zondi pressed one ear into the pillow and covered the other with his forearm. This did not cut out all of the noise, but kept it down to a minimum until it was obvious that the children had left to attend the first shift at Kwela Village school.

Shortly afterwards, Miriam came in and told him there was a municipal policeman waiting to see him.

"Bring him to me," he said.

In marched Argyle Mslope, who halted with a great thump of boots on the rammed earth floor. He saluted.

"Greetings, Detective Sergeant Zondi!"

"Greetings, Argyle."

"Your wife is a buxom woman, Detective Sergeant Zondi."

"I thank you, Argyle."

"She will bear you many brave sons."

"She has done that already."

"God bless you," said Argyle.

One of the old school and no mistake about it; mission-educated, a stretcher-bearer with the white soldiers in the deserts of North Africa, a perfect Zulu gentleman, and—at times—a fearless fighter. It was a great pity, though, that Argyle had not progressed very far at the mission or he might have been an asset to the South African Police itself. However, he seemed happy enough in the municipal force, guarding beer halls, hospitals, clinics, hostels, and townships. He played the bass drum in its band and put a shine on his brass buttons that contrasted as strongly with the tatty-quality uniform as fresh blood on a stray's fur.

Zondi could see himself stretched out and elongated in the belt buckle just three feet away.

"Why have you come, Argyle?"

"Your superior officer desires you to use the telephone."

"Straightaway?"

"I regret that is the case."

So did every God-fearing passer-by within hearing of Zondi as he hurried up the dirt roads to the township manager's office.

The African clerks there were quick to smile and greet him—and had an outside line ready waiting. Zondi glared at the number the manager had noted down. It was to a call box and that was always an ominous sign.

But ten minutes later he was back telling Miriam that he had been given the day off.

The lieutenant was taking his gun up to the boy's school, he had been told. In the meantime, he was going to sleep where he was calling from—the bird sanctuary. Mystifying.

"That is good, my husband," said Miriam. "Now you will have the time to put a plank across the bottom of the lavatory door outside. How does the corporation think a modest woman likes to be on that squat pan with everyone looking in under?"

"I have heard," replied Zondi with a leer, "that the corporation thinks it is part of our culture."

He artfully lowered the door eight inches.

Probationer Detective Johnny Pembrook stood outside the Colonel's office making sure he had no wind left to break. His gut had been in an uproar all night through sheer nerves. The order to report to the divisional commissioner had reached him in the barracks as he was turning in after a long, fruitless search for an old woman's purse. The awful thing was that only the time had been stated and he had no idea what he had done. Not specifically, that was. It had really churned him over. A probationer detective makes a lot of mistakes. One too many and he goes back into blue for the rest of his days. And Pembrook wanted to join CID more than he wanted to play for the A team—although he would never admit it. That was the worst mistake he could make. God, how his stomach fluttered.

Then, having almost fired a live round, he decided to quit playing Russian roulette with himself and find out what it was all about.

The Colonel was surprisingly cordial.

"At ease, Pembrook," he said in English. "How are things in CID?"

"First class, sir."

"Good! You're making nice progress."

"Thank you, sir."

"It is time you did some paper work, though."

Pembrook's chin came up.

"Sir?"

"We want you to take some statements. These are the addresses—Swanepoel, Steenkamp, it's all there."

"What case is this, sir?"

"Oh, something of Lieutenant Kramer's."

"*Murder* Squad, sir?"

"He'll be the one to brief you."

Pembrook could not help it.

"Why *me?*" he blurted.

"I'm buggered if I know, Pembrook."

The deputy headmaster usually acted as starter for the

races at the annual interhouse gala because he had an old revolver left over from the war. So, with him away ill, it had been one less thing for Mr. Marais to worry about when Miss Louw's friend offered to take his place.

But having now come face to face with the volunteer, and having been introduced, Mr. Marais was no longer too sure about that.

"This is very kind of you, Lieutenant Kramer," he said in his smoothest headmaster's voice, "yet is it very wise?"

"How do you mean, Mr. Marais?"

"Well, it might just cause an—er—awkwardness. As you can see out there, most of the parents are here this afternoon and some of them are very upset about what happened to Boetie. We even thought of canceling but we've got the interschools next week and this is how we choose our team. Also, it could make the children nervous."

"Oh, I'm sure nobody will know who Trompie is—they're all railway folk," said Miss Louw.

Mr. Marais took off his rimless spectacles, polished the lenses, and replaced them over his rimless eyes.

"I'm held responsible for everything," he said plaintively. "Bad language . . . Smells . . . You've no idea."

"Look, if you don't want me here, I'll go. Only I can't leave the gun behind for you because it's government property."

"Please don't take that attitude, Lieutenant! We're very, very happy to have you. An honored guest, you might say. I just needed to think a moment. No, I'm sure Miss Louw is right: nobody will know who you are."

"That's the beauty of it, man," Kramer murmured, as he acknowledged the wave Mr. Marais gave him from the French windows opening out on the pool. Then he turned to Miss Louw.

"Why did you suddenly call me Trompie just now?"

"You forget—I told him we were old friends."

"*Ach*, of course. And you may just have something there, Lisbet. Now what must I do?"

It was all very simple. He was given a box of .38 blanks, a program annotated to show him from which side each event began, a whistle to impose silence, and a pat on the shoulder for luck. He was also entreated to keep things moving, as there was a lot to get through.

A starter using a firearm is always regarded with some awe by children in bathing suits. There is something about that chunk of ruthless metal being carried so casually between their unprotected bodies that induces respect. A boy's fascination for weapons plays its part as well, as does a girl's dislike of loud bangs. With all this on his side, and his innate ability to have commands obeyed instantly, Kramer himself set an unofficial record.

Mr. Marais made a feeble joke about it over the loudspeaker. And then he explained that as it was only four o'clock, the ice cream had not yet arrived for the party after the prize-giving. Therefore there would be a short interval of fifteen minutes' duration.

Lisbet had already pointed out to Kramer where her class sat in a block on the grass. He wandered down there, reloading his gun.

Although the first boy to speak was a good six years older than Mungo Nielsen, his response was the same.

"Let's have a look, sir!" he pleaded.

Kramer made a show of reluctance.

"Come on, sir!" said some others.

He sat down.

"Don't touch," he warned. "You must never play with guns."

"Blanks can't kill you, can they, sir?"

"The wad would hurt, all right. You'd get a bad burn, too. Anyone know what kind of gun this is?"

"Smith & Wesson .38 service revolver, six shots, muzzle velocity of four tons."

"Not bad! How did you know that?"

"The police have them."

"Oh, yes?"

"He's a Midnight Leopard! Big show-off."

The black-haired boy with a harelip frowned at the girl who had spoken.

"I'm not," he said. "You know I'm not anymore. Nobody is."

She stuck out her tongue at him and then smirked at Kramer.

"I know what you are, too!"

"What?"

"Our teacher's boyfriend."

The whole class giggled—except for a sulky-looking miss out on the fringe. From the description he had been given, he was sure this was Hester Swart, Boetie's romantic lead.

"So what? I bet *you've* got a girl friend!"

Kramer flicked a pebble into the lap of the boy who had stopped him.

"Me?" he hooted.

"That's her there," said the cheeky girl.

"All right, then here's your darling little Dirk Botha!"

Accusation and counteraccusation rent the air like a dozen premature domestic disturbances rolled into one. Finally, however, the whole group had been paired off, with Hester again the exception.

"But what about this little lady?" Kramer asked, as guilelessly as he knew how.

"She's—"

"Go on?"

The speaker glanced at his fellows. They all looked away, very uncomfortable.

"What's the matter, kids?"

They all turned to Hester.

"I've never been *anybody's* girl friend!" she declared fiercely.

Harelip appeared as horrified as the others yet managed to speak.

"You can't say that, Hester! You even put his initials on your desk."

"Rubbish. I *hate* him!"

"Hester Swart!"

"I don't care! I hate him. I'm glad Boetie's dead. Glad."

Dear God, not another.

Seated on cane chairs in the Colonial Hotel's courtyard, Kramer and Lisbet compared notes. The tall glasses of lager were a great help.

"Man, you got to her just in time," Kramer said. "I thought she was going to have hysterics."

"She did. In the staff room."

"Slap her face?"

"No, let her have a go at mine. When she realized what she'd done, she was so startled that she shut up like that."

Kramer laughed. He hoped it would be infectious. It was. How edible she was.

"Well, it gave me the chance I'd been waiting for, anyway," he said. "I got Harelip—"

"Jan?"

"Yes, Jan—to one side and bought him an Eskimo Pie. Chatted him up about the Midnight Leopards. I think we can definitely rule the others out now—they packed up when the new sergeant put his foot down. And Boetie kept all his secrets to himself, too."

"Not from Hester, though."

"I gathered that. Hell hath no fury?"

"You've said it."

"I thought so. But even then, why the big reaction?"

"The new girl was English."

"*Hey?*"

"English-speaking, I mean."

"God Almighty! No wonder she took it badly."

Lisbet waved over an Indian waiter and ordered two double brandies with orange juice.

"It's my turn to pay," she said softly, pushing across the money when the waiter had gone. Kramer stopped her by placing a hand on hers. And left it there. The rest of him was miles away.

"I want to pay," Lisbet repeated. "Now that we're sharing things together, Trompie."

That brought him back with a bump.

"Sorry, Lisbet! I don't know what happened. Just all of a sudden this whole case seemed . . ."

"Do you want to know her name?"

"Please."

"Sally Jarvis."

"*Jarvis?* Why does that ring a bell?"

"It does?"

"Somewhere. Go on, meantime."

"I've had to put it together from all sorts of bits and pieces but the main gist of Hester's story was that Boetie gave her the boot without warning last month."

"When exactly?"

"On Tuesday the eighteenth. She went to the dentist

97

that day so she had the date fixed in her mind long before."

"I interrupted you."

"It seems this was a terrible shock for her. They'd been going to the bioscope to see cowboy films on Saturday morning ever since the middle of last year. He'd also written her letters that she'd shown her friends. Maybe it's hard for a man to understand the disgrace, but I can tell you it's very real."

The brandies arrived.

"What did she do?"

"What any woman would: asked him who her rival was. He denied this was the case. There were exams coming and his parents were pushing him. Hester didn't believe this—her Boetie was much too clever to have to swot. So she waylaid Bonita outside the high school two days later and discovered, without giving anything away, that Boetie was allegedly seeing *her*, Hester, most evenings. That really made her mad and she challenged him again."

"Did he tell her about Sally then?"

"Oh, no, he claimed Bonita was a spiteful liar, a typical big sister. Hester had to find out the hard way."

"How?"

"By being told what was happening by someone else. And not someone she liked: a self-satisfied young lady called Doreen West who lives in Railway Village but, because of her parentage, goes to the English medium school in town. Doreen stopped Hester outside the sweet shop and asked when she was going to take up ballroom dancing, too."

"No, this I can't take! You're not going to tell me that Boetie was going to dancing classes?"

"Why not?"

"Because—well, it's an *English* custom, isn't it? You don't get hundred-percent Afrikaners like Boetie going in for that bloody nonsense; long trousers, jockstraps, and quiffy hair styles!"

"Jockstraps?"

"Never you mind about the worries a young boy has—just tell me where this fits in."

"Sally was English, wasn't she?"

"*Ach*, I can see it must have been there he got pally with an English girl—where else? But what made him go in the first place?"

"There is a simple answer to that."

"Uhuh?"

"To meet Sally. Specifically. As you say: where else?"

The ice had melted away, ruining the taste of the brandy.

"You're a proper schoolmarm, do you know that?"

"Sorry, I didn't mean to squash you. I'll give you marks for neatness, though."

"Oh, yes?"

"I know you weren't thinking when you asked the question. You were off wondering just how much of a liar Boetie really was. He could have lied to Hennie, too, about those patrols he claimed to have been making up in Greenside—just to cover up the fact he'd been fooling round with an English girl. It also fits very nicely that he might have been going to see her that night for a secret meeting in the woods."

"You're psychic, Lisbet."

"A little."

"But only half a mark for me, I think—for effort. Because it doesn't tie everything up. There's the toffee tin and the papers inside it, for a start."

"And the fact that Boetie was not a natural liar. If he lied at all, I would think it would have to be for a very good reason."

"Yes, that's an important aspect of all this; he does seem to have been behaving out of character."

"Or was he?"

"I think the whole thing rests on that. Another drink?"

Lisbet nodded and a snap of the fingers activated the waiter, who stood, motionless between orders, like some kind of robot conserving its batteries, against a far pillar. He glided over.

"Brandy and telephone directory, Sammy."

The waiter's name was not Sammy, but his race had been divided by the whites into Sammy units and Mary units to facilitate friendly relationships.

"Horange juice last time, master," he intoned carefully.

"That's right—the directory's separate."

Kramer made his reply poker face and was rewarded when Lisbet smiled. If only the damn case could be set aside for the rest of the evening. Perhaps—

"Come on," she said. "Where had we got to? And what's the phone book for?"

"That, too, has a simple answer. Boetie went to the dancing classes because he wanted to meet someone, namely Miss Jarvis. Right?"

"Yes . . ."

"Therefore there was a connection between them *beforehand*. He must have come across her—heard of her even. Where, though? And why couldn't they meet there?"

"What we've already decided—it depends on where she lives. Normally Afrikaner and English kids don't mix."

"Exactly."

Kramer took the directory off the tray and flicked through to J. There were nine Jarvises listed. Two had Miss in front of their names. Another two were businesses. Leaving five, of which no less than three were in Greenside.

"Greenside!"

Kramer jumped up. Lisbet grabbed her handbag and ran after him.

"What's the panic, Trompie?"

"I'm going round to that dancing school!"

"How do you know which one?"

"They're only two—we've got a fifty-fifty chance of being right first time."

"But why not just phone all the Jarvises and ask if there's a Sally?"

"Because, my girl, I like to keep myself downhill when I'm stalking."

"You mean . . . ?"

"Nothing. It's a matter of principle."

It was exhaustingly boring just sitting there in the lieutenant's office hour after hour. There was nothing to look at, nobody to talk to, not even a shortwave radio Johnny Pembrook could tune across to Lourenço Marques for some pop.

Yet he dared not leave it. His orders had been explicit: get the statements, get back to headquarters, stay put.

Well, he had got the statements, all right, and felt rather proud of them. He was sure that the various parties concerned had been most surprised to find so young a man entrusted with their solemn declarations. Probably his age had had a lot to do with it. The adults had acted as though they had detected his anxiety to do well.

Johnny began reading their words once again. Midway through Bonita's recollections—God, she had frightened him, that one!—he realized he knew it all by heart.

"Bloody hell!" he said.

How silly that sounded.

But the whole setup was ridiculous.

Only a probationer detective would tolerate it—any other rank would have long since left a note and buggered off to the mess, lieutenant or no lieutenant. Johnny Pembrook suddenly had his first, perhaps second, insight into why Kramer asked for him.

The ever so gentle English gentleman, a real Londoner no less, who owned the Sadlers' School of Dancing, positively writhed at the implication that he taught the tango to teen-agers. Or any other such vulgar step to anyone, for that matter. He would have none of that. Things had changed enormously since he had taken over the lease at the beginning of November. Absolutely enormously. What a reception the city's wonderfully artistic people had given him! So starved of culture, poor creatures. It made him so happy. But now, of course, his whole evening had been totally, utterly ruined. And he had such dear friends in. How thoughtlessly cruel.

"Jesus, I don't know how they get into the country," Kramer said loudly to Lisbet as they turned away in the hall.

"Probably come in those crates marked 'British Made,'" he quipped on the stairs.

Phonetically, the pun was viable in both languages—the Afrikaans word *meid* meaning "maid," too, if you had to spell it all out. But Lisbet did not show any sign of amusement.

"I felt sick the way he was looking at you," she said quietly.

101

"Oh, Yes? How was it different to the way *you* look at me, then?"

"It wasn't," she said.

Kramer pondered deeply all the way round to the Trekkersburg Academy of Dance and Deportment. Where, to his considerable relief, they were received by a slant-eyed, fierce little woman in a black mantilla.

"Lat Am tonight," she said at the door.

"Pardon, lady?"

"Latin American, and you're not coming onto my floor in those shoes."

"Cha, cha, cha," Kramer replied, handing her his identification card and walking in.

Lisbet hesitated a moment and then followed them into the small office wallpapered with photographs of knob-kneed little girls in tutus, seedy Valentinos fully extended, and an incongruously obese Pekingese. There was a roll-top desk, two chairs, a coat stand; paper, mostly sheet music, lay everywhere.

"Name, lady?"

"Madame Du Barry."

"Uhuh. I'm Holmes and this is Dr. Watson."

"Mrs. Baker, then. Priscilla. Nothing immoral goes on in my studio."

"That's nice. But how about the ballroom classes held here on Friday nights?"

"It's enough trouble getting the spotty little sods down from their end of the room to the girls! I'd never need to tear that lot apart, I can tell you. Here, what do you think you're doing?"

"Inspecting your receipts."

"What for, may I ask?"

Kramer tore out a page and handed it to Lisbet. She read: "To: Sally Jarvis, 10 Rosebank Road, Greenside. R4 with thanks." Then Mrs. Baker snatched it away.

"So that's it!" she said, moving round them like a boxer. Kramer was reminded of that wog Cassius he had seen on a newsreel—only then they had called him a dancer. His mind would do these things at critical moments.

"What?" he asked.

"Old Calamity Jane again. You're working on the sex killing. He was also a pupil of mine, as you no doubt know. A nice boy, Boetie, quite a surprise considering he was an—"

Nearly a nasty blunder. Mrs. Baker sat down and made herself look very cooperative.

"Was he here long?"

"It'll be in my register. Just a mo. Here we are: Boetie enrolled on the twenty-first of last month. That means he's been here four times in all. A real little romance that was."

"Him and the Jarvis girl?"

"Calf love at first sight. Took one squint at her and he was across in a flash."

"How about the competition though? From the other boys?"

"For Sally? You must be joking! If ever there was a plain Jane, she's it, poor kid."

Kramer frowned, then began a smile Lisbet finished for him. Quite obviously Sally had an appeal for Boetie that set aside all normal prejudices. One that must have been very strong indeed.

"May I ask you a question, Mrs. Baker?"

"Please do, miss."

"You say Sally's a plain Jane. Why did you also call her 'Calamity Jane'?"

"Did I? I suppose because this is the second boy she knew who's died in a month. Both right here in Trek-kersburg, too."

Chapter Eight

THE BELL RANG and rang inside Kramer. So loudly that Lisbet had to raise her voice an octave above the rumba record to catch his attention.

"Trompie, do you know who Mrs. Baker means?"

"Of course he does, miss. That American student who was staying with her family and drowned in their swimming bath."

"Him? But that was—" Lisbet faltered.

"An accident," Kramer said. "A bloody fatal accident. I only check serious crimes."

"Weren't you away then in Zululand?"

"Heard a bit about it on the wireless. Didn't listen properly, it sounded such sentimental rubbish."

"And I read just the first piece in the papers. Who he was staying with didn't mean a thing to me but I think his name was Andy."

"Andrew K. Cutler, full out," added Mrs. Baker confidently.

Kramer noticed her again.

"You've got a memory!"

"Oh, I felt I should take a personal interest, you see. I've got all the cuttings in my scrapbook. Scrapbooks are part of my life."

"May I see them?"

Mrs. Baker was delighted to oblige. Then she asked them to excuse her for a while because the Lat Amers were probably wanting their money's worth.

"Gladly," said Kramer.

Man, the press had really gone to town. There were columns of the stuff, with only the report of the inquest showing any degree of professional detachment. As

Kramer preferred his news without comment, that is where he began. It was in English:

TREKKERSBURG, Monday—An American Field Scholarship student, 18-year-old Andrew K. Cutler, whose body was recovered yesterday morning from a Greenside private swimming bath, died accidentally, it was decided at an inquest here today.

The presiding magistrate, Mr. J. S. Geldenhuys, said after delivering his verdict that it was a tragedy one of the Republic's young guests should meet his death in such a way. He asked that his own condolences be added to those sent to the bereaved family.

Captain Peter Jarvis, who was Andrew's temporary guardian, gave evidence of identification.

He also stated that, following a report made to him by a servant boy, he had gone down to the swimming bath in the grounds of his home at 10 Rosebank Road, Greenside, at 7:30 A.M. He had seen Andrew's body on the bottom of the bath. There was no sign of life.

He noticed Andrew's clothing—a pair of jeans, a shirt, and some beads—lying beside the bath on the patio, and concluded that the youth had decided on impulse to take a swim.

Questioned by Mr. Geldenhuys, Capt. Jarvis said this swim could have taken place at any time after 10 P.M. on Saturday. That was when he, his wife, Sylvia, and his two daughters, 17-year-old Caroline and Sally, aged 12, had gone to bed. Andrew had told them he was going to "be around for a while."

The rest of the family, although present, were not called to the witness box.

Sergeant W. W. Brandsma then told the court that he had responded to a telephone message from Capt. Jarvis. He was shown the body and took charge.

The district surgeon, Dr. C. B. Strydom, said he had seen the body *in situ* and had later examined it in his mortuary. Andrew had been a "fine specimen."

Mrs. Jarvis collapsed at this stage and there was an adjournment while the Jarvis family left the courtroom.

When Dr. Strydom resumed his evidence, Mr. Geldenhuys asked him to state very briefly, in layman's terms, what he considered to be the cause of death. "A typical drowning," he replied. Mr. Geldenhuys then asked to see his post-mortem report.

The report was filed and Mr. Geldenhuys delivered his verdict.

Andrew's home address was given as 320 Pike Street, Teaneck, New Jersey.

Lisbet had been running her finger down the same cutting. She paused at Dr. Strydom's evidence.

"That's a funny word to use—typical?"

"*Ach*, some reporter who can't translate from Strydom's Afrikaans properly. I suppose what he meant to write was: 'Ordinary drowning.'"

"Of course."

They glanced over the rest of the headlines: TRAGIC FIND IN TREKKERSBURG; A CITY MOURNS; U.S. STUDENT'S BODY FLOWN HOME; LOCAL WREATHS AT NEW YORK FUNERAL; PARENTS THANK THE CITY THAT CARED.

Yech.

"Coincidence?" Lisbet asked lightly.

Kramer picked up the register.

"Certainly some lines of inquiry now coincide."

"Such as?"

"The dates. Boetie's been here four times, including last Friday. That takes us back to the twenty-first of November ... confirmed. Three days before that, on the Tuesday, Hester Swart got the boot from him. On the Monday, this inquest was held."

"Just a minute."

"What now?"

"I remember that Monday. It was the day he hadn't done his homework and really let me down, as Mr. Marais took my first lessons so I could do some organizing for the gala."

"So he started behaving oddly then, hey?"

"More important than that was what happened at lunchtime. You know how the kids go down to the sweet shop? Well, they came back teasing him because he'd spent his money on a newspaper!"

"Christ!"

"I asked him about it and he said it was to help him with his English. He was very peculiar all afternoon."

106

"Pity you didn't think of this sooner, my girl."

"It was only the one day—I forgot."

"Which paper?"

"The afternoon one from Durban."

"This one, in fact."

Kramer pointed to the inquest cutting and she nodded.

"And another thing, Lisbet: Hennie told me Boetie said nothing more about Greenside for a whole month. That's also about Monday—or the weekend before."

"The drowning—is that what he saw?"

The music stopped.

"Let's get going, Lisbet, before the mob reaches us. We'll say thanks another time."

They hastened away together.

But when she saw what the time was, Lisbet had to very reluctantly ask to be dropped off. She had forty compositions still to mark. Equally reluctantly, Kramer escorted her to the lift, promised to ring, shook hands, and departed in search of Dr. Strydom.

He found him in the surgery at Central Charge Office examining some pompous idiot who had been arrested while in charge of a motor vehicle he was trying to park in the mayor's civic goldfish pond.

"But I *am* a fish!" the driver insisted. "Pissed as a newt and fed to the gills. Ha ha. But I don't supply—suppose you could understand that in your bloody Dutch patois, hey?"

His jibes at sixty percent of the white population went ignored. Everyone was too intent upon what the district surgeon was up to next.

Kramer looked over their heads.

Dr. Strydom had his piece of chalk and was drawing a long, wobbly line with it across the floor.

"Right now, sir," he said with a showman's grin. "I've drawn a straight line from here to the wall. All I want you to do is walk along it without stepping off."

The drunk studied the challenge before him.

"God, I *am* sloshed!" he said and collapsed.

"Help him up," Strydom ordered the young constables who were staggering about themselves, hooting and slapping their thighs. "I've got to take a urine sample."

"What's that?" asked the drunk.

"Urine."

"Ah, number ones, you mean. Who—*whom* do I have the pleasure of doing it on?"

"Yourself, if you're not careful!" giggled the ubiquitous Constable Hendriks, who had grown a new patch of pustules.

"Cut this bloody rubbish out!"

Even the drunk was sobered somewhat by Kramer's harsh voice. Strydom most of all.

"Lieutenant! I didn't know you were here."

"What's all this in aid of, Doctor?"

"Well, you know, all work and no play makes—"

"Rubbish, man. This sort of conduct is dangerous and you know it."

"Spoken like a gentleman, sir!"

Kramer grabbed the drunk by the lapels.

"Call me that again and it'll be blood samples! Understand?"

Hendriks flinched.

"May I have the recep-tickle?" the drunk asked meekly.

Strydom obliged.

"Now get him out of here," Kramer ordered when the messy deed was done.

In seconds he and Strydom were left alone in the room. Then neither spoke for a full minute.

"I'm sorry, Doctor."

"Oh, you were quite right."

"It's just I wasn't in the mood—I need your help urgently."

"Indeed?" Mollification set in.

"Come up to the officers' mess and I'll buy you a brandy."

The dreary room was empty. Kramer went behind the bar and poured two stiff ones. Then, having put his name in the book, he joined Strydom in a corner.

"It's about the Cutler drowning case," he said after a sip.

"Now there's a coincidence!"

"How's that? Something new?"

"Oh, no, not the boy, I meant the family—Captain Jarvis. We had him treading the white line not so long ago. A

108

fortnight, maybe. Banned for a whole year and I wasn't surprised. What got me started on that?"

"I mentioned the Cutler affair."

"Sad, sad business. That's right, Jarvis said in mitigation it had led to him taking too much. I suppose the Yankee insurance companies want something from you?"

"No."

"What then?"

"Boetie Swanepoel."

"I don't follow you."

"Listen, and I'll explain."

Strydom listened. First with one ear, then with the other, twisting and wriggling in the soft armchair, becoming progressively more uncomfortable. His lobes turned very red.

"Damn it, man, you're implying I made a mistake!" he finally exploded.

"Only might have made one, Doctor. Let me finish first, please. Yes, suppose Boetie was nosing around Greenside, heard a suspicious sound from inside 10 Rosebank Road, and investigated. He goes in quietly and comes across something he later describes as being of great interest to the police. Was it young Andy drowning?"

"Why keep quiet about that?"

"Exactly."

"I see. You think it may have been a bit more dramatic in reality. A fight maybe?"

"Something along those lines."

"Impossible."

"Why?"

"Because he died of cardiac inhibition."

"That isn't what you said in court. Ordinary drowning, you told the magistrate."

"Never!"

Kramer opened the scrapbook and pushed it across the coffee table. Strydom found his spectacles, read the line pointed out to him, and grunted.

"Bloody young fool," he said. "I even gave my evidence in English and the reporter still gets it wrong."

"Then your words weren't: 'a typical drowning'?"

"*Atypical*. One word. It means almost exactly the opposite."

109

"Come again?"

"I was asked to be brief."

"But Geldenhuys read your report!"

"What does he know about it? I'd said drowning and that was enough. Everyone wanted the thing over as quickly as possible."

"So it seems."

"Be careful, Lieutenant. I'd like to tell you something now. Before Cutler was cremated in New York, he had to be examined again by a pathologist over there—his conclusions were exactly the same as my own: cardiac inhibition due to the stimulation of the vagus nerve."

"I need another brandy," Kramer said.

"Medicinal? Allow me."

An officer from the Security Branch, the one who never removed his high-crowned felt hat, was now behind the bar reading someone else's letter over a beer. He served Strydom without missing a word—you could tell that because his lips never stopped moving.

"There you are, my dear Kramer, get that down you."

The whip hand held out a well-charged glass.

"Ta. Now tell me how it was Andy Cutler really died."

"Cardiac inhibition," said Strydom, relaxing in his chair, "results from stimulation of the vagus nerve and, in drowning, this can arise in one of several ways."

"You're quoting, of course."

"Naturally. All you need is a sudden rush of water into the nasopharanx or larynx, it stimulates the vagus, and *phut!* Imagine the vagus is a brake on your heart you push down just so much to keep the revs right. If you cut it, that's like taking your foot off—the heart speeds up until it just burns out. On the other hand, if you stimulate it, that's the same as slamming on anchors; it clamps down, the heart stops, and loss of consciousness is usually instantaneous. Death comes at the most a few minutes later. There are none of the usual signs of drowning."

"Such as?"

"No foam at mouth or nose, great veins not engorged, no asphyxial hemorrhages, the skin's pale."

"What do you look for, then?"

"A good point—all these are negative findings. With

110

Cutler I checked for barbiturates, injuries, other primary causes."

"And there were none?"

"Only small grazes on the elbows and heels—consistent with the rough surface of the surrounding area including the bottom of the bath. Ah, another important thing is the element of surprise or unpreparedness. It can happen 'duck-diving'—if someone splashes your face."

"Or if someone creeps up behind you and gives a sudden shove?"

"I told you: there was no indication of violence, however slight."

"It wouldn't take much if he was near the edge."

"Perhaps not—but would you expect to kill somebody that way?"

Kramer almost shuddered at the thought of how many childhood friends he had sent screeching indignantly into the deep end.

"A joke, Doctor?"

"By whom? The family were all in bed and the place was locked—the gates, everything. Don't tell me it was Boetie playing the arse!"

The Security Branch man left with a secret smile. He moved like a shadow.

"There's one other bloke we've been overlooking," said Kramer, reminded of something.

"Who's that?"

"The burglar himself."

"If Andy had tangled with him the old fright-and-flight would have been working. You know, adrenalin—it would have boosted his heart so hard the vagus wouldn't have stood a chance. He'd have done ten lengths easy."

"What I had in mind was the bastard suddenly seeing this young guy out in the garden after all the lights have gone out. So he makes a run for it but his bunkhole— probably the same one Boetie used—is visible from the patio. What does he do? Creeps up behind Andy, chucks him in, and escapes in the confusion."

Strydom raised his glass and studied Kramer through the refractive distortion of his liquor. This made the eye that was not screwed up appear hideously large from the other side.

"If that was what Boetie saw happening, Lieutenant," he murmured, "why didn't he come running to you blokes for his medal?"

There Strydom had him.

At last came a diversion; the scuffling and shouts in the passage had Johnny Pembrook on his feet and across the room in two strides. He whipped open the door.

And was irrationally enraged by what he saw there: a bandy-legged Indian boy in a T-shirt being dragged along between two members of the Housebreaking Squad.

"We've got him," they both said together.

"Who?" asked Johnny.

"The Greenside burglar."

"Him? That thing? You're joking!"

"Caught him red-handed."

"What with?"

"A spade."

Johnny slammed the door on their laughter. Then he opened it again.

"Where in Greenside?"

"Orange Grove Road, trying to hide with his bike when we went by. Won't tell us where you got it, will you, you bugger? We'll find out, never you mind."

"Big deal. Anyone seen Kramer?"

"Right behind us."

So he was—but thankfully absorbed in thought.

"Evening, sir!"

"Who the hell? *Ach*, so you're Pembrook. Got the statements?"

"Sir."

"Good lad. Here's money; I want you to go round to the pie cart and fetch two curry suppers, coffee, and ice cream—just the one. I'll give you until I've finished reading through your bumf. Go."

There was a message waiting, propped up against the telephone. It gave the Widow Fourie's number and asked "Please ring."

Kramer sat down and opened the docket. Resting his head on the first page of statements, he closed his eyes and dozed. Dreaming.

112

Lisbet stood before the wardrobe and considered her bare body from another angle. How strangely remote it seemed, caught cold as a cameo in the oval glass.

The last time she had done such a thing was the day she discovered that breasts had started to grow. What wonder there had been in the realization *That's me!* Yet as she gazed at herself now, at a full-length profile far more varied in outline, she felt no sense of personal involvement at all. If that was her, so be it.

But there had to be some reason for the examination. She kept looking.

Lisbet twisted full-on.

Her face she knew of old. It was there every morning at the dressing table like a dollmaker's first task of the day. All it needed was a steady hand and five touches of color. Then it disappeared for hours at a stretch, popping up now and then, just a section at a time, in the lid of her powder compact: details from a portrait of a pedagogue.

The neck did its job; lifting the head well clear of the trunk and providing secure mooring for a coil of pretty beads.

The shoulders could have been less square. They made her arms begin rather suddenly and not know quite where to finish up when she was flustered.

A deeply tanned skin was always attractive.

She stared at her breasts. They stared back, with an albino's pink eyes through the white mask left by her bikini top. Neither blinked. The confrontation finally ended when, pressing them in at the sides to assess volume, she accidentally induced a squint.

Lisbet giggled. She and the image had communicated and now she felt self-conscious. It made her snatch up a petticoat.

Then her mood changed abruptly. She was entirely alone and yet had an audience. She would shock it a little.

By setting her legs well apart and having her hips experiment with a slow, clockwise motion. They balked, swung jerkily, then got rhythm with a grind that could clean tar barrels. The bump was born of a momentary loss of balance. Amused, she put the two together: three left, three right—bump! bump!

Her audience raised an eyebrow.

The petticoat came next. It had turned her from naked to nude and now suggested a few other sly little tricks. Like remaining smoothed over her without being held, solely by virtue of the static charge in the nylon, until a bounce too many brought it slithering down. To be caught at waist level and gradually gathered on either side into an ever-narrowing belt of lilac that sawed back and forth, lower and lower, becoming more opaque and yet less of a garment.

Three left . . . three right . . .

Up from some cerebral basement came strains of a boozy band steaming into a strutting number just made for the routine. The throbbing entered her and began to set its own pace, always progressively faster, although pausing intermittently to tease with a twang of silence before the downbeat. She abandoned herself to it. She was lifted to her toes and the peticoat fell away forgotten.

Lisbet was aware of only one thing: a sense of wonder as she looked into the mirror and realized *That's me.*

Bump-bump!

God, yes, and she would share this discovery with the next man of her choice; an older man, a proper man who would rejoice with her—not shrink back startled and fearful of Sin.

Crash.

Her foot had snagged the cord to the table lamp. It lay on the floor with its china base shattered and its shade off but still working. The harsh light, striking upward, made her recoil.

Or rather the exaggerated shadows did, for they were vindictive in their illusion of aging; drawing muscle, sinew, and knobs of bone to the surface, while molding the swell of the stomach into a potbelly beneath the hollowed rib cage.

She barely recognized the face with its jutting chin, high cheekbones, and—

In that instant, Lisbet knew whose hard blue eyes had stared from the reflection all along, considering her body from every angle. They were his.

"I won't change," she whispered. "I'll never change as much as this. Some people don't."

Knowing a lot about bodies, the eyes stayed steady.

Zondi wound up his gramophone and was reaching for the "Golden City Blues" when the twins came pelting in, shrieking something unintelligible. Miriam gave them a clout apiece and they calmed down enough to pant in unison, "Uncle Argyle is getting killed!"

Their father ran straight out into the night in his shirt and underpants without pausing to as much as slip on his shoes. There were no street lights so he had to rely on sound to indicate where the trouble was. That was easy, however, as short, weak blasts on a police whistle were coming from the next street.

He sprinted around the corner and found a crowd jibbering in high excitement outside the home of Nursing Sister Gertrude Dhalmini, an expensive whore when she was not on duty at the clinic advising on birth control.

"What's happening?" he asked.

Everyone wanted to tell him, but by beginning at the beginning. He listened only for as long as it took him to push his way through. Even so, they conveyed a great deal.

Apparently Sister Gertrude had been entertaining an enormous witch doctor of incredible wealth—that was where his Lincoln had been parked—and unbridled savagery. All had been perfectly amicable until he had removed the trousers of his tweed suit, whereupon Sister Gertrude's training alerted her to a definite public health hazard. She told him this and refused to run the risk of infection. Out of personal or professional pique, nobody was quite sure which, he had then beaten her brutally before leaving. Sister Gertrude, whose job gave her an extension line, rang the check-out gate and had him arrested for assault. She was just telling her neighbors about all this when the witch doctor returned on foot—having escaped custody with the declared intention of dissecting her. The neighbors had scattered. Argyle Mslope had gone in alone.

The whistling had stopped.

Zondi approached the door with one slight advantage: every house in Kwela Village was identical so he knew it would open into the living room and the bedroom would be to his left. The very nature of the case suggested he would find her—and the others—in the latter. He found

115

her in both. The witch doctor had been as good as his word.

And was about to behead the reeling figure of Argyle with the same ax when Zondi leaped upon him from behind, clamping an elbow around the massive, fat neck. He could hardly encompass it.

Like a cheetah on the back of a maddened buffalo, Zondi realized that he had bitten into a lot more than he could chew. With a toss of his horned headdress, the witch doctor broke into a short charge, spun round, slammed backwards into the concrete-block wall.

Zondi collapsed with the breath knocked from him. He saw the ankles start to turn and grabbed them, leaping to his own feet and heaving. The witch doctor sprawled, letting the ax fly out through a window. A roar of delight came from outside.

Argyle blew his whistle and fell over a chair, dazed, bleeding badly. His spear was nowhere to be seen.

The quick glance around cost Zondi dearly. The witch doctor brought him down with a kick from the floor to the groin. Then tried to bite his nose off—the foul spittle pouring into Zondi's own gasping mouth as he held him up and away.

Zondi was fighting for his life. It was not the first time, so he knew what to do. The problem was finding the right opportunity.

The prospect of which diminished almost entirely when the witch doctor relaxed his enormous weight, pinning him down as effectively as a pile of cement bags, and shifted his grip to the throat.

In a pink blaze of light Zondi saw—or thought he saw—the lieutenant enter the room.

"Shoot!" he gurgled.

But what made him uncertain was the fact that the ghostly blond figure failed to fire the gun in its hand. Instead it disappeared into the bedroom.

"Die, die, die!" the witch doctor bellowed, oblivious to any further intrusion.

This, too, led Zondi to believe he was going faster than he supposed. The pain was excruciating. He was no longer able to squeeze back. A wave of nausea swept up him and, finding the way blocked, spilled into his lungs. They

116

tried to burst. His brain burst instead and everything went black.

For a very long moment, in the middle of which he heard the most terrible scream and wondered how he had managed it, he counted his children.

Then he sat up and was sick. He was alive and the witch doctor was dying.

That was all he needed to know until he ceased retching. And then he took a proper look.

The beast's massive body lay on its side in a heap, heaving in spasm, with its tail sticking out straight. Not a tail at all, but the shaft of Argyle's spear. And holding the end of it, Argyle himself, out cold.

Kramer preferred to sit outside in the Chev, so Miriam brought his tea out using her washboard for a tray, disguising it with a dishcloth.

"Pity I missed the fun," he said to Zondi, raising his cup in salute. "Might have evened up our score a little. I still owe you for that time at the brickworks—that bugger with a knife in his bike pump."

"So the score isn't even, boss?" Zondi asked with a slight smile.

"No, man, and I'm glad it wasn't this time. If I'd got mixed up in that business it would have been statements and inquests and all that rubbish right in the middle of this other job."

"Argyle Mslope is a brave man to go on fighting with such wounds."

"You've said it. A brave man to go in there in the first place."

"I spoke with the doctor, boss."

"Oh, yes?"

"He said he did not know how Argyle could do such a thing."

"I don't think that's a problem. The bastard had his bum stuck in the air—must've done. Easy enough target even if you are half out."

"Because, boss, Argyle's right hand was nearly cut off already."

"*Ach*, no! I didn't notice. So much blood about. Did the doctor say what his chances are?"

"Not very good."

"Of course this will make sure his widow gets a proper pension—in the line of duty as they say."

Zondi sipped his tea slowly.

"What are you thinking?" Kramer asked.

"Nothing, boss. Just that Argyle didn't have his spear in the living room."

"Christ, Kaffir! I tell you we're not getting sidetracked onto this case. There's a lot you've got to hear from me and a lot we must do. That's why I came by your place tonight—I want you to start at Greenside first thing. It could be we're at last making some progress."

The mortuary van passed by to collect together Sister Gertrude, a good nurse notwithstanding.

Chapter Nine

WHILE WAITING for Zondi to report back, Kramer had Pembrook fetch the toffee tin from the safe so that they could study its contents afresh in the light of a drizzly morning. Little wonder people caught colds in such an unpredictable climate.

"Pull over Zondi's stool but don't sit too close to me," he said.

Pembrook complied with a sniff.

"I went round to the Swanepoels' at breakfast time, sir," he said. "That reference the father made to Boetie oversleeping one Sunday and missing church for the first time—it was on November the sixteenth."

"Fine! Now we have narrowed it right down to the morning after, so to speak."

"And that reminded Bonita that Boetie had been in high spirits the morning before. He'd exchanged his bike for a better one with a dynamo lamp—said he'd be out late testing it."

"Even better. But it still beats me why his parents never asked him what he was up to."

"They keep saying the same thing: they trusted him and—"

"Who, man?"

"God."

Kramer wrote the name on his blotter. Then he opened the tin, giving two of the squares of tissue to Pembrook and opening the other one out himself.

"I have a feeling," he said, "that these things might tell us a lot about what our young friend knew. The trouble is finding out how they work."

"Well, isn't the first thing deciding whether it's a code or a cipher, sir?"

"Hey? Come again? And stick to Afrikaans this time."

The probationer squirmed.

"I'm sorry, sir, but I don't know the word for 'cipher.'"

"What does it mean, then?"

"That you give each letter of the alphabet a number or something, perhaps switch the letters around, and write like that."

"Bugger it, Pembrook, that *is* a code!"

"No, sir—at least not according to what I read once. A code is where one letter stands for a whole word—or where a drawing, say a circle, stands for 'battleship.' The trouble is you can't write just anything and you must have a codebook to do it."

Kramer made a show of peering into the tin.

"Nothing there," he said.

"That's also the trouble, sir," Pembrook went on, rather apprehensively. "You can't get anywhere without one."

"Uhuh."

A prisoner from the cells shuffled in to sweep the floor and was waved out again.

"Seeing you know so much about it, my boy, which one is this in?"

Pembrook caught a sneeze in a tissue and spent some time folding it away.

"Couldn't we ask them through in Security, sir? They're supposed to know all there is to know—more than me."

"What? And make a bloody fool of myself if it's a lot of twaddle? We're dealing with a kid of twelve, remember."

"Sir."

"Well?"

"I think it's in code, sir. You'll notice how each line of letters stays straight and keeps inside a sort of square. There's a pattern to it you wouldn't need if you were just switching letters around. It must match up with something."

"Of course! That explains the tracing paper!"

Pembrook flushed with embarrassed pride.

"Shall I have another go at his room, sir?"

Kramer did not hear him. He was closely examining all four slips, putting one on top of another and holding them to the light.

"No good," he said finally, "can't see anything that way. But I can help you in your search a little. You'll notice that although he used tissue paper and a sharp pencil, there are no tears in it—no dents along his lines either. He must have done these on a very hard, smooth surface."

"A book cover?"

"Much harder than that. Probably some sort of plastic or tin."

"And the bedroom's a likely place?"

"Why not? A job like this would have taken time and he'd need to be private."

Pembrook reached for his raincoat but Kramer stopped him.

"Wait to hear what Zondi has to say first," he said. "I'm sick of repeating everything."

Grandfather Govender was being very tiresome. Short of telling him he was a senile old fool, the rest of the family could find no obvious way of explaining why he could not understand what had happened to Danny. There he stood, clutching his staff like some latter-day Gandhi in the corridor of the magistrate's court, toothlessly sucking on an orange and shaking his head.

"All rubbish!" he muttered once again.

"Listen to me, Grandfather," said his son Sammy. "Last night Danny was arrested by the police and today he must go to a place of safety until they find out what it was he has done."

"They remanded him," said the half-cousin.

"They say he was carrying a housebreaker's tools, Grandfather," went on Sammy. "Do not make another noise here or it will go badly for all of us—Danny, too."

"What tools?"

Sammy winced.

"A spade," said the half-cousin.

"Rubbish!" shouted Grandfather, expelling a seed with the word.

"They can get you for just having a nail file sometimes," said an uncle with unhappy experience in these matters.

"What's the matter with you all?" Grandfather spluttered. "Do you think I'm senile?"

All Zondi wanted to talk about were the dogs. To avoid any complications, he had left the Chev some distance from 10 Rosebank Road and gone on foot the rest of the way, dressed as ordered in his worst. Within a matter of yards he felt like the star attraction at a jackal hunt. One haughty old bitch in a floppy hat, cutting a rosebush down to size with secateurs, had actually encouraged a toy poodle to join in the chase.

"Shame!" laughed Kramer. "Did you show them your warrant card?"

Zondi patted his Walther PPK in the shoulder holster.

"Next time, boss," he growled.

"Don't let the Colonel hear you, Kaffir. He's always saying he doesn't ever want a Sharpeville in his area."

Pembrook seemed ill at ease in their company. He would have to grow used to the idea that CID work made such partnerships necessary and therefore fairly common. Kramer felt himself curiously irritated.

"Why the look?" he asked sharply. "Are you a liberal or something?"

"*Pardon*, sir?"

"Forget it. Now, Zondi, my heart bleeds for you, but tell us what you found out. We're all busy men here."

Zondi began, in the way of his people, at the very beginning. He told them how, in his ragged jacket and trousers, he had slunk up to the door of the back veranda at the Jarvis house and informed the maid he was a *togt* boy. She came back and said there were no odd jobs going. Then he had pleaded for a morsel of food. This had brought him a doorstep of stale bread, spread thickly with apricot jam, and a can of black tea, well sugared. He had been given permission to eat in the compound.

There he had encountered one Jackson Zulu, the head cookboy, who was resting from his labors and idly planning the midday menu. He looked askance at the stranger and ordered him into the coal shed. Jackson had such a grand manner, Zondi almost obeyed him.

Then he had shown Jackson his handcuffs and suggested a confidential chat. Jackson was a wily old bird, though. Before agreeing to anything, he had asked if Zondi, who would have to be educated if he really was a detective sergeant, could spell "asparagus." Oddly enough, he could.

122

Jackson added it to his list on the back of an old bill and pronounced himself ready to be of any service. He had a great respect for the police, as had any man with something to lose.

They got on tremendously after that. Shrewdly, Zondi had started with the staff, leaving his questions about the family to appear polite afterthoughts to make Jackson feel important.

The Jarvises employed a head cookboy, a head maid who cooked in his absence, a housemaid, a wash girl part time, a garden boy, and a youngster who helped him. They had all been with the family some time and had arrived with first-class references.

"Get on with it," said Kramer, tossing a cigarette to Pembrook. The smoke might dry up that damn nose of his.

Zondi seemed mildly aggrieved but continued. Captain Jarvis—that was a captain of an army—was regarded as a good master. He was very particular about everything, and sometimes he swore terribly in a language nobody else understood, but he was just. The remarkable thing about him was the fact he never went out to work. Jackson had once asked tactfully for an explanation from the missus and she had told him a long story about sharing petrol that he could not understand. Still, it did not matter, as the wages were better than most.

Jackson liked his missus very, very much. She was much younger than her husband and never got angry. She forgot many things, too, and that was why she let Jackson run everything and even order groceries by telephone himself. It was a great honor to be so trusted. One of which, of course, Jackson was eminently worthy. Zondi had entirely agreed with him.

That loosened things up a bit. Jackson then admitted that there were times when the Jarvis household was not a pleasant place to be. There was the night of the elder daughter's birthday, for example. There had been a dinner party with ten guests and no less than six delicious courses which Jackson had served personally, resplendent in his red sash and white gloves. He had thought the missus very happy and talkative. Why, she had raised her voice like their own women did when they were enjoying themselves.

123

And yet, afterwards, there was a quarrel in the missus's bedroom—his employers slept separately—that became so bad that he and the other servants were told to leave the washing-up. The master had shouted that the visitors would say things about her that could do the family harm.

Jackson had shrugged. He could follow the ways of the Europeans so far and then . . . Perhaps the Captain had taken too much spirits. Any sober man would have seen how attentively the guests had listened to the missus—and have heard how loudly they laughed.

This elder daughter? She was not so bad but a bit cheeky. Also very lazy about getting up and usually had her breakfast on a tray. He put this down to the fact that she had a lover called Mr. Glen.

The younger daughter, Sally, was a different calf altogether. More like her mother although she was not the pretty one. *Hau*, she had been so sad until she, too, found a little lover. At first he had come to the house just to swim, and then he had been invited to lunch.

That was another bad meal, Jackson remembered. Hastening to add that the cooking had been, as always, fit for a paramount chief. The thing was the boy had eaten his fish with the meat knife and fork. Then, when the meat was served, he tried to cut his steak with a fish knife. The little missus had been so angry when the others laughed because he complained the knife was blunt. She cried afterwards, too, when he had gone. Only the missus seemed sorry for her and asked that Jackson make some ice cream. After this incident he had given them their meals separately on the back veranda. There was talk, he added in hushed tones, that despite speaking English, the boy was actually an *amaboona*. A Boer.

Zondi relished echoing, by example, a degree of restrained horror. Kramer took the recollection better than Pembrook, who seemed, for some reason or other, acutely embarrassed.

Then Jackson had tried to get back to the garden boy, about whom he harbored certain suspicions. There was this curious habit he had of going to sleep immediately after his evening meal. But Zondi wanted to know if the story of the little missus had a happy ending.

The boy had been up at the house on Saturday, Jackson

said. No, not since then, because the little missus had gone away suddenly to stay with her grandparents in Johannesburg. That was on Monday. Oh, yes, of course, a driver was also employed now. He had taken her with the master.

"What about the American?" Kramer demanded.

"Jackson did not say much, boss, because he was at home in his kraal for the month. He could only tell me the maids thought he was very strange in his ways. He cut up all his food before—"

"Please, no more bloody table manners, man!"

"I was also going to say he spoke to the maids like they were white. They were afraid his mind was dirty."

"That's all?"

"*Hau*, one more thing. They told Jackson that one morning the maid who makes the beds found a sock in the older daughter's sheets. The laundry maid helped her return it to the proper place."

"Young Andy's chest of drawers, no doubt?"

Zondi laughed, nodding.

"You bastard," said Kramer. "Why not start there with your story? Still, we've learned a lot, hey, Pembrook?"

"Yes, we have, sir."

"Still not happy about something. What is it?"

"Must I answer that, sir?"

"Zondi, push off outside a minute."

He left, closing the door carefully behind him.

"Come on, Constable, speak up."

"It's just—well, this doesn't strike me as—er—a very wise procedure, sir, sending in Zondi. I'm sorry, sir."

Kramer turned his back on him and then went over to look down into the street.

"Orthodox, you mean? What happened to Boetie Swanepoel wasn't orthodox, Constable. Remember that. And to help you get your job into its correct perspective, I'm ordering you to go down now to the mortuary and ask to see the body. I want you to touch it with your left hand. I will then sign that hand in ink. You will not wash that hand until this docket here has some red tape around it. Understand?"

"No, sir. I mean—"

"What the hell do you mean, Constable?"

125

"I've already seen Boetie, sir. It's not that. I'm worried about what will result if the cookboy tells his employers. If we're wrong—"

He was interrupted by Kramer's chortle.

"*Ach*, Pembrook, let's have our storyteller back in and see if he can't put your mind at rest. You've got the aptitude for CID but still a lot to learn."

Zondi entered warily.

"Sergeant, did you speak to any other of the servants?"

"No, sir."

"And how did you end your interview with Bantu male Jackson Zulu?"

"I asked to see his room, sir."

"For what reason?"

"To admire it, sir."

"And what transpired there?"

Instead of answering, Zondi took an official envelope out of his jacket and emptied out of it two silver fruit knives marked with a crest. There was not a servant's room in the land that could not reveal some sign of petty pilfering.

"You gave Zulu a receipt for them?"

"He did not want one."

"But he took it?"

"Yes, Lieutenant. I told him to put it in a safe place while I considered making further inquiries."

"How was he when you left him? Talkative?"

"Very quiet, sir."

Pembrook, whose youth had made it impossible for him to disguise his astonishment at Zondi's sudden command of formal Afrikaans, laughed out loud for the first time.

"It sounds very orthodox to me, sir!" he said.

"Naturally," replied Kramer. "Now I think we'd all better get about our business. You to check the room and me to pay a call on the Jarvises. Zondi here has to tidy up his part in last night's ax murder."

They began to move towards the passage.

"Why are you taking that stick, sir?" asked Pembrook.

"To be honest, man, I don't like dogs myself."

"But there isn't one at No. 10," Zondi reassured him. "It's dead."

126

The last lesson before midmorning break induced the teeth-gritting feeling Lisbet usually associated with a piece of hard chalk squealing on the blackboard.

Finally she gave up trying to instill any enthusiasm for the onomatopoeia in early Afrikaans poetry, and told her class to read.

Immediately every hand shot up. She would kill the lot of them in another minute.

"What's the matter now, Jan?" she asked.

"We haven't been to the library this week," he replied earnestly. "We've all finished our books."

"Yes, miss," chorused the others, suddenly anxious to receive the best education possible.

Little swine. Kids were quicker than anyone to smell out weakness.

"Have the magazines come?" asked Jan.

"That's a good idea. They're in my desk. Just a minute."

Lisbet brought out the parcel, tore the paper off, and divided the pile into two.

"I'd like Dirk and Hester to hand them out, please. Be as quick and quiet as you can. Then you must all read until the bell."

"Can I do the crossword puzzle instead, miss?"

"Yes, you may, Jan."

Sometimes she suspected, rather nastily, that he took full advantage of that harelip of his, knowing that few had the courage to shut him up. You felt it might be likened to tripping a cripple.

Peace.

Lisbet began to do what she had wanted so badly all morning: to read through Boetie's compositions in the hope of finding something there of significance. Her courses at teachers' training college had included elementary psychology and she had learned something of the mechanism of projected thoughts.

"Miss?"

"Jan! Didn't I tell you I wanted silence?"

"I want to show you something, miss."

He looked very hurt. Realistically, too.

"What? It better be important! Tell me from there."

Jan pointed in Hester's direction without letting her see him do it. Lisbet took the hint but frowned.

127

"All right then, come up if you must."

He tiptoed onto the platform and spread his copy of the magazine before her. His finger jabbed at a letter in the Detective Club section.

"See, miss? It's signed by Boetie."

Lisbet read the letter in a gulp.

"Jan," she said softly, "I don't think it'll do Hester any harm to see this. But I think I'd better make a phone call. Can I leave you as monitor in charge?"

"If you like, miss."

She shot from the room.

The constable handling the switchboard at police head-quarters turned to his companion working on canteen accounts and said: "Hell, what are you buggers putting into old Kramer's coffee these days?"

"He doesn't drink our coffee. Why?"

"Then it must be that Greek over the road."

"Doing what?"

"Putting something in his coffee."

"Christ, I'm taking these things into the other office if you're going to go on like that all bloody morning!"

"*Ach*, don't be like that, hey? It was just a joke. I mean a bloke like that isn't my idea of a ladykiller—he needs a little extra."

"Look, just tell me what this is all about."

"That's two dollies now, both different, both wanting to speak to him. Very sexy voices, I can tell you."

"And so?"

"They keep ringing but I can't put them through. He's out and as usual I don't know where. Feel like introducing myself—they sound hell of a anxious, if you know what I mean."

One of the pinafored Bantu maids admitted Kramer to the hall and left to inform her master and missus of his arrival.

If she had been white, it would have convinced Kramer he was on a film set. Even the weather contributed to the uncanny feel of the place as rain hissed against the diamond-shaped bits of glass in the narrow windows on either side of the great wooden door. Not that he had seen more

128

than two films about England in his life, but they had made a strong impression on him—largely because the strange girl who insisted on going to them was too ladylike to allow herself to be unbuttoned.

Kramer removed his raincoat and hung it up with some others on a thing made of antlers. Curious to know the name of the beast, he peered at the small silver plate beneath it and read: "Subalterns' Mess, Fort George." A lot of use that was.

He went back and wiped his feet on the mat again before stepping onto the rich pile of the Persian rug. The ceiling was very low. He tapped one of the brown beams and confirmed it was painted concrete, as befitted such conceits in the land of the termite. The original purpose of a long row of brass disks with pictures cut in them was quite beyond him.

But he understood the prime function of the rest of the decorations, while wondering idly if some were properly licensed. There were old pistols, swords, a crossbow, a daisy of daggers, and a battleax; an enormouse gong, a vase as high as his waist stuffed with bull rushes, and paintings of horsemen in red blazers jumping over farm fences—in one the farmer was waving his stick at them.

Much as he looked, however, he could not find anything from Africa. All the smaller stuff was the sort of junk that Indians tried to sell you from cloth-covered baskets on Durban beach, although not as nice and shiny. With so many servants about you would think they—

The maid had returned with a maidenly giggle to announce that her master would see the boss now in the drawing room.

Having carefully surveyed the large, thatched house on his way up the drive. Kramer had worked out its distribution of rooms well enough to open the correct door in the corridor.

Captain Peter Jarvis stood with his back to the gigantic fireplace, which had a one-bar electric fire poised for winter in its grate, at the far end of a gleaming floor. In spite of the distaince separating them, Jarvis's features—and particularly his mustache—were defined with exceptional clarity; they were sharp, in the physical sense, but it was the strong coloring that gave such an edge. The face was

129

deeply tanned, from a line just above a normal collar, the cheeks had circles of red on them, the mustache itself was pitch black, while the hair fringing the pate was shark gray; the eyes were brown, the teeth whiter than a new golfball. The first thing Kramer thought of was a model soldier, dismissed it as too trite, and then could not think of a better comparison. That was what the man looked like, and he stood like one, too, making the best of his five-foot-ten heavy build, and no visible scars or tattoos.

He wore a tailored suit as muted in its tone as the furnishings, offset by a single carnation.

"Gentlemen generally make an appointment," Jarvis remarked in military English with a militant edge to it. "However, seeing as you're here, come in, Lieutenant. I'm afraid I do not speak Cape Dutch."

"That's all right, sir. I'm paid to be bilingual. Just a casual inquiry."

Kramer made his way over, using the many rugs like stepping stones, and was waved diffidently into a leather chair.

"Drink?"

"Later maybe. Is your wife not here this morning?"

"Mrs. Jarvis is about the place, but I am sure that there is no necessity for troubling her with whatever you have come about."

"I thought that might be obvious, sir."

"Is it? I would have thought our connection with the boy hardly warranted your attention. It was very much a passing phase on Sally Ann's part."

"Surely that's an assumption?"

"Made himself unpopular, I'm afraid, rather inevitably really. He was not quite our—"

"Go on, sir?"

Jarvis eyed Kramer carefully.

"Shall we say, cup of tea, Lieutenant?"

"Uhuh. And yet he came to your house very frequently."

"Got that off his school friends, did you? I'm afraid he must have exaggerated to impress them. I would not place his visits at over half a dozen at the most."

"So you're not sorry he's dead?"

Jarvis reddened. "That is a most outrageous remark, sir! You will withdraw it at once!"

"I was only asking, Captain. You're not the first person to seem—you know. Far from it."

Jarvis took a decanter from a tray and poured a whisky.

"Think I'll join you, sir, after all," Kramer said.

"Good man."

With them both seated, the tension eased slightly. They raised glasses and drank.

"I imagine you prefer a Cape brandy?" Jarvis said conversationally.

"To tell the truth, Captain, I usually order Pernod."

"Remarkable," Jarvis muttered to himself. Then added quickly, "Is there anything specific you want to know about the boy?"

"Yes, we'd like to know when he was last here."

"On Saturday afternoon. He came to bathe, I believe."

"So your daughter was friendly with him as recently as that?"

"That was when it happened, Lieutenant. He overstepped the mark with some of his schoolboy smut. My elder daughter was not amused. Sally tried to defend him and realized, during the kafuffel that then took place, how dreadfully—er—common he was."

"Smut? You mean a joke?"

"I do. A deplorable piece of filth, so I was told."

"By whom? Sally?"

"No, Caroline, my eldest daughter."

"What happened then?"

"He left under a cloud."

"I see."

"May I emphasize something, Lieutenant? When I use the word 'common' I refer to a chap's breeding. I have the greatest respect for the forefathers of this country. The Boers were the finest mounted warriors since the Huns—Winston himself says so in one of his books."

A pretty speech.

"You mean you were lucky to win?" Kramer asked with a laugh.

Jarvis reddened again—he was better value than a performing chameleon.

131

"Perhaps so, Lieutenant. I must say your people were a surprise after the peasantry we were used to scrapping with."

Oh, very nicely done. However, Kramer was not there to settle old scores, but a new one. And he still had no idea who the enemy was.

"Did any member of your family see Boetie again after his incident?"

"No. I'm quite sure they would have mentioned it."

"Nevertheless, could I have a word with your daughters this evening, Captain. After school?"

"Caroline is in the nursing home having a cyst removed. I wonder if you'd not—"

"Sally, then?"

"I sent her up to her grandmother on the Witwatersrand."

"When was this?"

"On Monday, directly I saw the news in the paper. It would have upset her dreadfully. I know what I said about their little liaison, but the child's had enough to contend with recently."

Kramer got up and put his glass on the tray. He had the air of a man who had suddenly lost interest in the matter in hand and just wanted to beat a friendly retreat.

"Of course, I'd forgotten," he said. "You also had that sad business concerning the American youth. I was in Zululand at the time."

"Lovely part of the world, that," murmured Jarvis, accompanying him over to the door. "I'll show you out myself."

"There was one thing I never quite did understand about that accident."

"Really, Lieutenant? This is your mackintosh, I believe."

"The bit about the American's clothes. The story goes he was stripped down and probably about to have a swim when he fell in accidentally."

"That's what happened."

"But where was his swimming costume? I've never seen that mentioned."

Kramer took his raincoat from the hands outstretched

to help him on with it so that he would be able to keep his eyes on Jarvis's face. A slight tremor.

"Then your colleagues have kept their word," Jarvis said quietly.

"Not that I've been asking questions, but I'd like to know out of curiosity."

"You're an astute man, Lieutenant, but the explanation is simple: he often swam alone without one. He was rather given to that sort of thing."

"Walking round nude?"

"Something of that order. Surprising what American youth considers normal these days. Even so, we felt obliged to be discreet in the matter for his parents' sake. Sergeant Brandsma was most understanding. We didn't want the papers calling Andrew a hippie either—it's such a vulgar expression—and they would have leaped at it. As it was, the press wallahs did rather overdo—"

"But was he a hippie, in your opinion?"

"Sheer affectation! Came of excellent stock—told me his father liked his pimp's trousers no better than I did. Never could get him to have a decent haircut, but we did calm down his clothes a bit. His manners themselves were remarkably good."

"What did your daughters and their friends think of him?"

"Sally and Caroline were all right, but I'm afraid the others suspected him of being—er—sissy. Hair that length *is* effeminate by South African standards."

"No girl friends, then?"

"Hardly had time, old boy. Poor little blighter."

"He had a month, Captain. I've known a bloke set himself up in a week."

"The devil he did."

The great door stood wide and the rain tapped its way towards the Persian carpet.

"One more thing, if I may, Captain."

"Fire away."

"Was 'sissy' really the word for Master Cutler?"

Jarvis looked wary, then broke out a man-to-man smile.

"Deuced difficult to tell 'em apart these days," he murmured. "But that's not for publication."

They shook hands silently.

As Kramer ran through the wet to his car, he turned once to look back at the house. Remembering then that he had, in fact, seen a third English film: one about a country mansion which became haunted. Not, however, by the ghost of a clean-living boy who told dirty stories—nor of a homosexual youth who left his socks in girls' beds. Man, it had been dull.

Chapter Ten

LUNCH BREAK WAS almost over when the call finally came through. Lisbet snatched up the receiver, aware that the secretary had paused for only a brief exchange with a raucous pupil outside the office door.

"Trompie? Listen hard because I haven't got time to repeat anything. It's the magazine—Boetie has a letter in the latest issue. No date but you can work out roughly when it was written. This is what it says:

" 'Dear Sir, I think the Detective Club is very good. But I have a complaint. The new station commander has chased us all away. He says it is not children's work. Now there is just me left of the Midnight Leopards. Of course he is wrong, but he will not listen. I think I have found a way of proving to him a big mistake has been made. Only I do not have all the right information yet. Respectfully yours,' et cetera.

"And underneath it says: 'Leave this matter to me, old pal. Send me the name of the police officer concerned and I will pass it on to the brigadier for his attention. Keep up the good work!' "

Lisbet nodded.

"That's just what I thought, Trompie. Yes, I'll be in all evening. Why?"

The line went frustratingly dead.

Pembrook, who had been typing to Zondi's dictation, dragged the sheet of paper out of the machine and handed it to Kramer.

"Word for word, Sergeant?"

Zondi, still toying with the telephone's extra earpiece, shrugged modestly; it had not been much to memorize.

135

The mission where he had been educated could never afford to issue textbooks.

"That's quite a trick he's got there," Pembrook observed. "Where did he pick it up?"

"*Ach*, from a nun."

"Hey?"

"Back to work, Johnny—what do you make of this letter?"

"It's ambiguous, isn't it, sir? I can see how the magazine read it so the 'big mistake' was referring to the station commander's attitude. I can also see Boetie could have been referring to some other 'big mistake.' "

"Like the wrong verdict at an inquest?"

"Yes, sir. But we have no evidence to—"

"Look at his last line, man. That could mean he didn't have, either."

Pembrook rubbed his brow and gave it a couple of thumps.

"Sorry, I can't think straight," he said. "This cold is a bastard. Can Zondi go out for some tissues?"

"In a minute. First tell me if you have any ideas, Mr. Memory."

"Many, boss."

"Let's hear them, then."

Kramer offered a cigarette to Pembrook, which was politely refused, and tossed another over to the stool in the corner. Zondi caught it in his hat and lit up. He enjoyed an audience but kept his tone respectful.

"My woman gave me two boys at one time thirteen years ago, boss. I have studied their ways—and the ways of others. From when they suck the breast until they are so high, there is no trouble for them in this world. It does not matter if their singing is like a dog crying to the spirits. Or if the drawing they make in the sand is like where the dung beetle has been running. Then one month they are not children. Because why? Because soon they will have time to find their own bread; we have told them this is so, we have said you must learn well in school now, we have shaken our finger at childish things. There is a big exam for the high school and they must pass it. This is the change, boss, they do not like to try something un-

136

less they can do it nicely. They do not like people to laugh at them."

He paused.

"Is it the same for white children, boss?"

"Can't remember. Certainly they lose confidence for a while."

"But it is the laughing that is the big matter here. You have asked why the little master did not go to the police straightaway—maybe this is what he feared."

Pembrook sighed, caught Kramer's eyes, and turned it into a dry cough. Zondi clicked his tongue sympathetically before going on.

"There is also another idea I have been thinking. If the little master had seen this foreigner being killed, he would have to admit to the policemen that he was trespassing on private property."

"So what? That would be overlooked under the circumstances."

"Unless they knew already there had been a murder, boss. They would laugh and say, 'What the hell were you doing there, you little bugger? Didn't we tell you to keep away from Greenside?' "

It was an impertinent bit of mimicry.

"Wait a minute!"

Kramer jumped up with an expression of dawning comprehension. He dithered a moment and then disappeared from the room.

Zondi took it very calmly, concentrating on smoking his cigarette right down to the pinch of his forefinger and thumb. Pembrook watched him do it, wincing once, and then blew his nose on a piece of notepaper.

The rain stopped.

Nothing else happened.

Until Kramer returned with a box of paper tissues that he flung at Pembrook.

"Hell, sir! But you shouldn't have gone out for—"

"Oh, belt up. I wanted a walk. Why not? You owe me thirty-five cents."

"I'll—"

"Later, man. I've got it all worked out."

"*All* of it?"

"Enough. One thing I want to check first, then I'll tell

137

you. Meantime you book yourself a seat on the five o'clock plane from Durban."

"Where to, sir?"

"Jo'burg—where else? Got a nice little girlie lined up for you there. Try not to give her your cold."

Providence did Kramer proud. The house and grounds were completely deserted, apart from the driver; having dropped off Captain and Mrs. Jarvis at their weekly bridge party, he was taking his time over waxing the Rover round the back. The other servants were out visiting.

Kramer left Zondi to have a quiet word with him, and began his tour of the property's perimeter. This established that it was completely secure except for an almost invisible hole in the wire fence hidden within the high hedge alongside the road.

He stood with his back to it and studied the lie of the land. There was a long stretch of lawn, a flower bed, more lawn, some large shrubs, the tops of the tennis court poles, and, out of sight, but very much in mind, the swimming pool. The house was also impossible to see from this point—and, presumably, impossible to be seen from.

It was an excellent access for the uninvited. Kramer headed in a straight line for the shrubs, taking the flower bed in a single stride, and not halting until forced to by the shrubs. There was a gap in them slightly to the left and he pushed his way into it. The sun had been out for an hour but the leaves were still very wet. He scowled but persevered.

Finding he had not far to go. Quite suddenly the tennis court lay before him, and—beyond its walls of wire netting—the pool. He examined the ground at his feet. Nothing.

The patio was on the far side of the absurdly blue water; a pebbled wedge of concrete on which stood some cast iron furniture painted white, a furled café umbrella, and a child's swing missing its seat. He could take in every detail. Even the oyster shell ashtrays.

Another, more careful, examination of the ground where he stood revealed nothing.

Then Kramer had an inspiration: he bent at the knees until he approximated Boetie's eye level. The patio was

138

now blotted out of view by some azalea bushes in the foreground.

So that was it. Edging along like a bad case of piles, to keep his head at the right height, he discovered a gap in the azaleas through which he could see very clearly.

Still nothing on the ground. But a sapling just to his right caught his eye. Someone had been tearing the twigs off it. Someone who had not seen it bore an important-looking botanical label. Maybe because it was dark.

And anyway, a Midnight Leopard probably did not give a damn where it sharpened its claws.

The dispatch manager at the *Gazette* finished his day at two in the afternoon, having had to be there before sunrise to supervise local deliveries. He was about to take a farewell ogle at the new filing clerk when Grandfather Govender hobbled in.

"Out!" shouted the manager.

"Master, one more time I am asking you to come help by Danny's side. That poor children, master, he—"

"I dont want to know."

"Please, master. God blessing you. I can see you are a kind man in your heart."

"But I won't be so kind if you come back again, Sammy. I've already told you the kid was too good to be true—always knew he was up to something. Now the cops have him and I'm not interfering with them for you or anyone else. Bugger off."

Grandfather Govender struck the floor with his staff, in the manner of Moses installing a plague, then withdrew with patriarchal dignity.

Whereupon the new filing clerk said he had given her goose pimples all over.

And the foreman asked to see them.

Three cups of coffee from the Green café were very welcome. Zondi poured one into his tin mug and retired to the corner.

"Too bloody hot!" said Kramer, sucking his upper lip. "Any milk?"

"No, boss."

139

"*Ach*, I'd better just get started then. But first, did Zondi give you Sally's address in Jo'burg, Johnny?"

"It's 39 Woodland Drive, Parktown."

"Or Avenue—the driver was not positive about that."

"I'll find her, sir. But what line do I take?"

"There is one thing about Boetie we know for absolute certain," Kramer said, "and that is he behaved out of character for the four weeks before his death. Or seemed to."

"Sir?"

"I don't believe anyone changes so much so fast. What we have to do is keep both Boeties in mind and see how they can work together. Okay?"

Zondi gave a nod of understanding.

"Right. The next step is to pinpoint when this—shall we say—apparent change took place. Any suggestions?"

"On Sunday he overslept."

"Perfectly normal if he was very tired. Nor is there anything really remarkable in the fact he didn't do his homework and seemed somewhat peculiar on Monday morning. This was all very *passive*, if you get me."

"Then what about when he bought the paper?"

"We're getting closer, but even that action appeared acceptable when he said he wanted it to better his English. The first time he actually *did* anything that shocked anyone was on Tuesday when he gave Hester the boot."

"Yes, it was crazy, that. He could easily have two-timed her. The girls lived worlds apart."

"What about spies like Doreen West, who saw him at dancing?"

"Just a chance he had to take, sir. Anyway, he could have lied. Hester would believe him sooner than a spiteful English dame."

Kramer shook his head.

"But this is Boetie Swanepoel you're talking about," he said. "Lying and two-timing are not part of a strict Christian upbringing—and we know he had a hatred of cheats. I think he would have taken steps to avoid having to do either if he could."

"Huh! And what about the lies he must have told Sally?"

"Perhaps they could not be avoided. Some lies make

140

you feel bad; others don't, if you feel you have good enough reason for them."

The coffee was now cool enough to drink. The three of them sipped in thoughtful silence.

"Even so, sir, if Boetie was the upright bloke you say, then it couldn't have been easy to drop Hester without telling her why."

"I'm sure it wasn't. Not something to be done on the spur of the moment. I'm sure Boetie gave it a lot of thought. How long would you make it?"

"A day, sir?"

"Agreed—although it's purely arbitrary. The interesting thing is to count a day back from Tuesday lunchtime and see where you end up."

"With him buying the newspaper?"

"And whose name appeared in that story?"

"Sally's?"

"It also gave her age."

Zondi tipped his head sideways like a puzzled jackal.

"Age was the common denominator, you see," said Kramer. "Something he could work on if he wanted an 'in' to the Jarvis family."

"But why—"

"Once upon a time," Kramer interrupted, "there lived a bloke called Boetie who wanted to catch a burglar.

"Bonita told us that on Saturday, November 15, he went out at night on his bicycle; Hennie told us he was still patrolling Greenside; Mr. Swanepoel told us Boetie overslept; and so Boetie was out very late on patrol in Greenside on the night of Andy's death.

"There are not many street lights in Greenside and most of the properties are difficult to see into. Boetie was going along, relying on his ears to alert him to suspicious circumstances.

"We have one address in Greenside with which we can connect him—10 Rosebank Road. He also claims to have seen something. This couldn't have been at No. 10 unless he entered the property.

"So what we have is Boetie passing by when he hears a sound or sounds that make him curious. He finds a hole in the fence inside the hedge and crawls through. All he sees

141

is lawn—and it's dark, too, remember. He makes for the next bit of cover."

"The shrubs where you—"

"Shhhh, man. He forces his way through the shrubs and then finds the way blocked by the tennis court wire. Does he then go round sideways?"

"If he has any sense."

"Unless, of course, he can identify from where he is who or what is making those sounds."

"Naturally, sir! He can see all right and that's why he stands there, buggering up that little tree, looking right onto the patio . . ."

"Through two lots of wire netting. That's important because although your eyes put it out of focus—like when you're gawking in a zoo—it still blurs the vision slightly, particularly at night. I'll come back to that.

"The question now is: What does he see? Take the official version. Andy is walking about bare-arsed, falls in, and doesn't surface.

"Man, I doubt it. The first reason is we wouldn't have had all this nonsense afterwards. Andy would have drowned and there's an end. The other reason is that Boetie was good at swimming—remember what the Dominee said. If he had seen someone fail to rise in the water, it would have been his instinct to rush and save him.

"Which forces us to concoct an alternative version, and we start by asking ourselves why didn't Boetie go to the rescue? Either he was afraid to or he did not see the point. What does that suggest to you?"

Zondi was the first to answer.

"That there was another person there, boss."

"Or, sir, he knew Andy was dead already."

"Impossible, Johnny; he could not even begin to see the bottom of the pool from where he stood."

Pembrook glanced across to Zondi before answering.

"Then he must have made a judgment based on someone else's behavior."

"Ah, so Andy was not alone after all when he took his moonlight dip! And what's more, this third party made no attempt at a rescue or the body would have been dragged back onto dry land—you can't apply respiration in water."

"And that's what Boetie saw!"

142

"Plus what went before. If I tell you that a man has died mysteriously and there was another person there at the time, what are your conclusions?"

"Foul play."

"You could go a step further, in the light of what happened to Boetie, and say murder. But let's keep within the framework and just call it a crime."

"Why didn't he . . . ?"

"This is where what Zondi said comes in. Here we have Boetie witnessing a crime. He knows it's a crime and he knows the police will inevitably become involved in it because they must investigate all sudden deaths. He also reads the Detective Club column which praises the police to high heaven. Nothing can escape their watchful eye. Naturally he supposes the crime he sees committed will be no exception."

"Christ, sir, that's good!"

"Logical, nothing else. So what is there in it for him? If he tells the police what they already know, they will laugh. If he tells them what they will doubtlessly find out, they'll want to know where he got his information. He realizes that it would be best to keep quiet."

"That sort of cool thinking would take a hard-headed kid."

"Boetie in a nutshell, Johnny. Okay, so he sneaks out and goes home, but he's only twelve and he's seen a man die. This keeps him awake. Makes him oversleep. Perhaps by morning it is all unreal and almost a dream. He forgets to do his homework. On Monday he wants to make sure he saw what he saw—and he's also very curious to check on how the case has been treated. Crime in Greenside is big stuff.

"He buys a paper. What's in it? An inquest stating Andy Cutler died accidentally. He must have flipped. And I wouldn't be surprised if he didn't make the same mistake we made over that line. 'A typical drowning.' "

"But, sir . . ."

"Go on."

"Surely that was his cue to tell the police? Now he was in the strongest possible position."

"Oh, no, he could go one better. Here, the letter reads:

143

'I think I have found a way of proving to him a big mistake has been made.'

"You mustn't overlook Boetie's feud with the station commander. That had made him really sore. He didn't want to reveal the crime so much as actually use it to *prove* how useful he and his mates could be."

Pembrook pushed back his cuff from his watch and frowned.

"You see," said Kramer, leaning forward, "what Boetie had in mind was presenting the police not with just his eyewitness report, but the whole bloody thing tied up in a string. Real evidence like a real detective."

"Sorry, sir, that's too much to believe."

"All right, let's try another approach. Up to the moment Boetie saw the newspaper article he had no reason to doubt his assessment of the acitivity by the pool. Now he is confronted by what seems an incredible oversight. Or is it? Only an investigation can give him the answer and he prefers to carry it out himself."

"Then nobody can call him a fool," Zondi murmured.

"Well, Johnny?"

Pembrook had been turning the rubber roller of the typewriter in an irritating way. He jerked his head up.

"I think all he wanted was something to back up his word. One or two outside facts, maybe. If he had just gone to the station commander with his story, it could have been dismissed as a nasty piece of malicious hearsay—particularly as everyone was being so soft about the thing. I'm with you there, but now I can't understand why he put it in his letter to the Detective Club. Or why he wrote to it at all."

"A good point. My theory is simply that he felt he had to tell *someone*. You can see the kids take this club pretty personally."

"Hmmm. Where do we go from here then, sir?"

"Just a minute—the wire netting. There is a chance that it boosted any doubt that started to grow in his mind. At that range he might not necessarily have been able to give a good description of the other party. He'd have to see them again first, so he decided to get mixed up with the family. He notices Sally is twelve and somehow finds out she goes to dancing. Let's not trouble with that point too

144

much. In the first place, it's a reasonable deduction considering the type of girl she is—and in the second place, we know he was training down at the town baths with English boys. They could have told him.

"Hester is a snag. She expects him to go around with her, and won't be easily fobbed off with excuses. She'll get in the way. Then the conscience thing again, which I think is very real. And on top of this, the breaking-off committed him to his plan of action.

"Boetie gets all togged up and goes to dancing on Friday night. Naturally Sally is pleased when a boy takes so much notice of her for a change. She's probably so hard-up that it doesn't make any difference he's Afrikaans—or maybe she goes for being a rebel daughter. With an old man like that, I wouldn't be at all surprised. From here on, Boetie worms his way into the household, trying to find out what he can."

"Yet he still isn't any the wiser after how many visits?"

"Who said? He must have finally got somewhere because he implied as much when he asked Hennie to look after the toffee box."

Pembrook opened it.

"I bet these codes could explain a few things. Pity there was nothing in his room—I was there two hours, you know."

"That's what I'm going to work on as soon as you leave. Christ, the time! You'd better go."

Zondi handed Pembrook his raincoat and small suitcase, adding a little bow which did not go down very well.

"All right, sir, I'll ring in the morning. I think I know what you want out of Miss Jarvis."

"What's that?"

"Mainly if Boetie told her dirty jokes, too. That's the one bit that doesn't fit into all of this."

"You're my boy." Kramer grinned.

The padlocked Ford van carrying Danny Govender from the place of safety to the magistrate's court for another remand that Thursday afternoon was being driven by Constable Hendriks.

A very cheerful Hendriks, because he had once again succeeded in winning a transfer to a job he considered

145

more congenial—and this time he was confident of having found his true billet. Nobody else had transfers granted as readily as he did. He wondered again if, in point of fact, he did have a winning personality. A sergeant had once murmured something to that effect.

There was not a great deal of traffic, yet he kept his speed down. The whole secret of ferrying prisoners to and fro was in the timing; if you did the journey too quickly, the jail would find paper work for you; too slowly and the court cell sergeant would bawl you out in front of the wogs.

He looked into his mirror, noting with satisfaction that the sole occupant of the lock-up section in the rear was sitting nice and quiet. Now here was an interesting case, this snot-nosed Indian kid who claimed he had gone into a posh area to dig up a dog. What a story! And yet everyone felt there was an even better one somewhere if only they could coax it out.

Hendriks' thoughts homed in on himself. Actually, when he dispassionately reviewed his career in the force to date, he could detect only one minor shortcoming: a tendency to forgetfulness.

Which was one of the reasons he had for being so pleased about his present job. There was nothing to remember—no messages, no beats, no faces on the wanted list. All he did was count the prisoners as they hopped in, snap the lock, drive, twist the key, count them as they got out, and hand over the papers.

He hiccuped, tasting again the very strong coffee he had been given out at the place of safety by the housekeeper. A nice woman who always made him very comfortable, and it was good to put up his feet for five minutes.

Jesus! Some cheeky sod behind him was hooting to pass; he would bloody well—

A fire engine shot by, its siren coming on with a long wail of derision. Hendriks could have sworn that the baboon next to the driver had shaken a fist at him.

He would bloody well show them!

The van leaped in pursuit, its POLICE markings giving it the same immunity from the normal rules of the road, and all other traffic shrank towards the curbside.

To his delight, Hendriks started gaining and could spare

a moment to check his prisoner in the mirror again. The little devil was loving it. There would be no complaints, and if there were . . .

Just look at that, the fire engine was chickening out at the turnoff to Binswood Avenue. It might be a blind corner but there was no need to drop down into bloody first gear for it. Wait till *he* got there. The fire engine disappeared out of sight.

Hendriks braced himself against the door and gunned the van into a fancy four-wheel drift.

He came out of the corner into Binswood Avenue at thirty mph, which, while being a lot slower than it felt, gave him a thinking distance of thirty feet and a braking distance of forty-five feet. For the first ten yards he thought about the petrol tanker lying on his side, completely blocking the road, and its load gushing out of the fractured seams. For the rest of the way he braked.

As it happened, he traveled all of eighty feet from the corner—missing the fire engine by a coat of red paint— before denting his radiator grille slightly on the stricken vehicle. It was amazing how his all-weather tires kept their grip through the great spread of fuel.

A fireman wrenched his door open.

"Jump, you stupid bastard! This lot could go up any second!"

Hendriks wobbled out on trembling legs and was hustled to safety.

"Has he got anyone in there?" asked the fire chief, being answered with a nod. "Then give us the bloody key, mate, and be quick!"

Hendriks felt in his pocket. Then in his other pocket. All three other pockets.

"*Ach*, no! I forgot it when I had coffee," he mumbled. "You see, you don't need it to snap on—"

"Bolt cutters!" bellowed the fire chief, somewhat needlessly, as two of his men were already rushing towards the van with them.

The exhaust manifold on the police van ignited the vapor—or so it seemed, for the first explosion came from under its bonnet. There were nine others, and flames as high as the walls of hell.

Luckily for the pair with the bolt cutters, the initial

147

blast knocked them flying before they got their boots wet. But although suffering severe injuries, they did not lose consciousness and were able to hear, as much as they tried not to, the sounds that Danny Govender made as he was roasted alive.

A horrible death for a boy—but pure accident.

Chapter Eleven

IF THERE WAS one thing that bored the pants off Kramer, it was a fire story. He picked up the evening newspaper, noticed BLAZE in the main headline, and dropped the whole shebang into the wastepaper basket.

Then he continued to pace the office, varying his stride only when he turned or had to step over Zondi's outstretched legs.

On his desk lay the three pieces of tracing paper with their enigmatic inscriptions uppermost. All around them were crumpled leaves from the memo pad, each covered in various permutations of the letters. Three hours' work had proved nothing more than the fact Pembrook was correct in his assumption that a code, rather than a cipher, had been used. A cipher required that each character of the alphabet be given a substitute symbol—even another letter would do; but Kramer had been able to find only twelve different letters anyway and you could not make up words from such a limited number.

"What I am wondering about," said Zondi eventually, "is why Boetie was thinking in English when he wrote this thing."

He pointed to a *c* in the bottom line of one sheet he had copied down. There was no such letter in Afrikaans.

"Yes, I noticed that, too, man. But I suppose it's all part of making up a secret message—if you can do it in another language as well, so much the better."

"And another matter, boss—who was he writing these messages to?"

"Himself, I'd say. Case notes. Information he had picked up but didn't want known until he was certain. Kids like writing things down—I remember a bloke at

149

school who used to make huge lists of birds he had seen, even though he remembered every last one."

Zondi went over to the desk and examined the original.

"Did Boss Pembrook find anything hard in his room to write on?"

"Bugger all."

"Boetie could have used this toffee tin lid."

"I've tried that—it isn't as smooth as it looks. Pencil picks up tiny bumps."

Sighing, Kramer wandered over to the window. Suddenly he stiffened.

"Bring me a spare bit of tracing paper and a pencil," he said.

They were in his hands in seconds. He pressed the paper against the pane and wrote. The effect was identical.

"As smooth as glass." Kramer smiled. "He did it on his window because the light coming through made it even easier to trace."

"But this paper is quite thin, boss."

"Perhaps whatever he was tracing wasn't too distinct, then. Come on, man, what could they have been? What is about that size and shape?"

No good—they had been through everything they could think of.

"What would this code thing have on it?" Zondi asked. "Just words?"

"I expect so."

"Then wouldn't it be just as hard to understand as these things—and mean, by itself, nothing at all?"

"Like a dictionary?"

"Yes, boss, you cannot find secrets in those books. They are quite safe."

"So?"

"Why should he hide the code if he has hidden the message?"

"Christ, that's a notion!"

"Thank you, boss."

Kramer sat down and ate his pie, which had gone cold.

"Know something, Zondi? He could even have had the code *on* him for all that it mattered—I mean when he got the chop."

"You said there was just rubbish in his pockets."

"Let's have another look, though. I've got the stuff here in my drawer."

Kramer cleared a space before emptying the plastic bag. The penknife clattered out first, followed by the rubber eraser, which bounced away under the furniture. The khaki handkerchief was next and in its slipstream fluttered the three bubble gum wrappers.

"Big deal," said Kramer.

Zondi retrieved the eraser and, after looking at it closely, put it back in the bag.

Kramer absently smoothed out one of the wrappers.

"Boss!" exclaimed Zondi.

But Kramer had already seen it was the same size and shape.

"Chewsy Super Bubble Gum," he read out in English before turning over the wrapper. It was deep blue on the inside. There was also a joke printed on it in black.

He slipped one of the squares of tracing paper over it.

"Can't see a bloody thing," he grunted. "Let's try the window."

There the low sun made the sandwich of paper translucent enough to show the letters at least were the same height, and set across the same width. No sense could be made of them, however.

"There are a lot of *c*'s in that joke, boss, and one near the end like this other tracing here."

Kramer substituted it for the first tracing, and held it against the glass.

Still no luck.

The third tracing was matched up.

"We've got it, man! Look!"

Zondi took a little longer to grasp what Boetie had done. And then he realized that all the letters in pencil were random and irrelevant—with the exception of a very few that coincided exactly with the initial letter of a printed word in the joke underneath.

What he saw was in effect, this:

A bad-tempered cobbler was sitting working on a shoe one day when a little boy pointed to some leather and asked him: "What's that?" The cobbler snapped: "Hide! Hide!

151

The cow's outside!" "I'm not afraid of a cow," the little boy laughed.

Chewsy Chuckle No. 113

"Write this down quickly," Kramer said. "B-s-o-h-c-b. Hell, that doesn't spell anything! Here we go again."

Zondi peered over his shoulder.

"But if you read the whole word each time, it does make some kind of sense, boss. Bad-sitting-on-him-cow-boy."

"Cowboy! One word, I bet you. The bad man was sitting on him—of course, on the American. You see, cowboy is the nearest he could—"

"Then why not underline this word and make it clearer by saying 'the cowboy'?"

"True. It does seem to break there. What can he mean?"

"Like you said, he just writes down notes for himself, he doesn't need the pieces in between."

"Uhuh. Let's try another and see if it works the same way first. I'll have the other one with a *c* near the end and that tracing over there."

A very fat old man standing in the gutter was asked by a cheeky Girl Guide what he was doing there. "Would it be possible to see me across the busy street?" he said with a sigh. She grinned at him and replied: "I could see you a mile off, mister!"

Chewsy Chuckle No. 57

"It bloody does work! Was-girl-doing-it-with-him? You can bet your socks she was, Boetie my lad. Hurry and get this all down."

A judge to the prisoner in the dock: "So we meet again. Aren't you ashamed to be seen in court so often? I would be." The old lag replied: "What's good enough for you, m'lud, is good enough for me!"

Chewsy Chuckle No. 317

Zondi added it to the other two on his slip of paper and handed it over.

"You made a mistake in this last one when I read it out. No, maybe you're right after all—I'm certain Boetie meant that. One of the first things I learned about English was there were many words that sounded the same but were spelled different. It's so stupid it sticks in your mind. Here he's found a use for it."

The slip read: "Bad sitting on him. Cowboy/Was girl doing it with him/To meet in wood good for me."

Kramer was elated. He slapped Zondi on the shoulder and they each nearly broke a bone.

"See? This last one? He thought he would have it all wrapped up after this meeting in the wood."

"A good time to kill him, boss?"

"You're so right. What a fluke we did them in their correct sequence, although it wouldn't have taken much effort to sort out anyway."

An uneasiness stirred in Kramer as he said this—flukes were seldom to be trusted.

"Boetie must have worked hard to find good jokes."

"Ones that would carry his message? Well, obviously he had more than three hundred of the buggers to choose from—and all the rubbish bins at school to find them in."

"It is a shame."

"What do you mean?"

"That he did not write these things another way. Have you noticed that not one of these papers has a word that connects the case with the foreign boy?"

"Except for cowboy."

"But, boss, you said that—"

"*He*, Andy, could have been the one doing the sitting."

"Then why say 'bad sitting on him'? Surely the man who is bad is the one that does the deed that is evil? I tell you it is not a plain matter at all."

Zondi was right. The bastard.

Traveling at 400 mph toward the northwest, an agitated air stewardess reached the flight deck of the South African Airways Boeing 727.

"We're flying as low as we can," the first officer protested. "Who've you got in there that's making such a fuss? This isn't the first time we've lost a bit of cabin pressure, and never have I heard—"

153

"A policeman."

"They're as tough as bloody nails."

"Shame, he's got a bad head cold. Says his ears are giving him hell and he feels dizzy."

"Look, tell your friend that we're very sorry, but another two feet down and we'll be plowed in as fertilizer. Okay?"

"Cure all our troubles," muttered the navigator, a sour man.

So she returned to Pembrook's seat beside the starboard wing. He appeared to have fainted.

Argyle Mslope had a bed in the passage at Peacehaven Hospital—the wards were too crowded for critically ill patients. The noise out there did not trouble him, as he was heavily sedated.

And quite unaware he had a visitor. Zondi used the bandaged head for a hatstand and then made himself comfortable in a stray wheelchair.

The blood dripped very slowly from the suspended bottle, about once every four heaves of the great chest beneath the sheet. Whether the tubes up the nose were going in or coming out was a moot point. There was a needle taped to the back of one hand, ready for the next syringe, and a label around the other wrist.

It was good to see Argyle still had both hands.

"Can I help you?" a woman said in brisk, affected English.

Zondi swung round in the wheelchair and there was an African staff nurse surveying him with arms akimbo. She had been trying to bleach her facial skin and it was a sickening color.

"Elizabeth Mbeta! It is a long, long time. When did you come down from Zululand?"

"Zondi?"

"The same, my beauty. Are things going well with you?"

"Can't you see? I am a staff nurse."

"But you wanted to be a teacher."

"They do not pay you in the holidays."

"True, true."

"There is not much choice for an educated girl. It was

154

this or work in the prison. Here we have nice rooms—
even a tennis court."

"How do you like it, though?"

She made no reply, pointing instead at Argyle.

"He is strong, that one."

"He'll be all right?"

"If he . . ."

"Yes?"

A shrug, that was all.

If she had been any less of a bitch, she might have
thought of something comforting to say in Zulu.

Lisbet had not, as she pretended, just finished preparing
her own supper when Kramer arrived. The whole flat was
filled with the smell of food that had been in the warming
oven overlong. However, it still smelled extremely good,
and the demijohn of Cape wine on the table looked even
better.

"Was the letter any good to you?" she asked, heaping
his plate with mutton curry. "I was so excited at the time,
but afterwards I wondered why."

"Call it feminine intuition," he replied gallantly.

"What did you learn, then?"

By the time the last banana fritter disappeared and the
coffee was poured, he had brought her up to date on the
investigation.

"Mind if I say something, Trompie?"

"Hell, no."

"Then I don't think your explanation of why Boetie left
the coded papers with Hennie is very convincing."

"You have a better one?"

"Maybe, although it's along the same lines. I think he
was going to show off with them when it was all over;
give Hennie and the others the wrappers and let them see
for themselves what a smart guy he was. You hear it every day in the classroom, especially on Mondays. Someone
says he spent the weekend hunting buck with a rifle and
all the rest say, '*Ach*, we don't believe *that!*' There would
naturally be a gap before the papers say anything and
that's when he'd have shown them."

Kramer half-closed his eyes.

"You sound as if you've gone off Boetie a bit."

155

"Well, am I right?"

"Nearer the truth than myself? Probably. This is all guesswork. But what is it about Boetie that's changed your attitude?"

"I was looking through his compositions today. He was very self-assured, you know, and almost frighteningly correct in his outlook. You should see the one he did on his beach holiday—a long complaint about litter and girls indecently dressed. He even quoted the regulation they have in the Free State for keeping sunbathers at least eighteen inches apart around swimming baths."

"Really?"

"Oh, yes. All in favor of it. And then he—"

"What?"

"Had the cheek to do this—to carry on his own investigation. That card the club issued him with stressed cooperation with the police, but he didn't seem to take too much notice of that."

"Everyone twists the law a little at times."

"But he had no right to! He was a child."

"Quite right. Boetie was a bad boy but you can't blame him altogether. He was provoked by the station commander."

"The last time you were almost defending the man!"

How galling it was to discover that even Lisbet argued like a woman.

"Well, that's the sergeant off the hook now—nobody to write in with his name, rank, and number."

Lisbet smiled wryly.

"Jan has already seen to that. In fact, they all spent their free period composing flowery tributes for the letter section."

"Christ! The Colonel doesn't want the club to become involved in this stupid incident."

"Don't worry. I offered to post them all in one big envelope—it's behind you on the telephone table."

"That's my girl!"

"Oh, thank you, Lieutenant, I thought you would never say it. More coffee?"

It was virtually impossible to gauge how jocular that remark had been intended to sound. Kramer recognized its potential in terms of the elusive signals exchanged by the

156

more modest mammals during mating season, but decided to dwell on work a little longer until he was certain of pleasure.

"How about taking a look at what Boetie actually said in the coded message?"

"I wouldn't mind."

He slid the slip over and brought back his refilled cup on the return trip. The light from the two red candles gave her a glow that warmed his eyes. And, to be entirely honest, his heart.

For he had suddenly grasped she was the genuine article: the haystack girl for whom he had searched much of his life. Right from when he was ten and saw the archetype on a calendar in a garage workshop; a cheerful, tomboyish, smooth-limbed girl sprawled smiling an invitation to an energetic game. Part of his response had been envy—there was not enough grass on his father's farm to make even a small pile for jumping on—and part the curious precognition of a child who sees a Cadillac and declares it will ride in one someday. As he had grown older, however, compromise had smudged the image, like the greasy thumbs of the mechanics tearing off the months. The years. The long trail of discarded nylon trivialities leading only to the fear she would never appear in her checked shirt, freckles, and blue jeans.

Lisbet had freckles and wore blue jeans to relax in. Her blouse might be plain pink but the tablecloth was a bright red-and-white gingham.

Christ, she was frowning.

"What's up?" Kramer asked anxiously.

"You told me there was nothing in these to connect the cases. Personally, I don't see how Boetie could have made it any clearer than this, using the joke."

"Show me!"

She turned the slip around his way.

"The word before 'sitting on him,' Trompie—that's 'bath,' isn't it?"

Of course it was—in Afrikaans.

"Damn that bloody fool Zondi! It was his idea all this was in English and we never thought of it any other way. He said so even before we got the code."

"What gave him the idea, though?"

157

"The *c*'s."

"But that's clever, you've got to admit."

"Zondi's too bloody clever half the time."

"*Ach*, Trompie, don't get so angry. You should have realized that Boetie would probably have to use every language he could to make anything of such a small selection of words. You've got the connection now—it would be too big a coincidence to mean anything else—and that proves you're on the right track."

Kramer rose and went over to the telephone.

"I've got to put a trunk call through to Pembrook in Jo'burg before anything else happens," he said.

"What do you mean by that, Trompie?"

There it was again—only a fifth-rate comedian would try to capitalize on such a commonplace ambiguity of words, but the tone alone was suggestive.

"I meant—hello, is that the exchange? I want a call to Johannesburg. From Trekkersburg 42910—the Jo'burg number is 7723612. Two hours' delay? At this time of night? I don't care if you're having to route calls via Bloemfontein!"

"Tell them you're the police."

Kramer looked over his shoulder at Lisbet. She had closed the sliding doors across the alcove where they had eaten and was now sprawled smiling on the settee.

"Hello, exchange? Are you still there? Make it a person-to-person fixed-time call for eleven o'clock. The name's Kramer. I want to speak to Johnny Pembrook. Thanks."

"That was a funny thing to do, not to use your position," Lisbet said.

"There's wine left in the bottle, isn't there?"

She pouted.

"You're not trying to get me drunk, are you?"

"Is there any reason why I should?"

"No."

This time he was certain, the denial had been so softly spoken. She moved slightly to give him space to sit.

"You're strange," she said, touching his hands. "You seem so hard and tough yet you're gentle as well."

"What makes you say that?"

"The Swanepoels."

158

"Hey?"

"You've never once been to see them. You can't face the idea, can you? Not after seeing what actually happened to Boetie."

"*Ach*, no, I stay away because I don't like saying sorry for something I haven't done."

"No emotions?"

"They reduce efficiency."

"In private life, too?"

"I haven't got one," Kramer countered.

"Oh, dear," she said. "Am I wasting my time?"

Jan Smuts International Airport was agog with the discovery of a bomb on an Alitalia jetliner. All passengers on the flight had been hustled aside for questioning. There were police everywhere.

But, to Johnny Pembrook's relief, none of them had a moment to spare on assisting a colleague in distress. By waving his identification card at each checkpoint, he was able, despite being lightheaded, to reach the taxi rank within minutes of touchdown. The stewardess, who had been very quick with the sal volatile, was probably still searching for him.

He was obsessed with one thought: to see Sally Jarvis and complete his mission before falling over.

The taxi door swung open and he climbed in.

"Where to, sonny?"

"Parktown."

"It's a big place."

"Er, 39 Woodland Drive."

"What's that off? Woodland Avenue?"

"Could be."

"Never been there before?"

"Just drive."

"Hey ..."

"Get going. I haven't got all bloody night!" bellowed Pembrook, betraying his state of extreme agitation.

The taxi driver made a casual adjustment to his rear-view mirror. In it he saw a disheveled youth with a very pale face and the shakes.

"Just a minute, son, while I take a look at my map. You just got in?"

"Yes, on the Durban plane, five minutes ago."

"I see."

"Have you found the address yet, driver?"

"But what about your suitcases?"

"Just this bag."

"You can't have much in there."

"What the hell business is it of yours? Give me the map—I'll guide you."

"It's all right, we're on our way. As the bishop said to the actress."

Pembrook sat back and glared at the funny man who fully deserved to have ears that stuck out at right angles like Mickey Mouse. He hoped the sod got leprosy in them.

For this was certainly no time for idle chitter-chatter and pedantry. Pembrook felt terrible; he wanted desperately to flop down on a bed in the barracks—to see a doctor even, for the pain. But he knew such a move could bring immediate suspension from duty and that would not help the lieutenant. Hell, no, old Kramer was depending on him. Whatever the reasons, he had been given a chance to shine, and shine he would as long as he could. This meant he would be foolish to take a chance of being well enough in the morning to carry out his assignment as arranged. It had to be seen to without delay. His plan of action crystallized: extract fact from Sally Jarvis, telephone same reverse charges to Trekkersburg, find a cheap hotel to lick his wounds in. With luck, he would be fine come sunrise. If not, too bad—at least the investigation could continue.

Pembrook focused with difficulty on some flashing lights ahead. There were several vehicles parked on the highway itself and he spotted a policeman.

The taxi slowed down.

"For Christ's sake, don't stop," Pembrook said. "It's just an accident."

"That's what you think, you bugger," muttered the driver, suddenly accelerating and then slamming on his brakes.

Pembrook was flung hard against the front seat. His forehead struck a chrome ashtray and he slumped, momentarily stunned, to the floor.

160

"It's a roadblock!" the taxi driver shouted triumphantly as he leaped from his seat.

"Hey, what's going on?" an authoritative voice inquired.

"The bomber! I've got him in there—grab him quick."

The back doors of the taxi were wrenched open. Pembrook was dragged out and put on his feet. A couple of thick-set constables held him there, his arms pinned.

"Look," he said and got no further.

"Came out of the main building like a bat out of hell, Sarge," the taxi driver burbled. "All shaking and white, with just a bag. Very jumpy. Wanted to be taken to Woodland Drive in Parktown—there isn't such a place. Then he says he got straight off the Durban plane but it gets in an hour before that!"

"Pressure trouble," explained Pembrook.

"Huh! He's trouble, all right—isn't he, Sarge? Told me to drive like hell and not to stop for you either."

"He doesn't look like an intellectual," said the sergeant, unsnapping his handcuffs.

"Just shows you how clever the swine are! I was telling the blokes on the rank only yesterday that appearances meant nothing these days. Take pop stars, for example. They arrive here all dressed in—"

"What's your name?" the sergeant asked Pembrook.

"John Pembrook. This is all—"

"Where from?"

"Trekkersburg."

"Any papers to prove it?"

Pembrook thought fast. His driving license had his parents' address on it. It would do for identification and he could sort out the rest of the story without revealing his affinity. The cautious sergeant was just the sort of fatherly type to wreck his plans through an excess of charity.

"This is all a big mistake, Sergeant," he said very calmly. "The Boeing lost cabin pressure and made me sick because I've got a cold. It was late—ask the control tower. As far as the address goes, I stupidly didn't bring it along and was working from memory. It was 39 Woodland Avenue I wanted, I'm sure."

"I asked if you had any papers."

"If you'd let my arm go, I'll give you my driving license."

"Careful, Sergeant," warned one of the constables, "I can feel a gun through his jacket."

"Did you hear that? A *gun!*" the taxi driver announced excitedly to the crowd of motorists that had gathered.

"Hold him nice and tight and I'll help myself," said the sergeant, taking a wad of documents from Pembrook's inside pocket. He turned to read them in the beam of his riot van's headlights.

The crowd went up on tiptoe.

"Is he a saboteur, Sarge?" asked the taxi driver, adding, for the benefit of late arrivals, "It was me who caught him!"

"Are you really this?" the sergeant asked, turning on Pembrook and holding out his identity card.

The probationer detective constable said good-bye to all that, brought himself back into the present, and nodded.

"What's he?" begged the crowd.

"I'm entitled to know!" demanded the taxi driver, grabbing the sergeant's arm.

"A policeman, sir. Do you want to leave your name? For a medal?"

Even Pembrook found a smile to go with the ignominious retreat by a citizen who might still have won praise for vigilance if he had not gone about it with the gusto of a vulture.

Well satisfied, the crowd discreetly withdrew.

Leaving Pembrook very much alone.

"*Ach*, you are all done in, son," said the sergent. "I think I'll leave my questions for later. Best we get you to a doctor."

Kramer read the label upside down because he was loath to change his position.

The Ultimate in Comfi Sleepware—Summer Cloud—the Mattress that Makes your Night.

It also made one hell of a fine haystack.

His body, partially supported on cantilevered elbows over a dozing Lisbet, was entirely relaxed, emptied of striving, and no longer nagging for a piece of action. His mind was experiencing a state of tranquil detachment like having the moon for a head.

So he serenely surveyed what had come to pass on an

162

earthly plane and accepted it amounted to very little. His only achievement being the establishment of a nebulous link between Boetie's murder and the death of an American student. No more than that because his theories so far had been based on assumptions rather than deduction. While the decoded message went a long way to confirm them, there was still the possibility they could apply equally well to some other situation—or to nothing at all, being merely part of a kid's wild imaginings. What was needed was one tangible something that tied the two cases together, beyond a reasonable doubt.

Kramer slipped out of Lisbet and rolled over on his back. She cuddled up.

Everything rested now on what Pembrook could discover from the younger daughter in the morning. She was the sole member of the Jarvis family they could approach without arousing suspicion and, with the contents of the toffee tin exhausted of information, their sole source of fresh fact. Kramer hoped to God the Telex statement would come through before midday as the press would soon start getting restive. When that happened, bigger brass than the Colonel would dictate how the investigation was run—maybe take charge themselves. And as Zondi said, a man should share nothing but his bed.

Such thoughts broke his mood, making him restless again. Lisbet, however, had fallen deeply asleep. He decided to have a smoke.

What a gorgeous sight she made from the doorway. It was worth dwelling on—toasting, even, with the dregs of the demijohn.

He found enough to rinse out his mouth and, after another pause, went in search of his Lucky Strikes. They were there in the jacket with his other clothes stacked on the phonograph. It had been a ritual as solemn as any church ceremony. Then had come the extraordinary business with the jazz record. He had soon put a stop to it by teaching her instead a few healthy games.

The match flared brightly, hurting his eyes. He waited for them to readjust before going over to the drinks cabinet to pour something special. He opened the doors and looked in.

To see himself reflected dimly in the mirror that backed

163

the cabinet's interior. Hell, this was how that tennis player champ must have looked that night; a naked, muscled body in semidarkness with a cigarette tip glowing like an illuminated boil.

"Jesus!"

Kramer let go of his tumbler where he thought a table stood and it shattered on the floor. A startled sound came from Lisbet's bedroom. He was on his way over when she staggered into his arms.

"What's happening, Trompie?"

"*Ach*, I'm sorry, my poppie! It's just I've suddenly realized . . ."

"Oh, yes?"

"You're still asleep, though. Let me take you back."

"Please tell me."

"Come over here, then. That's right, sit. I'll put the little light on because I've got something to show you."

Lisbet battled to keep her head up as she watched him hurriedly sort through the junk from his jacket pockets. He bulged open an envelope.

"See this?" Kramer said gleefully. "It's the stub of a Texan found at the scene of the murder. I discounted it before, thinking it had been dropped in the glade by the young bloke who found the body. He told me he had one to steady his nerves after dressing and before going for help. What I overlooked was that his clothes were in the *other* glade—like mine were in this room."

She beat off a yawn with her fist.

"Couldn't he have gone back with it?"

"I'll check, of course, but under the circumstances, that's very unlikely. The girl with him had flipped her lid and I'm sure he'd seen enough of the body."

"Now you're *bleeding* on my carpet," she groaned.

So he was, having rushed in bare feet across broken glass without noticing.

Chapter Twelve

THE REPORT KRAMER received from the laboratory at eleven o'clock the following morning enabled him to be philosophical about Pembrook's misfortune.

"Jo'burg CID say he should be all right by tomorrow," he told Zondi, "so I said not to trouble themselves with the matter. Anyway, once we've seen where this lipstick thing leads, we might get a lot more out of that interview with Miss Sally."

"But what were you laughing at, boss?"

"Some cock-and-bull story about him being arrested. By the way, he'll be coming back by bus this time and so we'll have to fix for a van to pick him up at the station."

"When?"

"Late tomorrow night."

"Okay. You were going to tell me what was in the report."

Kramer opened it with a flourish.

"It says here that the sample of lipstick I took from the girl at the dance—Penny Jones—was a cheap brand on sale at bazaars, shops, and most chemists. Now, the lipstick on the cigarette looks the same color in artificial light, but is a much more expensive make and you can see the difference in daylight. It's called Tasty Tangerine. The maker's name is Rochelle."

"And so?"

"Rochelle is one of those swanky firms that make a big fuss about who sells their products. Their agent in Durban says the only outlet in Trekkersburg is the chemists' on the corner of De Wet Street and the Parade. That's where I'm going right now."

"And the cigarette?"

"Read that part for yourself, you lazy bugger."

From his high window, the Colonel stared down at the street and saw nothing. He had problems. Big ones.

A reporter had just left after spending half an hour coming as close as he dared to being forthright. It appeared his editor was receiving an unusually large mail concerning the police. Anxious as always to act in the public good, the *Gazette* had so far published none of it on the grounds that space was currently very restricted. But the leader-page columnist was getting fed up at having to churn out so many extra paragraphs—and, anyway, it would soon be obliged to use at least one or two. If only there was something about either the sex killing or the fire tragedy that was new they could print. People were getting the idea there was political significance to be found in the absence of news. Rumors about terrorists were even doing the rounds. The reporter himself had been informed in a certain bar that the Swanepoel boy had been found with the insignia of a guerrilla movement carved on his back. And as for the Indian burned in the police van, the grandfather had been in to the news editor to say he had heard the child was alive and well; which, when taken with the story that the charred body was that of a Nigerian midget trained to incite school children, made one think.

It had made the Colonel laugh—as it was supposed to have done. Not very heartily, though, because the message was still there, and such fears had a rational basis.

He was also able to deal with the matter of the Govender boy by declaring it *sub judice* as a departmental inquiry was being held that very afternoon. But all he could say about the other case was that a senior officer had it well in hand and particularly requested the press's cooperation in not interfering with the families involved.

In the end, all he could offer the reporter was an official denial that politics were involved—insisting, at the same time, none of the rumors were printed. Result: a muted howl of dismay.

The Colonel was not accustomed to being under pressure from a newspaper. It annoyed him considerably and yet he could not deny things were proceeding very slowly.

166

How unlike Kramer this was. He hoped the man's sex life with the teacher at Boomkop Lower School was not distracting him.

Speak of the devil, there he went now, moving like six feet of whirlwind—towards the Parade.

The Colonel decided he could afford to concentrate on his own work for another day, half of which was unavoidably going to be taken up by that idiot Constable Hendriks.

Zondi spoke to the Widow Fourie for ten minutes when she rang. Then he copied down a message and stuck it in the dial.

The report's findings with regard to the cigarette end were understandably limited. The Texan bore traces of Rochelle cosmetic, had gone out before having to be stubbed, and was—according to a test of the tobacco's moisture content—perhaps about a month out of its airtight packaging. The technician added in parentheses that the crinkling of the paper was the result of the handling received subsequent to being smoked. How obvious. A small amount of tobacco was also missing for the same reason.

Pity there were no such things as lip prints.

Then a really practical idea struck Zondi that occupied him for the next half hour, at the end of which he called in a Bantu detective constable to make an express delivery. He gave him a verbal message and said it came from the lieutenant—anyway, that was what he had to tell the doctors.

It was noon when Kramer came hobbling back into the office with a grin like a nymphomaniac's at a love-in. He waved a receipted invoice at Zondi.

"Got it," he said. "We had to go through every bloody carbon, though, because the Rochelle girl is on leave. A delivery made to the Jarvis home six weeks ago included an order for a stick of Tasty Tangerine."

"And how many other people have been buying it, boss?"

"Christ, don't give me that! What other people did Boetie know who were loaded enough to afford the stuff?"

167

Zondi laughed, moving out of Kramer's chair and back onto his stool.

"You know who you are like, boss? There was this old priest by the mission who used to tell us that God was the great spirit behind everything. With you it is Jarvis."

Kramer knocked his hat off as he passed.

"That's called faith, you bloody pagan. You've got to have it if you want to get anywhere in this world."

"The priest was eaten by a crocodile."

"You don't say."

His lacerated foot hurt so much from all that fast walking he had to rest it for a while. When he had more time, he would get Strydom to put in a few stitches.

"Well, what can you tell me?" Kramer said over the top of his shoes propped on the desk.

"It was as you said, boss. Sergeant Frans took a message from the tennis boy; he did not go back into the glade where the body was."

"Fine! Now all we have to do is sort out how the thing got there. Remember it had rained that afternoon for a short while. I think we can discount the actual murderer for a start: women don't kill like that and—"

"It was fake, though."

"Even so, the chances are nil. Also that branch where the sickle was left would make her about six feet tall to reach up. They would remember her at the chemists' if she was so big, but they don't."

Zondi had begun linking paper clips into a pair of miniature leg irons, and generally behaving nervously as if he was waiting for something.

"*Ach*, don't fidget, man! What was I saying?"

"That the murderer had to be a man."

"Ah, yes, and a careful one, too, because *he* took care not to leave anything behind. But what if he had an assistant?"

"Never, boss!"

"Stranger things have happened, I know that for a fact, Zondi. For example, they caught a young couple in England who had murdered about six kids altogether—and in much the same way. Got sadistic kicks from it. Just picked them up in the street and took them into the veld."

"But did they ask them to their house?"

Kramer was about to snap back at Zondi when his jaw mutinied.

"Holy Jesus," he said, "that's exactly what happened with the last one—they got careless! Even had a friend there. A couple not much older than this bloke Glen and the eldest daughter. Man, it could have been a proper sex killing after all. Only ..."

"Boss?"

"No, it can't be! Why have we been pussyfooting all round this case? Because we've got to be sure we're on the right trail, that's why. The Jarvis bunch are a respected family, not rubbish like these English ones, and there would be a hell of a stink if Boetie leads us into making a wrong move. What do you think? You haven't put forward anything so far."

"There are those who would say it is not my job," replied Zondi.

"Come on, you've got your hoof in something!"

Before Zondi had to reply, the Bantu detective constable clumped in and deposited Boetie's shirt on the desk. He handed Kramer a note.

"What's this? You had it dry-cleaned?"

The shirt was indeed very neatly folded inside its plastic bag.

Kramer read the note and dismissed the messenger. Then he walked over to Zondi and knocked his hat off again.

"You cheeky Kaffir! Sitting there, listening to me suck all that out of my thumb, and all the time you knew there were specks of tobacco in the little bugger's pocket!"

"Texan, boss?"

"Naturally. And the microscope picked up a tiny smear of Tasty Tangerine."

Ye Old Englishe Tea Shoppe off De Wet Street was crowded by office girls buying roast beef sandwiches with luncheon vouchers—and the smoothies who preyed on young lamb. There were also the usual parties of intrepid elderly shoppers who built laagers of parcels around them as if anticipating an attack by the Zulu waiters.

However, the Widow Fourie had booked a table, so Kramer was able to sit down and ease his extremity while

169

waiting for her. It had been sly on her part to leave simply the time and the place, and the rest to his conscience. Not that guilt had brought him there; it was more the excuse of having an engagement which would postpone confronting the Jarvis household.

For he still lacked the clincher. Some spark of insight that would arc between Boetie and Andy, galvanizing him into action.

Zondi, who had done well solving the Texan riddle, was understandably impatient for him to proceed. But he chose to largely ignore the fresh questions his deduction presented. While Kramer could accept that Boetie would hardly carry the Texan around unless he thought it important, and that it was probably a vital clue in the child's estimation, this did not account for the fact it had been found six yards from where the T-shirt lay. Zondi's argument that it fell out during the struggle was too feeble, as the pocket was deep and the T-shirt tight-fitting. Besides which, the medical evidence canceled out any rough stuff.

"Hello, Trompie."

Kramer pushed out her chair.

"Thanks. I hope I haven't kept you waiting long. We've got a sale on."

"Keeping busy, then?"

"Oh, yes—and you?"

"Never stop."

"Still on the boy up at the country club? There's been nothing in the papers."

"How are the kids?"

"Fine. They ask after you."

"Uhuh."

The waiter asked for their order.

"I'll have an omelet," the Widow Fourie said without consulting the menu. "A cheese one with no tomatoes. Bring the boss a rump steak, very rare, with some tossed salad and potatoes in their skins."

Kramer smiled.

"So you haven't forgotten my little ways?" he asked, watching her burrow in her handbag.

"After three years, I've got a lot to remember, Trompie."

She opened an affectionately inscribed cigarette case

170

and held it out. He made no move to take one. What a dirty trick.

"Come on," she said. "Your steak will be ages."

Perhaps there was no guile.

"What's this, then?" he asked flippantly, noticing she had changed her brand. "Smoke a Texan and cough like a cowboy?"

The Widow Fourie laughed.

Then frowned, bewildered. Kramer's chair was empty—he had left without another word.

The headmaster's secretary had the afternoon off, so Lisbet was at liberty to speak to Kramer as intimately as her waning modesty would permit—and for as long as she liked, too.

But when she got through, an unfamiliar voice answered the call in his office. The name was impossible to catch.

"Are you a Bantu?" she asked finally.

The reply was in the affirmative.

"Then where is your boss? It doesn't matter who I am, boy, just tell me what I ask. Oh, it's an order he's given you, is it? I'm Miss Louw from the school. Are you satisfied?"

Completely, and with apologies.

"*Ach*, don't waste time. Just tell me where he is and how long he'll be. *Three* hours? What's that?"

She listened attentively, occasionally interjecting a question.

"Thanks," she said at the end of it. "Don't worry, I won't tell him. You've done me a favor."

There was no point in stopping off for Zondi—the investigation had moved outside his terms of reference. But Kramer did manage a telephone call from the nursing home where Caroline Jarvis had had the cyst removed.

"So there weren't any messages? Fine. Well, I've made the breakthrough and now I'm on my way up to the Jarvises' place. No, she isn't—discharged this morning, but still must stay in bed for a few days, so she'll be home for sure. Argyle? That's good. Bugger off and see him if you like. *Ach*, I haven't got time, man, but I'll give you a

171

clue: the word 'cowboy' in the first code was Boetie's way of recording an exhibit. Exhibit A! Work it out for yourself."

He smiled nicely at the matron, who had insisted on vacating her office while he spoke, and limped fast for the car park.

Damn, there had been another point he wanted to try out on Zondi: his theory as to how the Texan came to be found six yards from where Boetie's clothes lay. It was based on the reasonable assumption the boy regarded it as a vital clue—and that, as the killer had not removed it from the scene, its presence must have remained undetected. Put the two together and it was plausible that Boetie, sensing he might be facing danger, had ditched the Texan to prevent it being found on his person. A simple test had shown he could have thrown it that far. However, this left him trying to explain how it was that such a throw had been missed by the killer, who surely kept a careful eye on his victim, and why, in the first place, Boetie had taken the clue along with him.

Kramer entered Redneck territory with a large locust riding shotgun on the Chev's bonnet. It had no difficulty maintaining a grip because, back yonder in the last of the skyscraper canyons, he had slowed right down to figure the odds for the last time. After all, he was about to risk his scalp. But they still looked pretty good now ten minutes later, provided he avoided shortcuts and went the long way round.

Having made his decision, Kramer pulled up outside the house at 10 Rosebank Road and rested the horses.

Captain Jarvis himself answered the door after the third clatter of the brass knocker.

"Damn maid was due back half an hour ago," he grumbled. "Didn't expect to see you again, old boy."

"Always a good sign," Kramer replied, not waiting to be invited inside.

"Can I be of service?" Jarvis asked stuffily.

"Your daughter Caroline—I'd like that interview."

"But if it's about that Swanepoel lad, I've already—"

"It isn't, Captain. I've handed that case over to a subordinate. I'm conducting further investigations into the death of Andrew Cutler."

172

"Good Lord! I thought that whole wretched business was over."

"So did we—until we caught this housebreaker who's been doing the rounds up here in Greenside. He's got some funny stories to tell."

Jarvis patted his pockets and drew out a gnarled pipe. He poked the stem at Kramer.

"But how does this involve Caroline?"

"It involves everyone in this house, Captain," Kramer answered solemnly. "But I'd like my first statement from her."

With a surprisingly swift movement, Jarvis positioned himself across the foot of the stairs.

"You will not proceed beyond this point, Lieutenant, until you make yourself perfectly clear. This is worse than the confounded Gestapo!"

Kramer had heard that one before.

"Has it not occurred to you, Captain, that Cutler's death was strangely sudden for someone his age—just falling in your swimming bath like that?"

"According to the police surgeon, your police surgeon, it could have happened if he had simply rolled in. A matter of chance."

"But he could have been pushed."

"By whom, sir?"

"By a housebreaker trying to make a getaway and finding the boy barring the path."

The ramrod snapped, causing Jarvis to subside suddenly onto the bottom step.

"This is appalling, Lieutenant. It never once crossed my mind that . . ."

"Ours neither. Until this suspect made us think twice. For a hard case, he seemed a bit too worried we had caught up with him—carried on as if there had been aggravating circumstances."

"I'm sorry, old boy, not quite with you."

"That's when housebreaking can become a capital offense. We checked back and discovered two interesting things: the first was he had not burgled a house since the night of November the fifteenth—"

"The night Andy died?"

"Yes, although it tied up only after we'd checked out

our crime sheet for that week. The other thing was a lipstick found among the recovered property; it is not a common brand, and we were able to trace the sale of a similar lipstick to this house."

"That's a damn funny thing to steal!"

Of course it was. Kramer, who had almost begun to believe the story, struck himself an invisible blow. But no harm done.

"You could say this wog is a damn funny bloke," he went on. "A bit crazy, if you ask me. He agrees to anything you say."

"Have you asked him if he did it?"

"Naturally."

"And what does he say?"

"I told you, he agrees to anything—but the prosecution expects me at least to attempt to find some actual proof."

"Will he hang either way?"

"Who knows? Personally, I think he'll be locked away safe in the loony bin."

Jarvis got his pipe alight.

"Then you might say this was nothing much more than a formality?"

"Off the record, yes."

"No real need to bother Caroline, then?"

"I would have thought, sir," Kramer said, "that you would realize that when the Colonel gives an order, you do your utmost to carry it out."

That brought Jarvis back on parade. He straightened up and nodded curtly.

"Quite so. I'd forgotten you chappies were really a paramilitary outfit. And a damn good thing, too, if I may say so. I'll tell Caroline you're here, and then you can go up to her."

Kramer clicked his heels together.

And spent the wait on a closer examination of the curious brass plates decorating the roof beam.

Pembrook had been so much better since lunchtime that he found himself given a clean bill of health just to get him out of the place. The decision was taken by the assistant district surgeon, who obviously thought his superior overcautious in ordering a day's rest.

174

"There's a good Rugby match at the Station Ground," he advised. "Go and get some fresh air."

"I will," Pembrook answered, heading straight for the car pool and cadging a lift to 39 Woodland Avenue, which turned out to be the biggest house he had ever been inside.

Not that he was allowed further than the hall until the mistress had been summoned by a Bantu maid of infuriating superiority. The black bitch had given him the very distinct impression he should have presented himself at the back door, and he deeply resented that.

But she must have been new and not the usual carbon copy of her employer, because Sally Jarvis's grandmother, Mrs. Trubshaw, was exceptionally hospitable—despite her natural concern that he should call. She ushered him into the drawing room and sent another maid for her granddaughter, adding an order for tea.

"And now," she said, taking up her embroidery, "*do* tell me about yourself. It's so unusual to come across one of *us* in your profession."

She had to be joking.

The girl lying demure and dainty between the candy-striped sheets might have made it a lasting impression if Kramer had not noticed the hockey stick and shin guards under the window. She had to be tough, to play goalie. For the rest, she was—her head at any rate—a typical adaptation of the current debutante ideal now the State President had permitted such things: shoulder-length blond hair, plucked eyebrows, pert nose, and arrogant chin. The eyes were green and unabashed. The mouth ever so slightly sorry for itself.

"Hello Caroline, I'm Lieutenant Kramer of the CID."

"Hello."

"How are you feeling—any better?"

"It only hurts a little, thank you."

"Uhuh. Mind if I sit here? I've got just a couple of questions to ask you."

"Daddy told me."

She was nervous despite appearances—it showed in her voice. But curiously, not as much as he anticipated.

"What did your father tell you, then?"

"You know, about Andy. Something to do with a burglar."

Kramer opened his notebook and wrote her name at the head of the page.

"The medical evidence suggests that Andy was drowned somewhere around eleven o'clock—where were you at this time?"

"I've already—"

"Please, miss. It's best we start from scratch again. Just answer my questions."

"I was here, asleep in my bed. I got in just before ten, had a shower and listened to pop on Springbok Radio. I must have dropped off before the advertisements because I don't remember hearing them."

"Say about ten-thirty, then?"

"Yes."

The old, old story: much too glib, much too swiftly phrased, much too earnest. She was lying. Gold dust at the first turn of his shovel. And the ready means to assay it.

"But what if I told you there wasn't any pop on Springbok that night? If you remember, it was the day of General Marais's state funeral—all stations were playing solemn music."

"Then it must have been Lourenço Marques. I didn't really notice. Does it matter?"

He put a tick in the margin.

"*Ach*, no! Us blokes just get in a habit of examining the facts. So you were asleep here. Did anything wake you? Did you hear any sounds?"

"Nothing at all until Jackson brought in my orange juice in the morning."

"Dead to the world," Kramer said, as he made a note.

"Pardon?"

"I said, Did you like him?"

"Who?"

"The American. Did you like him? Yes or no?"

"No," she said spontaneously, and then looked appalled at herself.

"Don't worry, your father's already said he was a bit of a you-know-what."

"Hell's bells!"

176

"What's the matter?"

"Daddy's a jolly sight cleverer than I thought. Me and my friends thought Andy was effeminate until we found out."

Kramer played for time by demonstrating his nasty smoker's cough.

"But surely he wasn't as bad as that?" he croaked.

"He was, though! A proper sex maniac with hands like hairy spiders running all over you."

"I don't believe it, miss."

Which made it his turn to lie; Caroline sounded entirely, perplexingly genuine about her allegation. He began to share the confusion of a snake in a tuba.

"It's true!"

"Then prove it. Tell me some more."

"Are you going to write this down, too?"

"No, and I won't repeat it either if you like. But it'll help to give me a picture."

The way she regarded him was probably the same as when she summed up a school friend before parting with a piece of juicy gossip. Even Lisbet had not managed to make him feel as young.

"Well," she said, "promise not to let my parents know, but one night I even found him waiting in my bed! Honestly, I'm not bluffing. And what was really awful was that I'd started to undress before I noticed him. I'd come in rather late and I didn't want to put on the light in case Daddy saw it under the door and there was a row. He's terribly strict about being in bed by ten—none of my friends have to be. It's really unfair."

"But what happened when you saw him?"

"You'd never guess. He pulled his trousers out from under the bedclothes and asked me to hang them over a chair!"

"Did you?" Kramer chuckled, showing willing.

"I'd jolly well think not! I clouted him as hard as I could with a hanger—that made him scoot. I had to throw his pants after him, he went out of the door so fast."

They both laughed.

"But why didn't you tell your parents, Caroline? He sounds he was dangerous."

"You don't know them, obviously. There would have

been a terrible scene. Worse than that, they'd have gone mad at what people would think if we got rid of Andy without an explanation. My father's spent half his life thinking about the Regiment and the other half about the Family Name. He can't see a difference. He said 'Welcome to the mess' on Andy's first night here and this made him a *guest*. Oh, something very special. It would have been a disgrace to the Family Name if he had gone, because people would think the thing was really our fault."

"So you didn't feel too bad when he drowned?"

She gasped.

"What a horrible thing to say! Of course I was upset—although it still doesn't seem real and I forget when I'm talking."

"My apologies."

"You see, he was much better when he knew where he stood with me and my friends. And, in some ways, you couldn't really blame him. America's so different to us. He got a letter one day from Puerto Rico and in it was a picture of his girl friend *pregnant in a bikini!*"

"Hey?"

"Yes, his mother, no less, had taken her down there for an abortion."

"What about the girl's ma?"

"Andy said she was too fed up to bother. It had happened once before."

"These Americans."

"Oh, they're not all like that. Tracey Williams, she's staying with the Flints, is quite different. She doesn't go in for free love and smoking dagga and all that; in fact, she said Andy wouldn't have had anything to do with her set at home."

"How was he chosen to come?"

"I think there was a bit of a mistake."

"I'll say."

But this was getting a little too cozy for Kramer not to have his suspicions. He put down his notebook and went over to the window. Jarvis was out there on the lawn, remonstrating with a garden boy.

"You don't seem to have had much luck with your guests," he murmured casually.

"You mean?"

The voice was apprehensive again.

"Boetie Swanepoel. He seems to have made a real pest of himself." Kramer swung round in time to see an expression of cold indifference on her face. "Your father also had a few words to say about him."

"Oh?"

"Were you surprised to hear what happened up at the country club, Caroline?"

"I think it's shocking."

"Apart from that? You seem pretty perceptive for a teen-ager. How do you suppose he was lured there?"

This forced her into making a reply.

"Well, he was the sort of kid who'd never miss an opportunity. A chancer, like Mummy says. He only took any notice of poor Sally because of the swimming bath, that stuck out a mile. Of course, we couldn't tell her. She was so defensive about him, especially because he—wasn't English."

"What did he do that particularly annoyed you?"

"I've told you, treat Sally like an admission ticket. And he was always prying about the place. I caught him here in my room once, going through my dressing table."

"Haven't I heard this story before?" Kramer said flatly. "Or did he keep his pants on?"

She blushed—but with anger.

"Well, really!" she said. "I think you'd better fetch Daddy."

"A joke. You don't have to laugh if you don't want to. Did Boetie tell jokes?"

"No."

"Then let's have your father up. He said Boetie told you a dirty story the last time he was here. Is that true? Or is everything you've been telling me just lies?"

"He'll kick you out when he hears!"

"Give me an answer or—"

"What?"

"He might be very interested in what was allowed to go on under his nose."

Caroline literally cowered—Kramer had never seen it done before in such surroundings. It gave him a warm sense of the brotherhood of man. Fear was the second great leveler, and a lot more practical.

"It wasn't a joke, just something—"

"Go on!"

"Something crude and horrid he said to me. It came out of the blue, too, and didn't even make sense."

"The exact words, please."

"He—he said he'd seen me fighting with Andy. In the garden. At night. I was sitting on him—and I hadn't had any clothes on."

"Fighting?"

She nodded, keeping her moistening eyes averted.

"When did he say this was? Caroline, I want an answer!"

"Do you think I'd stand for any more than that?" she flared. "I went straight to Daddy—but I didn't say exactly what happened because he'd have exploded. He took Boetie into his study and told him never to come back."

"And why do you think Boetie said this to you?"

"Because he was a nasty, dirty-minded bit of scum, that's why! I'm not at all surprised what happened to him."

"Young lady," said Kramer, "I'm sorry I've had to push you like this, but you've just given me an insight into Boetie Swanepoel that nobody else could have done. It'll help me a lot with the case."

Caroline could not help glancing round.

"But I thought you came to see me about Andy?" she said in a whisper. "Was it a trick?"

"Oh, no, a coincidence. The boy's none of my business but I'll pass on the information without naming names. Now I've taken up enough of your time when you're not feeling well. I'll say thanks and get going. There's nothing else about Andy to add?"

"I don't think so."

"Fine. Now if you'll just give me the address of this boyfriend of yours."

She sat up, wincing at a pain but not caring.

"What's Glen got to do with Andy?" she asked.

"Routine—corroboration of your statement."

"Please don't ask him! I'd rather tell you myself."

Kramer sat down and stretched out his legs. He signaled for her to proceed.

"You see, I wasn't being truthful about the night of

180

Andy's accident. I wasn't here—I sneaked out again when Daddy thought I'd gone to my bedroom. Glen was waiting in his car in the road. There was this party for Tracey— Sally let me in the back door."

"And that's the truth?"

"Yes, I promise. Honestly."

"Suppose I ask Sally?"

"You can, she'll say the same thing. I woke her up by chucking stones up at her window at about three and—"

"I believe you, Caroline." Kramer sighed and meant it. "Forget what I said about telling your father anything. Your secrets are safe with me."

Poor bloody kid. He tried to reach the door before gratitude engulfed him.

"Just a moment, Lieutenant," she called.

"Uhuh?"

"Weren't you going to ask me about my lipstick? That's what Daddy said."

"Oh, that."

"Mine did disappear that night because I wanted to wear it at the party. But it couldn't have been the burglar because I missed it before supper."

Chapter Thirteen

EVERYTHING WAS WORKING out perfectly for Pembrook. No sooner had he dropped off the statement for Telex transmission to Trekkersburg than he was traveling there himself in a flashy new sports car.

Thanks to old Mrs. Trubshaw, of course, a real lady for all her frills and fancies; one whose claim to being a "born arranger if nothing else" was entirely justified. First she arranged his interview with Sally so tactfully the little pudding showed no reluctance to talk, then she arranged a seat for him at the supper table because she realized what ages these things took, and finally she arranged—having heard a graphic account of the flight—for her neighbors' son to give him a lift back that very night.

This bloke, by the name of Pete Talbot, had agreed so readily to the idea that Pembrook experienced an attack of cringe, suspecting he was being offered a demonstration rather than a favor. And he was right: Pete, an engineering student at Durban University, had made the midweek trip up only to complete the running-in mileage and intended, on the way down, to really let rip. But Kramer was probably spitting buckshot and that had settled it.

"Fan-as-ic!" bawled Pete, having his *t*'s torn away by the wind as they side-swept into another tight bend.

Pembrook yelled back: "Star-ing oo izzle!"

So the car slithered to a halt for Pete to display his expertise by getting the top up in one minute flat.

"Bloody quiet, isn't it?" Pete said as he drove on.

"Yes, pity about the rain—I was enjoying that."

"You were? Great! Fantastic!"

"Buy this yourself?"

"Parents did."

Imagine that, enough moola lying around to pay Pembrook's salary for two years—or his old man's pension for six, come to think of it. Some people . . .

"I'll have to get a radio," Pete said. "Helps keep you awake on these straight stretches. What were you doing over at the Trubshaws'?" Sally gone and done something naughty at last?"

"You know her, then?"

"Oh, sure. Had a pash for her big sister once."

"And was she?"

"What?"

"Passionate, too?"

"Never got the chance to find out. That father of hers is a right bastard. Met her at Trubshaws' one school holiday, you see, just before term. So when I got back to Durban, I whipped up to see her in the old jalopy. Man!"

"Shall I light you one?"

"Thanks. Anyway, to cut a long story short, I chickened out the second time he caught me bringing her back late. I was expecting a bit of a sesh, not the bloody Riot Act. Christ, and who does he think he is, the bastard?"

"Here you are."

"Smoke Texan and—hey, it isn't him, is it?"

"Who?"

"*Captain* Jarvis—the one that's in trouble with you chaps?"

"Hell, no! The family are just providing background to a case."

"Pity."

"Uhuh?" More than colds were catching.

"Well, he could come down a peg or two. He isn't what he makes himself out to be, not by a long chalk. You should hear his ma-in-law, Granny Trubshaw, go on about him to my old lady. In the first place, that's only a war-time commission he's got. You can't blame the regulars who finished up captain or major or colonel from hanging on to their rank, I mean it's like calling yourself 'doctor' after years of hard graft. But our friend Jarvis was just a manager on a rubber plantation in Malaya until the Japs came. Whoever was in charge gave him some Malayan soldiers to boss around and that was how it happened."

"Did the Japs catch him?"

"POW for a year—then he escaped."

183

"I thought that was impossible."

"You're not the only one, my friend; Granny Trubshaw always avoids that part of the story. My dad—he was real army—has been heard to mutter dark things."

"Like?"

"A bit of the old collab, with the enemy, y'know. Wouldn't put it past him either, not after the streak of cruelty he dished me out with!"

Pembrook laughed.

"He could have you for slander, man. But what happened after the war?"

"Usual thing with his type; bummed his way around the disappearing Empire, complaining the wogs weren't grateful and they forgot to put ice in his drinks. Had a go at being DC—district commissioner—up in Kenya, spent a bit of time as a police chief somewhere else. I don't remember it all. Then got his windfall—old biddy died in England leaving him thousands—and came down here to have his brandy the way he liked it."

"But why not go back to England? I hear his house—"

"Servants? Tax? He wouldn't recognize an Englishman today, I can tell you—I've been there."

"Why—how, I mean—did the Trubshaws get involved in this?"

"Sylvia married him because he was the only white lay within forty miles—that's what my old man says. Granny Trubshaw says she even tried to get a witch doctor to stop it!"

"No, really?"

"Of course not. But I'll bet she spent some nights on her knees. Our Sylvia's quite a girl on her own account—another of the old man's dark hints, but he's past it. Much younger than the Captain, of course, and not bad. Sure she gave me the eye once, while they were up here."

"You mean she . . . ?"

"Good God, no! Sylvia's bloody petrified of him, everyone will tell you that; sometimes gets on her ear at parties and wham! confined to barracks. Forty days bread and water. None of the old slap and tickle either."

"You're bulling me," Pembrook chortled. "From what I've heard of the bloke, it could've happened between them only twice."

184

"You could have something there," Pete replied.

Then he suggested breaking the journey at Vryheid for a few beers. Pembrook, calculating he would still be back in the office before midnight, offered to pay for them.

This time Lisbet had eaten and stacked the washing-up ready for the girl without waiting for Kramer. And she answered the door with curlers in her hair and brown muck all over her face.

"*Sabona umfazi, epi lo missus?*" Kramer inquired in his best Kitchen Kaffir.

"Ha ha," she said. "You're late."

"Didn't say I was coming. Got any plonk left?"

He went straight through to the living room and opened the drink cabinet.

"Want one?"

"No, thanks."

"What's the matter with you?"

"*Ach*, nothing. Take what you want."

"Thanks."

Something was very wrong. Lisbet was moving edgily around the room like a cat at the vet's.

"Okay if I leave kissing you hello till later?" he said.

Lisbet ignored the remark. She sat down cross-legged plumb in the middle of the sofa, leaving too little room either side. Which meant Kramer had to drag over a stool to be near her.

"Where have you been, Trompie?"

"Seeing the biggest Jarvis girl. Man, now I've really got problems."

And he listed, briefly, all that had been said. Then took it point by point.

Caroline did smoke the odd Texan; smoking was permitted, she thought, because her father liked to have some moral support considering the number he got through in a day. Caroline had used, and still used, Tasty Tangerine lipstick because the color was fashionable among teen-agers. So if Boetie had tried to identify the smoker of a Texan stub smeared with Tasty Tangerine, she was the obvious choice in that household. Her mother, for example, occasionally took a puff, but wore magenta lipstick. Further-

185

more, Boetie had been poking about in Caroline's dressing table, where her cosmetics were kept.

Clarification had also been brought to the question of the sock in the bed—more than likely it had come off with the trousers; and the Captain saying Boetie had never addressed him: it was Caroline's belief the boy failed to get a word in edgewise when given his marching orders after the social gaffe. Nobody had ever succeeded in interrupting her father on such an occasion. Jarvis had verified this supposition as Kramer left.

From there on in, however, contradiction repeatedly banged together the halves of the brain, as what Boetie believed to be true collided with the actual truth of Caroline's admissions. The only resort was to concentrate initially on the one other common factor involved.

Boetie had written down the words "sitting on him" and had used them again, in substance, on Caroline. Clearly this made her the subject of his incomplete sentence; demonstrably, she was not. The conclusion had to be that Boetie saw someone sitting on Andrew at the bath, but not Caroline.

"*Who*, then?" Lisbet asked, momentarily upsetting the air of cool formality into which they had retreated.

Kramer shook his head.

"Funnily enough," he said, "that's not the question I'm most interested in at this moment. I want to know how Boetie, who was a smart cookie, made such a mistake. It would have been different if this was all based on one quick look—but he spent a month poking round Rosebank Road. Perhaps the best thing is to put ourselves in his shoes: start where he thinks he has seen Caroline doing something to Andy that ends up in a drowning. His proof of her being there is the cigarette stub he finds in one of those oyster shell ashtrays. Now he needs to discover the motive. He asks himself was the girl, Caroline, doing it with him? Sex is an obvious line to take."

"Then we know he spent a month on it, don't we? Caroline had nothing to do with Andy—apart from the bed incident she's told you about—so there was nothing for him to find. In fact, he could have spent longer if it hadn't been for what happened to him."

"Very nice, Lisbet. I'm Boetie and I've spent a month

186

getting nowhere—what do I try next? The old technique us blokes use: clobber the suspect with the knowledge you have and see what happens. He made his bid with this talk about fighting."

"All he got was the reaction any decent girl would have given him."

"Can he be sure?"

"No, but three days later he's dead."

"Naturally, if Caroline couldn't understand what he meant, somebody else could—and they took steps to make sure he kept it to himself for good."

"That makes sense of it all!"

"No, it doesn't," Kramer said, going over to refill his glass. "Firstly, why the hell did he persist for so long in thinking it was Caroline when he couldn't find any evidence? The light couldn't have been that good by the bath."

"I'll have a sherry, after all. What did you say? Oh, I suppose Boetie just couldn't think of an alternative."

"Why?"

"Maybe he didn't know of any other girl to pick on."

"Logical enough, but then we come to the really crazy part of his thinking. He said Caroline had nothing on when she was with Andy and that she was *fighting* him! Is that what any other boy would have thought? Come on, you're supposed to be the psychologist around here."

Lisbet took her glass from him carelessly, spilling some on a cushion and not noticing.

"After last night, that's a funny question."

"What the hell do you mean?"

"It's a commonly known fact that a child can mistake the act of intercourse for an act of violence. Some kids are scarred for life because they think they've seen pa knocking the hell out of ma."

"Christ, you can be sick."

"It's true!"

"I don't doubt that—it's the reference to last night I don't think is funny."

"What about this afternoon, then?"

Kramer stared at Lisbet, aware for the first time that she had been drinking before his arrival. She was slurring her words. His stomach hollowed out with foreboding.

"You tell me," he challenged.

"Have a nice lunch with your mistress? I know all about her—and how you've been double-crossing me, you bastard. I suppose she badly needed a rest."

"Jesus."

"Don't ask me who, because I won't tell you. Anyway, you should know by now that Trekkersburg is a small place when it comes to this sort of thing. They say you had her down three solid hours."

"I'll—that isn't true!"

"You weren't in the tea shop at one?"

"Only to tell her about you and me."

"I bet."

"Don't you believe me, Lisbet?"

"Course I do, lover boy! You told her all about me and my supple young body and made the old bag so jealous she took you and—"

"What the hell do you think I am?"

They were both on their feet and Kramer close to becoming his own customer.

"To be frank—my, look at those wrinkles!—a dirty old man."

"Like your father?"

Lisbet slapped him across the throat, being that much shorter. Another glass went to waste. Then she froze.

"The eyes in the mirror," Lisbet whispered.

"You're pissed."

Giggling, she collapsed back on the sofa, letting her skirt ride right up.

"My father image. Don't argue, I'm the psychologist around here. And don't go—your little girlie wants tickle-ickles!"

"Miss Louw," said Kramer, "I'd like to help, but incest is an indictable offense. Sorry, but you understand."

The ward into which Argyle Mslope had been moved was foul with the smell of a soiled bed. Zondi had asked him about it, astonished by such laxity.

"I regret that the staff nurse . . ." Argyle was a man who evaded speaking ill of his betters.

"Mbeta? The one who talks like a white church-woman?"

Argyle found the description so apt that he laughed out

188

loud and so did his neighbor, a factory worker minus a leg. It was he who explained to Zondi that Staff Nurse Mbeta was far more concerned about the welfare of the doctors than the patients. Right at that moment she would be trimming the crusts off tomato sandwiches for the houseman to enjoy in the duty room. Unless there was a critical case, the chances were he would no more than glance into the ward. Staff Nurse Mbeta could be totally engaging.

"Where are the ordinary nurses, though?" Zondi asked.

"Very few at night," said the neighbor. "The staff nurse calls them from the other ward if she needs help."

Zondi squeezed his way between the beds and went into the passage, intending to have a word with the slut. But, from what he could overhear, the houseman must have arrived early and that required a change of plan. He stood undecided for only as long as it took him to spot a wheeled stretcher left abandoned outside an operating room while its former occupant was inside being hurriedly stitched together. He carefully lifted from it a sheet.

The factory worker and Argyle saw him return with it and go to a patient near the door who was sonorously asleep. Zondi spread the sheet over the one already covering the bed, tucking it in all around in the approved fashion.

"Good night, my friends," said Zondi. "You tell me tomorrow what happens."

And he made for the ground floor. Relishing every step of the way the severity of the shock awaiting Staff Nurse Mbeta when the horrified houseman pointed to a man apparently bleeding to death by the bucketful. That borrowed sheet had received a spectacular soaking.

Kramer induced catharsis by imagining, in excruciating detail, just what he would do to the bandy-legged-yellow-faced-apparition-of-a-pox-struck-whore who had lost him Lisbet. It almost made his fingers ache.

This gave him back his reason and he had to concede that perhaps it was all just as well: the girl was sick—he should have realized that when everything happened too quickly, like in banned books. Someone had simply done

189

him a favor for the wrong reason. He would leave it at that.

A couple of blocks further on, he was still thinking about her—now in the strictly business sense of her observations with regard to Boetie's insistence he had witnessed fighting. It was a great pity they had not first finished that part of the conversation because she knew a lot about the twelve-year-old mind. He seldom, if ever, came across one.

The Chev knew otherwise. Without any conscious direction from him, it turned off at the next traffic lights and took the road leading to Hibiscus Court.

"Well, I'm buggered!" Kramer exclaimed. "Why didn't I think of Marie before?"

But the Widow Fourie had a disappointment in store for him: all four of her children, including Marie, were long since asleep. She caught hold of his sleeve and inquired very gently if this was not, perhaps, merely an excuse he dreamed up to explain his visit. And reminded him that she had never required excuses on previous occasions.

Kramer hesitated a moment before stepping inside. At least here was the mother of a twelve-year-old and, as such, she might know something useful. He was also able to lay before her all the salient facts relating to Boetie without fear of his confidence being betrayed.

Afterwards, she made coffee and brought through bone-dry rusks to dip in it.

"If you want my opinion," she said, "then I don't think what Marie might make of two naked people rolling about would help much. I've always been very straight with her in these matters. She'd know like a shot. But from what you tell me about Boetie and his background, I can see he might not be so well informed. His parents sound the sort who'd run a mile before they'd say the word 'sex.' They wouldn't have any juicy books in the house either—and you said he didn't seem to understand dirty jokes."

"I know, I know," answered Kramer, dunking his rusk with enjoyment. "Yet it still seems impossible he could not have guessed. It is out of character for him to be so certain of something if he had any doubts."

"Maybe he did ask someone then—and got the wrong

answer. A schoolmate, perhaps. Some of these kids have the craziest theories."

"He wouldn't have placed his faith in someone his own age."

"Who could he ask, then? Some other adult he knew? Can you think of anyone, Trompie?"

"Hey, how about the Dominee?"

"Ring him and find out."

Kramer did just that.

And came back from the phone to dance a small jig with the Widow Fourie. She pulled him down with her into an armchair.

"Come on, Trompie! Tell me what he said!"

"He invited me to the funeral tomorrow afternoon—the whole school's going to be there. The cadets from the high school are going to fire a salute."

She punched him in the stomach.

"Talk! Or there'll be trouble!"

It was a bloody hard punch, too.

"A whole load of humming and hawing to start with and then he admitted that about three weeks ago Boetie had come to him to ask about the birds and the bees. Seems he's quite accustomed to these requests. Anyway, he took Boetie through it all from start to finish—ovaries, little seeds with tails, the lot. Then the Dominee pulled up short again and I had to work hard on getting the rest out of him. You could see it was the sex killing behind his worries."

"Go on!"

With a right jab like that they could do with her on the squad.

"Seems Boetie shocked the good man by asking him *exactly* in what position it was done. He had to do a drawing which he assures me he burned afterwards."

"How sweet."

"Wait for it. Boetie then, and I quote, 'asked me a very strange question about the female taking the dominant position. Was this possible?' That's when the Dominee got very excited on the phone and said, 'I soon put him right about that! What could have put such a diabolical and absurd idea into his head?'"

191

The Widow Fourie blushed and never looked better. She was a simple soul at heart.

"So that's what was happening when he saw someone sitting on Andy by the bath!"

"Yes, and I might have reached this point sooner if I hadn't thought those coded messages were in order—the second one was obviously the other half of the first. Was the girl et cetera. He had his doubts, all right."

Kramer had gone over to drink the dregs of the coffee before it went cold.

"How did Andy die, then?"

"I've got a little experiment to make first before I say anything about that."

"Does that mean you get going straightaway?"

"*Ach*, no, plenty of time."

Even so, Kramer's impatience wrought miracles of reconciliation and within the hour he had the Widow Fourie spread-eagled like a charming guinea pig on a laboratory bench.

Chapter Fourteen

BATTLE STATIONS. The klaxon sounded precisely at 10:30 A.M. the following day outside the CID buildings, bringing Pembrook scrambling to his feet. Kramer saw him take a quick glance out of the window and then emerge seconds later from the main entrance. The nearside front door was already hanging open. He revved the Chev's engine again.

The door slammed and they were away.

"Where're we going, sir?"

"Country club."

"Did you read the statement from Sally?"

"Before you got in this morning, drunkard."

"Find anything useful, sir?" Pembrook persisted, still somewhat aggrieved that his devotion to duty had not won any acclaim.

"Bugger all, apart from her saying that she overheard Boetie talking back to her father and what she called a sarcastic line about his having to find himself another girl. What you picked up from the bloke in the sports car was a lot more to the point."

"I'm glad, sir. I worked the lift thinking I might be able to pump him a bit."

"Don't flatter yourself."

"Sir?"

"That sort of gossip is the easiest thing to get out of the buggers up at Greenside. We'd have got it anyway if we'd asked. I did just that this morning after I'd been to the Jarvises'."

"But what happened at the Jarvises', sir?"

"A lot."

"Is it in the bag?"

"Almost."

"Then you know who the mystery girl was?"

Kramer raised his head slightly to catch Zondi's change of expression in his rear-view mirror.

"It wasn't a girl," he said. "Now just keep quiet until we're clear of this traffic."

Over on the other side of the valley, three African gravediggers crouched behind a hedge and passed a cigarette between them; not one rolled from newspaper such as laborers made do with, but a genuine Peter Stuyvesant that came to them ready-lit. It was one of the perks, this being able to salvage the shower of good tobacco that fell when mourners arrived without an opportunity to finish their smokes.

They made sounds of deep content as each took his puff, and argued in low whispers over whether it was less work to make a hole for a child's coffin. The one who had been to school said it was obviously easier as there was not as much to shift. But the foreman pointed out that the more confined space made getting through the layer of shale more arduous. Their colleague sought a compromise by calling their attention to the fact there was less to put back in again. It was accepted and they looked forward to finishing the job by twelve and taking an early lunch. The hot sun had made them feel excessively lethargic. They saved the other cigarettes for the afternoon and dozed against the spade handles held upright between their thighs.

As their instructions were to keep out of sight at all times, they had not taken any interest in the funeral proceedings after their snatch-and-grab raid on the area where the cars parked. So the salute fired by a full platoon of cadets from the high schools, which was both deafening and alarmingly ragged, came as something totally unexpected: all three of them immediately fled down the hill, brandishing their spades like spears and yelling in fright—not knowing quite why.

Mrs. Swanepoel cheered.

This utterly astonished everyone but Dominee Pretorius. He, better than any, perhaps, knew what a terrible state her mind was in; and besides, the woman had a wonderful, deep-rooted sense of her historical heritage.

It moved him more than anything that day.

194

Pembrook could restrain himself no longer. He rounded on Kramer and begged to be put out of his misery.

"Then let this be a lesson to you," Kramer replied. "Always make a point of seeing everyone who might conceivably be involved in a case, however unlikely that possibility. Ah, that's better."

They had reached the dual highway.

"And another thing, Pembrook: beware of the mistake Boetie made when he tried to be a detective. Our job requires us not to make assumptions based on class, color, or religious belief. His set ideas cost him his life."

"But, sir!"

"I want that in your head before we start to confuse you."

Zondi gave a snort.

"Hey, you back there—stop that listening!"

"Straightaway, boss."

The Chev moved over into the slow lane behind a wattle truck and dropped down to thirty.

"Well, it was like this, Pembrook man. I left that note in the office for you and then went to Greenside. As I was coming up the drive at No. 10, I see Caroline out there in the garden cutting some flowers. Hell, I think, that's a quick recovery! So I stop and go over. Guess what? It's her ma."

"No!"

"At a distance, they've both got that wiry sort of body that never changes much. Hair style's the same, same color, and eyebrows all buggered about to nothing."

"Age?"

"Around thirty-seven. She must have reached desperation pretty fast wherever it was she met Jarvis. But that isn't the point, is it? She jumps nearly out of her pants when I say who I am, and that I'm investigating the Cutler case. Then she says, 'But it *was* an accident!' Why are you so sure, lady? I ask. She can't tell me but keeps on that I'm wasting my time. Hell! She should have known what big jumps my mind was taking."

"I'll bet! Did you—?"

"Stick around. When I was last at their place I told the Captain that we'd caught a loony housebreaker who admitted pushing Andy in. So when I ask her why she's so

195

anxious it was accidental, she says she doesn't want the bloke to hang for nothing. That's all right, I tell her, we know it wasn't him. And then I say, all calmlike, 'What happened, Mrs. Jarvis, did you and Andy roll over the edge?' "

"Christ!"

Zondi made a muffled sound.

"Next thing she's laughing crazy but quietly and asking me how I know. That was a good moment to get the hell out, but I waited. Then she asked me what happens next and I tell her, Nothing. Like she says, it was an accident. No sense in dragging up evidence that would not alter the court's verdict. I explain that was why I was calling by. Her relief, it was fantastic. The Captain had said he would kill her if it ever got in the papers."

"But wait a minute, sir; if the two deaths *are* connected, then what the hell did she think she was doing?" Pembrook said.

"She felt guilty about the mad Kaffir she thought we'd string up."

"Since when has guilt been stronger than self-preservation? She could have left well alone. All this implicates her in the other."

"Only if *she* connected them also. Think about it."

Pembrook looked round at Zondi. All he saw was the crown of a straw hat tipped well forward.

"Be fair, sir," he entreated. "You must have asked more than one question."

"*Ach*, yes, I'd forgotten. Just as I got back into the car, telling her not to worry, I said, 'Do you ever wear trendy lipstick when you want to feel younger?' And she answered, 'What woman doesn't?' Enough for you now?"

The wattle truck, laden with bark and a loll of plantation workers, one of whom was playing the concertina, slowed down even further as the long climb up the escarpment began. Delighted to discover he had a following, the musician turned on a special performance. Kramer found it amusing for three bars and then put a mile between them.

"Slow down a bit, sir. I want to know what's on or I won't know what I'm supposed to be doing."

"Let me just tell you then and no hard feelings. A lot of

196

this is still shots in the dark, but we'll be able to verify it before long—that much I promise you.

"We'll start with this bloke Andy—Randy Andy, according to the girls, but not getting any from them. We add to him our dear Sylvia, who sounds, from your mate's description, in much the same boat. What have we got? A bit of whatnot without any too great a stretch of the imagination. Follow?"

"Surely the Captain—"

"Go back to Jackson the cook. He told us they slept in different rooms. Caroline felt safe to sneak out again after ten so you have a fair idea of when the old man hit the sack. This left a lot of night for lovin' in—yes? And one night they're down at the swimming bath, probably had an hour of it already and trying out a few variations. I think a psychologist friend of mine might even say that Sylvia would go for 'reversal of roles' after being married to that bullying bugger for eighteen years. Anyway, there she was, sitting on Andy, right near the edge—"

"Why?"

Kramer shrugged.

"Maybe for a bit of extra excitement. Kicks? Or they could have moved across without noticing. *Anyway*, they climax and fall in. Andy doesn't see what's coming. The water slams into his vagus, he's dead. Now, don't start on adrenalin because, if you know anything about the subject we're discussing, you'll know how fast it sends you to sleep afterwards. Besides, it's been proved scientifically to my satisfaction."

"In America, I bet."

"Uhuh. Can you imagine what it must have been like for her? The boy was dead in an instant. That's why she didn't even try to get him out: the fact was so obvious that all she could think of was to run for help. She told me the Captain had said he would kill her if it got out. So she must have gone right to him, or had hysterics, or something, but the fact remains he was aware of the situation. He covered up, not for her sake, you can be sure."

"I know: the family name. Remember he got drunk and banned soon after?"

"You're learning fast. Now tell me, where does Boetie come into this?"

197

A short pause followed as Pembrook prepared himself for the test. He was sweating all of a sudden.

"Accepting what you have said as basically correct, sir, then we can start when Boetie was crouching behind the tennis court watching something going on between a male and a female on the patio. From the fact he made a mistake in his identification, we deduce he could only distinguish rough forms, length of hair, and so on. Suddenly they . . ."

"Heave?"

"Yes, heave, and roll in. Well, he sees the female surface and run away."

"She could have dived a few times but he'd think she was pressing her attack."

"Yes, sir."

"Go on."

"Boetie expects to—"

"Just a minute, sorry to interrupt, but I've just realized how I hit on the 'rolling in' idea. Jarvis quoted Strydom as saying so and it struck because the DS didn't—never mind."

"Naturally Boetie waits a little for her maybe to come back. By the time he gets to the patio, he is sure the male is dead. He looks around for clothing to identify the female with—all he can find is a cigarette."

"Gone out in one of the oyster shells."

"Hey? He takes it and zooms home, wondering if he should tell the police. Like someone said, he decides they will sort it out. But come Monday and the inquest verdict, he is sure a mistake has been made because—more than that—people are lying and that means something sinister is going on."

"What proof did he have?" Kramer asked.

"He knew one thing for absolute certain, and that was Andy had someone with him when he fell in."

"Be careful now and think as though you are Boetie—remember everything you know about him."

Pembrook, made irritable by so many interruptions, fought to keep a civil tongue in his head.

"Lying, to Boetie, implies evil. He appraises the situation again. His confidence in the police drives him to have his doubts about what he's seen happening—perhaps there is another explanation. It crosses his mind that it might have been a shameful act and hence the silence, but he's never heard of it done like that. Being a good detective, he checks this out with the Dominee."

"First class!"

"The dates made that one easy, sir," Pembrook said, very heartened. "The Dominee flips his lid and 'puts him right' and we all know what that means. Boetie comes away convinced he had seen a death struggle. Convinced he's a pretty smart cookie after all. Still, there is a little doubt remaining. If he tells the police and hasn't more than his story to back him up, then there could be trouble. He was a great one for the trespass laws himself."

"I favor the idea he did it to win the Midnight Leopards a big pat on the back."

"Or himself."

"Certainly. Thank God we didn't pull the magazine in on this—it didn't have any responsibility, the more you think about it. And then?"

"Boetie gives Hester the shove, chums up with Sally, and tries to identify the female. The lipstick on the cigarette makes Caroline Suspect Number One. You know, sir, that ciggie must have been still warm or something for him to link it so strongly."

"With Boetie, you can bet your boots on it. Caution all down the line."

"That's really shown in what happened next, sir, I would think. We know there was nothing between Caroline and Andy, so he hits trouble straightaway in trying to connect them. But he keeps at it for a *whole month* before trying out a bit of the old head-on attack to see what she does."

"Kramer gestured for him to steer while he lit up a Lucky. The turn-off to the country club was just beyond the next rise.

"No doubt, Pembrook, our friend Sally must have dropped a few hints about Andy's morals."

"I grant that could keep him hoping, sir, but—hell, that's as far as I can get. Sorry, sir."

"Why?"

"Because I'm buggered if I can see why Boetie didn't

notice the same thing as you right at the start—the similarities between Mrs. and Miss."

"He could have done."

"Hey? And not thought about it?"

"Unthinkable. What if it was unthinkable?"

"Sir?"

Kramer yanked the wheel over and the Chev skidded to a halt on the gravel shoulder.

"What the hell did I tell you to do, boy? I said keep your thoughts about Boetie characteristic! Were you brought up Dutch Reformed?"

Tact made Zondi spring out to relieve himself behind a portable lavatory dumped in the grass by a road gang.

"Many thanks, boss," he said as he climbed back in again, timing it all to a nicety.

Kramer drove on before addressing Pembrook in kinder tones: "It seems I must spell it all out. You have the Dominee's word that Boetie was a good little churchgoer who actually listened to his sermons. You have evidence that his parents are good, virtuous folk, who keep their house free from evil influences. And you have the *Trekkersburg Gazette* from the day before yesterday."

"Sir?"

"You must learn to read, man. Then maybe you would have seen what the synod is asking the government to do. There's a whole list but two are enough: it wants to have all Sunday papers banned—you know bloody well what I mean about their back pages, all those film star bust-ups—and it wants living in sin made a criminal offense. All right, so that was this week, but I bet you the Dominee's been preaching that stuff for years. Ever since Boetie was big enough to come out of the babe-in-arms room at the back. All in dark hints, mind you, that only the grown-ups properly understand. So what did he know of what went on in the world? Only one thing: you mustn't do anything to a girl until you're both married and the Lord gives his blessing."

"A good world to grow up in, I suppose."

"Boetie was very lucky. But in freak circumstances like this, it cost him his life."

The Chev slithered off the main road, clattered over the cattle grid, and started up the last stretch through the wattles, making a brace of guinea fowl catapult into the undergrowth. An approaching Mercedes and then a Peugeot pulled over to allow them to pass.

"*Ach*, no," said Pembrook, "even then I find it hard to believe. He must have heard somewhere that married women fool around."

"But is that how he saw Mrs. Jarvis? That's the crux of it. Whose statue stands outside the Voortrekker Monument? A mother's. Heroic mothers fill the history books in primary schools. And when you are still a kid, what woman is the one you can least imagine doing wrong?"

"Your mother?"

"And what was Mrs. Jarvis?"

"Sally's mother," Pembrook responded, very peeved with himself.

"Unthinkable." Kramer chuckled and stopped the car.

He had parked again above the third and last hole of the pitch-and-putt course. Straight across the other side were the trees in which Boetie had been found; to their left, and cutting off their view of the rest of the golf course, was a windbreak of firs.

"Maybe that was staring me in the face, sir," Pembrook said, "but do you know more?"

"We can guess. Here is Boetie; a month gone by, no corpse left to prove anything different from what Strydom found, and Caroline giving him a hard time. So, like we said, he challenges her and ends up on the carpet in Jarvis's study. Gets the balls chewed right off him and is told to get the hell out and not come back. Note, Jarvis did not know at this stage what Boetie had said to his daughter.

"Right; by now, I reckon, Boetie has had enough. Kids can fight bloody dirty when you push them and Jarvis's patronizing attitude towards Afrikaners no doubt got a showing. Also Boetie's personal investigation has been brought to an end: he had to hand the matter over to us or forget it. What would be more natural than for him to hurl the lot in Jarvis's face? Tell him what he saw his daughter doing. Tell him about the Midnight Leopards. Threaten him with what was to come when he got down to the station."

201

Pembrook, plainly pained to disagree once more, drew in the dust on the dashboard.

"If he'd done that, sir, Jarvis would have more than chewed the balls off him."

"Right."

This time Zondi's excuse for an exit was seeing a butterfly settle on a distant arum lily. He darted off after it.

"You must ride two horses at once, Pembrook," Kramer said, surprisingly mildly. "Jarvis knew that despite the fact Boetie had the wrong female, the substance of what he said was correct. The real police would not necessarily make such a mess of it."

"Hell, sir, but then why let him go?"

"Because silencing there and then could have led to a lot of suspicion—and have been very difficult. This man was once a police chief, your friend said. However ropey the force he was in, he would know how a detective's mind works: two fatal accidents so close together, well . . ."

"Accidents happen—"

"In the best-regulated families," Kramer said, continuing in English. "He also knew that a sex-killing investigation is generally conducted differently. . . ."

"I don't see why Boetie didn't tell us, though. How could he have kept him quiet in between?"

"You gave me the idea with what Sally overheard. The one when Jarvis said he'd help Boetie find another girl. Don't you see? Probably dragged out an old picture of himself in his police gear and offered to lend a hand. He could even claim to having been investigating quietly on his own. It couldn't have been difficult to convince Boetie he was barking up the wrong tree. And that's also how he could get him to meet secretly in the woods—by playing up to a twelve-year-old's sense of melodrama, especially this one's."

Kramer got out and beckoned Zondi over.

"I know what you're going to say next, Pembrook. You're going to say that he was mad to do it up here at the country club—he could have gone to any number of places in the bush."

They began walking towards the club entrance. The secretary, Pipson, who had been chattering to a member,

202

sidled indoors. It was a wonder he did not take the WEL-
COME mat in with him.

"I think I've got the answer to that," Pembrook said
suddenly. "He was banned from driving. He couldn't go
anywhere unless his wog took him."

"Or his wife. But she wasn't to know anything about
this, and he couldn't take the chance of being found driving—or having an accident himself—on the way back
from the deed. This was the simplest, cleverest solution.
There is only one thing left to decide."

"Sir?"

"If it was possible."

The inquiry was adjourned at the Colonel's request and he
hurried to the radio room to get through a call to
Kramer. Having already failed to get him on the phone in
the CID building, his only hope was the car.

"Sorry, Colonel, but there is no response," the chief radio operator told him.

"Then I want a call put out every five minutes to him,
understand?"

"Yes, sir."

"Make it two-minute intervals."

"Yes, sir."

"Tell him I have information to do with the conversation I had with him at eight this morning."

The operator wrote it all down.

"You wait till I get hold of those buggers in Housebreaking," the Colonel said, apropos of nothing.

Or so the operator thought.

Pembrook preoccupied the club secretary with perplexing
questions—his instructions were simply to ask any nonsense that came into his head—while Zondi tracked down
the African caddy who had carried the Captain's clubs on
the day Boetie died.

It was not a difficult job, as the Captain was notorious
for favoring an old-fashioned, heavy leather bag. Kramer
watched them talking from the terrace in front of the
clubhouse. The view of Trekkersburg was truly magnifi-
cent and the air so clear he could pick out the mosaic of
white headstones on the farthest hill. He wondered how

the funeral had gone off and if someone should not have been there to note any odd behavior. He still had nothing but theories.

The caddy came across, dragging his heels behind Zondi.

"He says Boss Jarvis was here middle of the afternoon and played all the way round the course," Zondi said.

"Did he play well?"

It was translated, mainly for effect.

"Not very, boss. This kid says he can do much better. He just play by himself for practice. There are few people on Monday."

"When did he finish?"

"Half-five," the caddy replied in English.

"Half-past five," Zondi informed Kramer.

"Then did he go into the clubhouse or home?"

There was a long conversation in lisped Zulu, a subdialect Kramer had never mastered.

"No, he was very angry that he had not played well. He went on to play on this little course here."

"Pish-n-putt," prompted the caddy.

"And did you carry his bags?" Kramer asked.

"No, suh. Boss *meningi* angry. No tip."

"Uhuh!"

The caddy whispered something and giggled.

"He says Boss Jarvis never wants them to take his bag up to the club because then people can see he gives no tip. He always does it himself."

"No time for jokes, Zondi man! Did he see him playing on the pitch-and-putt?"

More giggling.

"It seems, boss, that he had a bit of an argument with the chief man of this place before he started."

"The secretary?"

It was a relief to be spared the comedy and given a neat nod.

"No tip," said Kramer and stalked off.

Pembrook rose from the cane chair on the veranda and held out a long glass of lager.

"Yours, sir."

"With the club's compliments," added the secretary.

204

"Mr. Pipson? Yes, we should have met the other night. Just a few questions, please."

The drawn little man sighed silently.

"I believe, sir, that last Monday afternoon you played a round of pitch-and-putt?"

"Oh, God," Pipson replied. "I'm beginning to think—"

"Did you?" Kramer demanded, slamming his fist down on the tabletop. His foot was agony.

"I—er—always do of an evening, before the rush in the bar starts. Just a quick three holes with my nine iron—the committee don't mind. Yes, I played on Monday."

"Was there anyone else on the course?"

"That's difficult to say. I mean . . ."

"Have an argument with anyone?"

"Definitely not. Our members are—Do you mean the few words I exchanged at the first hole?"

"Who was that with?"

"Captain Jarvis."

"Who's he then?"

"One of these retired military wallahs. A bit of a rough diamond, but a good enough chap if you want a reliable partner in a foursome. See him here often, has shares, you see. Wonderful couple of girls he's got. Pretty wife."

"Why did you have words? Just as a matter of interest."

"Damn silly really. I was teeing up when he arrived and insisted I let him play through. Something about having to pick his family up. But I had my bar to get to. It was over in a second."

"I suppose you let him through?"

"One has to, hasn't one?"

"See anyone else on the course?"

"Just the Captain. I had to wait for him to hole first, of course. Same thing again on the second. Rather irritating. The obvious answer was to play two-up but it wasn't my job to suggest it."

"So you followed him right to the end?" Kramer asked casually, adding with a sympathetic laugh, "How was his game on a liver like that? Pretty rough?"

"First two weren't bad. As I said, he—"

"What about the third?"

"You've never played here, I suppose, Mr. Kramer?"

"That hasn't been my pleasure."

205

"Ah, well, the third is up the terrace through the windbreak. You can't see a damn thing from the second. I arrived just as he was walking off the last green. I called out to offer him a drink—you know how important good relations are—but he just waved and went up the steps to the car park."

"As you're facing the windbreak, is the wattle plantation off to the left there?"

"Butts on to it actually."

"And the last you saw of Captain Jarvis from the second was him going up through the firs?"

"Heavens no. He was lugging this ridiculous golf bag of his, so he went the way the ladies do—steady the Buffs! What are you getting at?"

Kramer pressed him back into his seat with just the tip of his right forefinger against the checkered waistcoat. Pembrook went round behind him.

"I'm not getting at *you*, Mr. Pipson," Kramer soothed. "That's all you have to worry about. Now tell me about the way the ladies go."

Pembrook cracked his knuckles dramatically.

"Don't do that, it's a nasty habit."

"Sorry, sir."

"It's not so steep, you see, Mr. Kramer. You go round the edge of the terrace, so to speak. Just a few yards into the wattles and out again on the top level. Quite a natural thing to do with a weight to carry."

"And did you see Captain Jarvis on his way through the wattles?"

"I couldn't have. There are a lot of saplings there; they tend to swallow you up."

"But you saw him again on the last green, after he'd gone round this way. How much later was that?"

"Let me see . . . Three, four minutes, I suppose. The second's the shortest hole and I managed it in two. I give myself about quarter of an hour to get round."

"If it's the shortest hole, weren't you surprised to see Captain Jarvis had already finished? His hole should have taken longer and left you waiting like before."

"That didn't strike me. My handicap's very poor and he could have had a lucky drive right up to the flag. Hole-in-ones are common enough anyway."

206

"Okay, back to the time element again. Captain Jarvis was out of sight for a maximum of four minutes—right?"

"Perhaps five."

"Why's that?"

"Well, the time I took to get up through the firs. Although I suppose it would take him even longer round the other way. Say four."

"Got a nine iron handy, Mr. Pipson?"

"Y-yes."

"Fine, I'd like you to do the second hole in two for me. Have as many tries as you like."

Central Control were receiving complaints from every car and van within a ten-mile radius.

"I'm sorry, Major," the chief operator apologized. "These are Colonel Muller's orders. The call must go out every two minutes. I'll see the ambulance is sent immediately."

He swiveled around in his chair and called over a subordinate.

"Dawie, you have a turn now, I'm bloody sick of all the trouble this is causing. Come on, man, I'm going for a pee."

"What is the Colonel's message, sir?"

"Don't try that one! If you're stuck, just call in any one of them; they know it off by heart by now. Get Major Dorrell if you prefer it loud and clear. Won't be long."

What a sod the chief operator was. He was gone until long after Major Dorrell had come all the way in to make a personal matter of it.

Kramer's foot gave him a perfect right to make Pembrook do all the running under the hot noon sun. Zondi had been disqualified in the first heat for having too short a stride. But the man really suffering was the secretary, who, he confessed, always played damnably badly on an empty stomach.

In the end, however, it was established that the secretary took five minutes to complete the second hole in two and reach the trees for the third. And Pembrook proved that it took a total of five to reach the glade, wait there two minutes, and then walk to the final green. He did it in four on one occasion but was sent back for moving too fast, without making allowance for a load. Which was all very surprising, as the distances themselves seemed quite considerable until Kramer realized that five minutes from a cigarette machine on a wet night was a very long way.

"Well, sir, where does that leave us? Any good?"

"Manners, please, Pembrook. Thanks very much for your help, Mr. Pipson."

"I can go?"

"You're a free man in a free country."

The secretary made sure Kramer knew he was amused. They shook hands in a most friendly way.

"Ah, one thing, though, Mr. Pipson. Please keep our little game to yourself. I don't think Captain Jarvis would care to be told about it."

"I wasn't going to phone him, if that's what you mean!"

"Hey? That didn't enter my head. I just meant when he next came up. Just cause needless trouble, perhaps."

The secretary beamed with relief.

"I see," he said. "I'm so pleased. The club's suffered enough as it is. You must come up for a proper game sometime. Cheers."

Pembrook grinned as he watched him retreat with a spring in his step.

"That was neat, sir," he said.

"But I meant what I said," Kramer replied grimly. "Jarvis is out of the running."

"Oh, bloody hell, no! Why's that?"

Zondi moved in closer.

"Did you think," Kramer asked, "that Jarvis took advantage of the secretary for a nice little alibi? I did at first. But the problem is that he just didn't have enough time to get it all done and be certain of being in sight afterwards. Not unless he knew, down to almost a split second, how long it would take to have Boetie dead, mutilated and in the right place for the ritualistic touch. The bloke who did this wanted the job to look right—he couldn't take the risk of a rush job. Strangle, slice with the sickle, and prop in the tree? He'd never have tried it unless he did a test run."

"A *practice*, sir?"

"No, a test, I said. And if he had, there'd be *two* bodies on our plate, not one."

Chapter Fifteen

SQUARE ONE WAS an appalling prospect —coming, as it did, so soon after Kramer's heady exposition. They stood about the flag on the third green like three mountaineers who had planted it on the wrong peak.

"Sodding bloody hell," said Pembrook after much deliberation.

"Too right," Kramer concurred.

Zondi said nothing.

"Anyway, would two minutes have been enough for the killing, sir?"

"Huh? Well, there was that lift murder down in Durban."

"Oldroyd?"

"The same. He got in with the tart on the ground floor, escaped at the fifth, and the people buzzing from the sixth couldn't believe she was dead already."

"Then couldn't—"

"*Ach*, man, for Christ's sake! Oldroyd wasn't setting anything up, he wasn't trying to fool anyone. A crime of passion and he was caught the same night. The only relevance is the time factor."

"But—"

"All this is beside the point, Pembrook."

"You misunderstood, sir. I was going to apply what you told me earlier and suggest we take a look at this bloke Glen. He was there when Boetie spoke to Caroline; you never know what his reaction might have been. We seem to have overlooked him all down the line—not that he struck me as important before."

Kramer had his notebook out and open before Pembrook finished speaking.

"Glen Humphries, of 24 Leafield Road, Greenside," he

209

read out. "Articled clerk with the law firm of Henderson and Blackwell. Shall we go?"

"Where, sir?"

"To the secretary, of course—find out first if this bugger also belongs to the club. Get some background. Better come along, too, Zondi, in case we want a check with the caddies again."

Still Zondi said nothing.

"Wake up, Kaffir! What the hell's the matter with you?"

"I was listening to all the noise from the car, boss. Never have I heard so many messages."

"You don't say. If it's worrying you, go over and see what's happening."

Without further delay, Kramer made for the clubhouse with Pembrook marching smugly by his side.

Zondi shrugged.

The inquiry was over. Constable Hendriks, somewhat dazed, had been allowed to sit down.

Colonel Muller stood up and stalked out. He entered the control room just as the call to Kramer's car was acknowledged.

"Give," he ordered, grabbing the microphone away from the chief operator. "Receiving you, Zondi. Where is the lieutenant?"

Zondi's voice replied from the speaker on the wall: "He is not here, Colonel; he is very busy."

The Colonel kept his thumb off the SPEAK button while uttering an imperative unfit for broadcasting. As guest of honor at the Rotary luncheon, he could hardly afford to be any later.

"Then take this down very carefully, Zondi," he said, "and give the message to the lieutenant as soon as you can."

"Sir!"

"It concerns a dead dog," the Colonel began.

And frowned as the chief operator, strangely overcome by mirth, blew a mouthful of tea through his nose like an elephant.

In a state of acute distress, the secretary left Kramer and Pembrook to themselves in the office.

"Fits, sir, doesn't it?" Pembrook said gleefully. "Glen was here in the morning as well as the afternoon—with Jarvis the nearest we got was that he had played a round on the pitch-and-putt the night before. Must say, these articled clerks do all right, don't they? Tuesday's a working day for most people."

"They get time off to go to lectures," Kramer replied, resting his foot on the old-fashioned safe. "Wait until we see him before jumping to any more conclusions. He could be on holiday, for all we know."

Pembrook continued to pace about, leaving his fingerprints on the vast array of silver cups and his ash all over the carpet.

"Oh, come on, sir! If you hadn't got the same feeling about this that I had, you wouldn't have asked the secretary so few questions."

"He said Glen was just out there in the car, so why should I?"

"Can I go and get him, sir? I mean, he might try and—"

"Sit down!" barked Kramer. "If my foot wasn't so sore, I'd give you a good kick up the arse. How many times have I told you we have to go carefully in this sort of case? This isn't one you're going to solve with rough stuff. Any violence and we've made a mistake and that's us finished. We play it cool all the way."

From inside the winged chair Pembrook was heard to mutter, "It all bloody well fits."

"What does? We've heard Glen was here and that he's a fiery-tempered, spoiled little bastard who once clobbered a caddy for whistling. Huh! I bet you I could find ten others like him in this place any night of the week."

"Then there was Caroline's attempt to keep you from interviewing him, which—"

"Say no more, Pembrook. I'm noticing quite a lot myself now but from here on we work strictly with facts. Fact one: Where was Glen on the night in question? Let him tell us that."

The door opened and Glen Humphries, a very frightened-looking little bastard, was led in.

Zondi was caught napping, stretched out full length on the

back seat and snoring softly. Not that anyone gave a damn what he was doing, but the double slam of the doors brought him round quicker than a kick. And the Chev's almost instantaneous takeoff had him startled into an apology.

"*Ach*, shut up, will you?" Kramer snarled. "If you want to sleep, sleep. I don't care."

Down through the plantation they bumped and skidded.

"That was the last thing I expected," Pembrook said, making out he was addressing himself.

Kramer fumbled a cigarette into his mouth and accepted Zondi's light for it without thanks. Probably it was the same two guinea fowl which reached safety only by turning themselves into polka-dotted cannon balls. At the gate a delivery van sidestepped into the ditch. Its Indian driver turned away, with his eyes screwed up, as the Chev plunged on to the dual highway behind him.

They reached the far lane safely.

"Christ," whispered Pembrook, again to himself.

"Hey?"

"Nothing, sir. Just—"

"Look, Pembrook, don't play around with me in this mood. Tell me what the trouble is."

"Well—er—can we be sure that it was really there on the day?"

Kramer had never been asked a more fatuous question. Forgetting all about the routine checks that would doubtless confirm the claim made by Master Glen Humphries, the plaster cast encasing the fractured hand had been signed and dated by a score of inane acquaintances. It was in itself an affidavit, testifying that, for a period extending back at least three weeks, the bearer had been incapable of tying his own shoelaces—let alone strangling someone with a stout wire.

"Pembrook?"

"Sir?"

"If you don't like the way I drive, you can get out and bloody well walk."

Dismayed at being found so transparent, Pembrook shrank back, mumbling denials.

"Can I speak?" asked Zondi. "I have a message from the Colonel."

212

"That's all I need!"

"Boss?"

The rage in Kramer was having an effect on him more pronounced than half a bottle of peach brandy before breakfast. He no longer cared what he said or did. It was really quite pleasant, although potentially very dangerous unless he soon found some means of channeling it to advantage.

"Don't tell me—the killer's gone prancing in and confessed everything. Was it the Mayor?"

Zondi grinned into the mirror.

And Kramer eased back on the throttle.

"Okay, you tell me," he said.

"Colonel's radio message as follows: 'It concerns dead dog mentioned during inquiry into death of Asiatic juvenile Danny Govender, arrested on suspicion by Housebreaking in Greenside area, Rosebank Road, three nights ago. Was held because story believed to be rubbish made up to cover real purpose there. Anyway, Govender alleged he was investigating the death of a very big dog, a bitch as big as himself, at the weekend.' "

"*You're* not making this up, Kaffir?"

"True's God!"

"Go on, but I warn you . . ."

"Then the Colonel says: 'I took an interest when told Govender alleged dog had been strangled by prowler.' "

Zondi paused for dramatic effect and then continued with a passable impersonation.

" 'Housebreaking made no attempt to verify this story at the time, but contacted the licensing department this morning at my request. I consider it more than a coincidence that the biggest dog in the neighborhood was a ridgeback Great Dane cross bitch belonging to Captain P. R. Jarvis. Suggest you now follow my advice, drop farfetched theories, and switch investigation from family to the criminal element. One last point: Housebreaking has apparently overlooked the burglar's success despite number of watchdogs kept. This could indicate we should be looking for a white—even one living in Greenside.' "

Something odd happened to Pembrook's expression. Kramer noticed it at once.

"You look as if you know about this?"

213

"No, sir! First I've heard about it."

"Then how come the Colonel so obviously knows that the Jarvises have no dog at present?"

"He—he could have got the license people to make a casual inquiry. By phone."

"Hmmm. Possible, I suppose. Always knows more than you think, that bloke. What do you make of his theory?"

A catch in Kramer's voice made Pembrook swing round surprised. There was a disturbing smile on the face he examined.

"Pretty farfetched, too," he said cautiously. "If the prowler was white and didn't have trouble with dogs, why did he do this one in?"

"Some dogs won't be friendly with anyone," Kramer reminded him.

"Even then, the more unfriendly they are, the harder to get near their throats. *Ach*, I can see what the Colonel is getting at, all these factors strung together—dog strangled, Boetie strangled, prowler surprised a white burglar, a white murderer, coincidences—but it doesn't hold together when you think about it. For a start, we know now what the Colonel doesn't know—and that is what Boetie saw at the swimming bath. It wasn't the prowler that time and Boetie was at home when the dog was killed. Makes your head spin."

"No, it doesn't," Kramer replied. "Like you say, the Colonel's got it all wrong. He's been sitting at the inquiry with his mind on other things, just slinging together a few ideas. But it's all there."

"Hey? I can't see anything to work on."

The Chev slipped off the highway down a byroad. Half a mile later it was in Greenside.

"I've got you, boss!" Zondi exclaimed as they turned in to 10 Rosebank Road.

Which left Pembrook very indignant indeed, so indignant he rounded on the other passenger.

"Come on," he snapped, "you tell me what I'm too thick to get from all this!"

"*Hau!* But you are not stupid, Boss Pembrook. You said this thing yourself: that it is hard to get near the neck of a bad dog."

214

"Unless," Kramer intervened, "it's your own dog—and it's probably expecting you to put its collar on."

"Not back to Jarvis again!"

"Why not? Doesn't this give us our other body? One as big as a juvenile?"

The Trekkersburg Rotarians never got to hear the Colonel's speech on the primary role of the police force as guardians of the security of the Republic, although they came very close to doing so.

The empty dishes had been whisked away, the cigars brought round, and the coffee served; he was about to stand up, curiously niggled by a feeling that he had not got that hunch of his about the dog quite right, when the hotel's manager rushed in.

"I'm sorry but you're wanted urgently at police headquarters," he said.

"What on earth for?"

"Somebody's running amuck there with a gun. Two shot already!"

"Nonsense!"

"That's what the sergeant on the phone said. They've got him cornered in the billiard room."

The Colonel's second hunch of the day was fully substantiated: Constable Hendriks had cracked.

A bumblebee in the hollyhock beside the great wooden door fizzed no louder than the fuse to a bomb, and yet Kramer heard it. All of Greenside lay hushed; the beginning of a drowsy afternoon in a suburb so civilized that everyone rested indoors until the heat wore off and servants could serve tea.

But, for now, the heat was on. Kramer could feel it there in his belly, too, burning like peach brandy.

"Let's get this over with," he said, making a crude, brutal gesture with his hands.

Zondi gave a growl of approval.

"Surely you don't mean that?" Pembrook asked.

"Nice and quick, boss," Zondi said, smiling.

"Think I'm mad?"

"Then what . . . ?" faltered the apprehensive Pembrook.

"There is more than one way of skinning a cat, son.

Watch and you'll find out. Know your job?"

"Keep the women away and try to get a statement from Mrs. Jarvis."

"And you, Zondi?"

"Find the garden boy."

Kramer knocked hard, once.

The maid opened up so promptly she gave herself away. Those diamond-shaped panes of glass had blobs in their centers like the lenses in peepholes.

Zondi questioned her. Captain Jarvis was in his study. Mrs. Jarvis was in her sewing room. Caroline was still in bed.

"Forget the daughter, then," Kramer said to Pembrook. "I'll be with you as soon as I can. Zondi, get this woman to take you to the garden boy."

He led Pembrook in by the arm, unaware that his grip accounted for the brawny youth's sudden pallor.

"For Christ's sake don't go soft on me," he hissed.

"I'm okay, sir."

"Sewing room's on the landing. Keep it quiet as you can or Caroline'll only complicate things. Now move!"

Kramer watched him start up the stairs, then he began opening every door in the passage, other than that leading to the drawing room, which he remembered was first on the right.

Third time lucky—Jarvis rose in surprise from behind his desk.

"Please don't get up, sir. Just a few questions."

"Really, this is getting beyond a joke!"

All the same, Jarvis lowered himself back into the chair. Maybe his legs had weakened.

"First question: Do you own a firearm?"

"Several."

"And where are they?"

"The guns are locked away—my revolver's in my bedroom. What's all this about? They're licensed."

"And your dog—is it licensed."

"I don't have one."

"I see."

Kramer took out an invoice he had received for a dozen red roses.

"What's that?" Jarvis asked.

216

"The counterfoil of a dog license issued in your name by the Trekkersburg Municipality. It's expired."

"So I was informed this morning," Jarvis said coldly. "But as the wretched animal itself expired about a week ago, I don't see the point of all this. As a matter of fact, I—"

"Yes?"

While awaiting an answer, Kramer wheeled over an easy chair and then commandeered a small table for his foot. He made himself comfortable. And noted that now he was closer to Jarvis, the man reeked of strong drink.

"This is intimidation!" Jarvis declared.

"Asking about a dog license?"

"The hell with that. What are you really? Special Branch?"

"*Ach*, no, just a bit of an all-rounder."

Kramer lit a Lucky.

"Well?" challenged Jarvis, bringing a small tumbler out from behind a pile of books.

"Cheers!" said Kramer.

Jesus, it was bizarre. Only a genuine psychopath could have lasted as long in a situation engineered to disorientate a suspect and now having much that effect on Kramer himself. You had to be mad to treat it anything like normal—and to rationalize so fluently, as with the Special Branch remark. On another level, these were the responses of a man entirely confident of his position; nothing would be achieved by trying Boetie's trick of flushing out fact with a well-aimed fistful of surmise. It would clatter off the cold-blooded bastard like pellets off a croc. The most Kramer could hope for would be a cynical, private admission of guilt, without any indication of where concrete evidence, fit for public judgment, could be found. For that sort of information, the abandon of high passion was required; this in turn meant a change in metabolism, something that would raise the body temperature high enough for careless talk. Kramer had a plan, based on first reverting Jarvis to basic behavior, that might or might not work. It was worth a try anyway.

"Going to sit there long, Lieutenant?"

"Just giving my foot a rest. I cut it yesterday."

"Always a nasty business. What on?"

"With a sickle, actually."

A gleam shone momentarily in Jarvis's monocled eye. Then he leaned across his desktop.

"Isn't it time you ran along, Lieutenant? It does seem as though we were just going to waste each other's afternoon."

"I'd hoped . . ."

There were slithering footsteps in the passageway outside.

"Just a minute, Captain Jarvis, I've got a small surprise for you before I go."

Kramer went quickly over to the door, took a large zinc bath from Zondi, and returned with it to the desk. The stench which suddenly filled the room was incredibly awful.

"Good God! What have you there?"

Kramer let the bath fall on the desk with a thump.

Inside it was a shape, a long shape as shiny as a prune, only hairy in parts, and acrawl with a mass of maggots more numerous than the grains in an orphanage rice pudding. A snarl of teeth gleamed at one end.

But it was undoubtedly the smell that made Jarvis spew violently over himself as he turned his head away, ruining the right sleeve of his smoking jacket. Some of his lunch—barely digested—splattered more considerately into the wastepaper bin. If the stuff had its own smell, it was certainly not discernible against such competition.

Kramer switched to autopsy breathing and concentrated on the next phase of the operation. He tipped the bath up a little and shook it. The dead dog released gas bilaterally.

"Oh, my Christ!" gasped Jarvis, doubling up to dry retch.

Meanwhile, Kramer resumed his seat, sick to the stomach with the pain in his foot. He should have foreseen that carrying over the bath would place an agonizing weight on it every other step. But somehow he managed to maintain an air of bright interest in the proceedings.

"Sis, man, you're disgusting!" he said finally, with a laugh. "Where's the pride of the regiment now?"

This brought back the color to Jarvis's puffing cheeks—and then some. His head became engorged with blood until it threatened to seep steaming through the pores. He gave a hoarse shout and lunged.

The black pupil of the Smith & Wesson stared him back to the far side of the desk, yet it could not silence Jarvis.

"You swine!" he said. "You filthy Boer bastard! Bringing a thing like that into a man's house!"

Come to think of it, the incongruity alone was powerfully disturbing. There squatted the servants' bath, smack in the center of a rosewood veneer clean enough to eat off and surrounded by such elegance as a silver inkstand; a crystal goblet containing a single, immaculate rose; an ivory paperweight carved with great delicacy; and a picture in a leather frame of a young woman with her two little girls.

"*Ach*, yes, it would have been nicer to bring Boetie along, but his ma wouldn't let me," Kramer replied.

Jarvis jarred, as if struck a blow by the words.

"My God! Is there no limit to the way you Afrikaans scum behave? First the Junior Gestapo and now you."

"But you wouldn't have killed him if you'd really thought he worked for us," Kramer said quietly.

"Oh, no? Prove it!"

And there it was: that incautious bravado Kramer had planned on producing.

"Mrs. Jarvis is already being a great help."

"*Sylvia?* She wouldn't tell you a damn thing as long as I live."

"Don't tempt me, Captain."

"I see, you're going to build a case on bluff and bullshit."

"How come I decided to dig up this dog, then? You didn't notice her at the window? Take a look at its throat now the fur has fallen off."

"But she couldn't know anything else anyway—that's not enough and you know it."

"I've got plenty. You should have treated her better."

"*Me?* Why, I—"

Jarvis struggled out of his jacket, hurling it into one corner.

"How shall I put it, Captain? Mrs. Jarvis has promised to help us with the Swanepoel case if we don't reopen the Cutler one."

"The woman's mad! It would all come out in court anyway."

"Not necessarily. She was expecting, for the sake of the family's name, that you would—well, you know."

"And get strung up as a sex killer? Good God Almighty, what help would that be?"

"The medical evidence is against that for a start—and the element of premeditation. If you like to fill in a few more details, maybe I'll be able to think of something."

It seemed Jarvis was no longer aware of the seething corruption before him as he collapsed into his chair, shattered with the realization he had already talked too much. He was not his abnormal self.

The sewing machine refused to keep a neat stitch. Pembrook, whose mother was a dressmaker, assured Mrs. Jarvis he could repair it in a trice.

"You're such a nice boy," she said.

All along she had been struggling to contain her hysteria with her stiff upper lip. But she had refused adamantly to make any statement, for fear of what her husband would do.

"Be nice to us, then," coaxed Pembrook. "We can't help it if there is this order from New York through Interpol. It won't be in any of the local papers."

"Will it work now?" she asked, putting an arm over his bowed shoulders.

Kramer had Zondi remove the bath and then drew his easy chair up closer to the desk.

"From what you tell me," he said to Jarvis, "you planned the whole thing too well. Take the sickle, for instance, chucking it out of your car window where a wog would find it means we'll never trace it now."

"Newspaper appeal?"

"When not one in a hundred can read? That's a fat hope. And then again, the way you carried the sickle off the course in the hang-down lid of your golf bag—using a plastic bag in there cut out all traces of blood, as you say."

"I was very careful," murmured Jarvis, half a size smaller now, it seemed. "Was a police wallah m'self once, you know."

"I suppose, with a bit of luck, we might find the wire from the dog with a metal detector."

"I'm pretty sure I didn't put it in the dustbin—threw it in the hedge, I think. After all, I hardly expected you . . ."

"How did you get Boetie up to the plantation?"

"Piffling. Informed him I had my suspicions but I couldn't afford to reveal them where we might be overheard."

"So that's how the cigarette got on the ground," Kramer said softly. "Boetie chucked the bloody thing away—deliberately. Discarded it as irrelevant."

Jarvis toyed with a paper knife.

"There's no way of doing it without connecting the two cases, Lieutenant."

A short while back Jarvis had been ranting and yelling, and now he was sitting there discussing his future so dispassionately it could have been that of a stranger. Mad as a rabid bloody meerkat. Apparently quite unaware he had been sprinkling around enough information for Kramer to have the whole thing sewn up by nightfall—providing, of course, both cases *were* used in conjunction. No, wait a minute, Kramer had him anyway so he, too, was becoming confused. It was the corroborating statement about the Cutler case that needed attention. Plus the compulsion Kramer felt to make this double-barreled bastard suffer for all the trouble he had caused. Quite suddenly, a most satisfactory idea occurred to him.

Kramer stood up.

"Captain," he said, "we have overlooked one certain solution to your problem. In its way, it is also a solution to our own. Let us treat this as a matter of honor, as you would in the regiment, if you get my meaning. It would cause the least amount of damage to the family name and you will be required to undergo no indignity."

He picked up his revolver, which had been lying on the desk, and broke it open. Jarvis leaned forward and saw each chamber was loaded. The revolver was snapped shut.

"In passing," Kramer said, "I might point out that head injuries cause immense distress to those left behind. Now, having chatted amiably with you, as I shall tell the Colo-

221

nel when he arrives in a minute, I'll go up to the lavatory. Have I your understanding?"

He placed the revolver nonchalantly on the desk.

Jarvis got unsteadily to his feet—Kramer had encouraged him to drink freely during their lengthy discussion.

The two men stood looking at each other in silence; shoulders back, stomachs in, chins out.

"Spoken like a gentleman, sir!" said Jarvis.

Kramer shook hands and left.

Pembrook was very proud of his repair work and equally peeved when he found Kramer so inattentive while he gave a full explanation of what it had entailed.

"He was sweet about it," Mrs. Jarvis said. "Far, far better than that little man I usually get in when things go wrong."

"I think you'd better get down to helping him with his statement then," Kramer said.

"Oh, I can't! I've told you why, I simply can't."

"Come on, madam, sit down and Constable Pembrook will make it all very simple."

"But, sir— *Christ!*"

A single shot had sounded from downstairs.

Mrs. Jarvis began to laugh in that crazy way once again. When she overdid it, Kramer slapped her.

"Was that Peter?" she asked, her broad smile remaining.

Kramer nodded.

"But how the—"

"When you feel up to it, your statement, please, Mrs. Jarvis."

Pembrook looked in amazement from one face to the other.

"Oh, but I must first go and tell Caroline it was nothing to worry about," she said. "Don't go away, young man."

"And I'd better go down and see what has happened," Kramer added.

They parted company on the landing.

Zondi, who had run in from the servants' quarters, met Kramer at the bottom of the stairs.

"*Hau!* Who is shooting?" he asked, bewildered.

"Boss Jarvis. Let's inspect the damage."

Kramer seemed absurdly jolly and this left Zondi considerably apprehensive. He followed him down the passage and into the study.

There, on the far side of the big desk, Captain Jarvis lay slumped in his chair, a huge powder burn on his shirt front over the heart. From his right hand hung a .38 Smith & Wesson with distinctive ivory embellishments.

"It's your gun, boss! How can this be?"

"Must have left it behind after our nice little talk—stupid of me. Can't remember doing that."

"He's breathing!"

"I should bloody well hope so."

"Boss?"

Unable to restrain himself, Zondi rushed forward and then realized there was no blood to be seen.

Kramer worked the trigger guard off Jarvis's finger and broke open the revolver. He cleared the chambers and a stunted spent cartridge, plus five others with curiously crimped noses, jumped into his hand.

Blanks.

"I've had them in there ever since the gala," he admitted, winking.

Then Zondi recalled that, when locked in mortal combat with an oversexed witch doctor, he had seen a blond phantom making no attempt to use the firearm it carried. Sudden comprehension slid icily like a hailstone down his spine. He shuddered.

"You're crazy, boss!"

"Why so? There was never any real likelihood of violence in this case. All kid gloves and romance in the bloody moonlight."

So saying, Kramer put the rose between his teeth and poured the contents of the crystal vase over Jarvis. It was too warm for an immediate effect but they did not have to wait overlong.

"Where'm I?" Jarvis slurred—nobody expected for a moment he would come out with anything original.

"Guess," said Kramer.

Jarvis's lids parted briefly.

"My study," he mumbled.

"Wrong," said Kramer.

223

"Where then?"

"Hell," replied Kramer. "Just improvising, you understand, until we get the noose on you. After that, who knows? I never take chances."

This time Jarvis opened his eyes wide and kept them open.

"You Afrikaner scum," he said, with such hatred Zondi feared for the worst.

But Kramer laughed. "Don't blame me, Captain—blame Professor Aardvark."

And he thoroughly enjoyed his little in-joke.

Zondi was able to share his amusement. It was he who had shown the lieutenant that the first word in any English dictionary was, in fact, Cape Dutch.